THE
CALF
THE
CALF
THE
CALF
THE
CALF

Deep Vellum | Fum d'Estampa Press
3000 Commerce Street, Dallas, Texas 75226
www.fumdestampa.com

Deep Vellum is a 501c3 nonprofit literary arts organization founded in 2013 with the mission to bring the world into conversation through literature.

Originally published in Norwegian as *Kælven* by Det Norske Samlaget (Oslo, 2019)
First English edition, 2025

Support for this publication has been provided in part by grants from the National Endowment for the Arts, the Texas Commission on the Arts, the City of Dallas Office of Arts and Culture, the Communities Foundation of Texas, and the Addy Foundation.

This translation has been published with the financial support of NORLA

Library of Congress Cataloging-in-Publication Data
Names: Høghaug, Leif, 1974- author | Smith, David M., 1982- translator Title: *The Calf* / by the author Leif Høghaug ; translated from the Norwegian by David M. Smith. Other titles: *Kælven*. English Description: Dallas : Deep Vellum, 2025. Identifiers: LCCN 2025021635 (print) | LCCN 2025021636 (ebook) | ISBN 9781913744243 trade paperback | ISBN 9781913744526 ebook Subjects: LCGFT: Black humor | Novels | Fiction Classification: LCC PT9072.H574 K3413 2025 (print) | LCC PT9072.H574 (ebook) | DDC 839.823/8--dc23/eng/20250604 LC record available at https://lccn.loc.gov/2025021635 LC ebook record available at https://lccn.loc.gov/2025021636

Cover art and design by Douglas Suttle
Interior design and typeset by Douglas Suttle
Printed in the United States of America

THE CALF

by the author

LEIF HØGHAUG

Translated from Norwegian by

DAVID M. SMITH

D
D
D
D
D
D
D
D
D
D
D
D
D
D
D
D
D
Down, down, down. Would the fall
never *come to an end?*

Lewis Carroll

These past few days I been thankin an' thankin bout a late summer night I tried a long time to fergit. I's a-settin here a-thankin an' a-writin an' soon enuff you like'ta realize that everthang I's a-thankin an' a-writin . . . naw it's these voices, man . . . it's these chaintooth voices, way down inside this ol' wore-out metal warsh-tub noggin o' mine, it's them whut's talkin an' talkin, churnin an' rattlin, on an' on they go.

But okey. It's okey.

Man, I tell ye whut . . . this here rotted-out man-husk I still believe has got to be *me* . . . yessir, *still*, even after they got him to take a journey jaunt down to the unnerworld fer to begin agin . . . an' so down he goed an' they seated him to a desk an' they put him to work sharpnin pencils an' shreddin paper an' fiddlin wi' the coffeepot . . . man, I tell ye, he done learn'd he better breathe slow, nice an' slow, an' he ain't too hard to please an' if you was to call upon yer goodwill e'er so little it *might* just be possable to portray him as a ordnary ol' barn gnome, native to Hadeland, Gran, an' all.

Might. It might just be possable. An' ye'll call upon that goodwill, won't ye?

Yessir. He'll be fine, that gnome. He can keep on pretendin, actin the optimist, tho' he'd sooner hear tell when he might git to see calm daylight agin.

Light. Just a jag of light. Just one sliverin skiver of light, but still a trusty courier from the sun whut heaves an' swells fer many a lively night-wrangler over an' above that hill in the east, a-heavin an' a-swellin an' chasin them satanical shadows you says you remember too, them shadows swingin round an' round in a tralalalala trollin hoedown, once upon a time in the year nineteen-eighty-and-thereabouts, one forestclad late summer night?

An' mightn't there have been one you'd allow you done seen before? One o' them satanical shadows in pertic'lar?

Okey. He'd a-been right pleas'd with a little daylight, that there man-husk. An' that sun, she chas'd away them cadgy unnerworldly fellers . . . but that there meckanickal barn gnome, boy . . . he can spook around up here in the daylight jest as well.

Meckanickal? *Meckanickal* barn gnome?

Durn straight. If that ain't a ittybitty deetail. About that there feller I still believe must be me . . . he is an' always has been meckanickal, just a fairly ordnary meckanickal barn gnome. Cables, connectors, fuses, plugs, screws, an' nuts. Push-puppet man. A stop-moshun push-puppet gnome-doll man, right outta Ivo Caprino. An' a ol' metal warsh-tub where ye ought ta've found a gnome-noggin on yer usual dimestore dollie.

Remote-controll'd? Nuh-uh, boy. This here model's one o' them self-operatin types, accordin to the manual. An' that late summer night? Well, he just up an' operated his own self an' he was a nimble lil' booger too considerin he's a meckanickal barn gnome an' all. But now? Now he's all rotted out. Plum rotted out. Naw, he ain't much good no more, an' dadgum if it don't hurt him a right smart to go runnin around operatin hisself sometimes.

An' these voices. They's a-talkin an' a-talkin, sayin: *Naw, start all over agin? No-ho-hooo boy. Done to a fare-thee-well. Done.*

Listen to him. Listen to him. Listen to how talkified he is all of a sudden . . .

We tried gittin him to talk too. But talk to us? Durn'd if he won't.

Bout two-three days ago last we tried. Tractor putterin about. Wheat stalks a-bulgin. An' a chaintooth voice tolt us to skeer him real good. We diked ourselves out good, boy. This one feller, he put on one o' them gashly-lookin yulegoat masks ya gotta yank down over yer mug to put on, just like them factory-stitch ski-masks. Then we toddl'd on over. Masks an' overcoats an' boots . . . An' it turn'd hot out. The daydown-sun, she's havin herself a good ol' time. Daydown-sun . . . sun . . . Ha ha. Better not make no menshun o' her, ah? Anyhow . . . We git right down unner the feller's kitchen wender an' set ourselves to howlin an' hollerin like a bunch o' wolves who cain't hardly hold in the howlin no more. Naw, hold it in? Hold it in all the way till the moon come out? We stood there a-howlin. Tractor putterin off yonder, ye could hear it putt-putt-puttin away in betwixt all the howlin. But they wutn't nary a sound comin outta his house. An' the daydown-sun . . . sun . . . ha ha. Light. Just a jag of light . . .

Talkin? I tell ye I heard plenty o' talkin. In the way-back-when. Past few days, too, natcherly. These past few days in the unnerworld.

They. They was talkin an' talkin, churnin an' rattlin, on an' on they goed. They.

Ain't no matter.

Cause it was the Dead Feller, ye see, it was that there *Dead Feller* sangin . . . Sangin. Not talkin.

The Dead Feller'? The cloudcuckoo. The cloudcuckoo coo-coo-cooin, they said.

Nuh-uh, buddy. Wutn't no cuckoo. Wutn't no nightowl, nuther. Dead Feller. That was the Dead Feller, sangin.

Dead Feller Dead Feller Dead Feller.

Down in the Mare Cooter Canyon that late summer night. Down in the overgrow'd Mare Cooter Canyon o'er by the Lunnerworld. It was *there* the meckanickal barn gnome finally heard the Dead Feller sangin. *Fust*, he heard the cows an' the cow concert an' *then* the Dead Feller hisself, boy . . .

> O the girlie, the girlie, she went out a-walkin'
> An' the foxie, the foxie, in wait was a-stalkin . . .

More. More to come, I tell ye'. More. As 'twere woven in an' out o' this here norration, this tellin from a time they says is over an' done with an' that's why they call it the way-back-when.

The way-back-when. Over an' out. Them voices in the warsh-tub noggin says so. An' the menfolks down here in the unnerworld, they say so too, th' whole herd o' suit-wairin, fine-smellin, buff'd-up menfolks. They says the same thang as all them swaggerin pissants, them swaggerin pissants way up yonder, on the surface. Up there an' down here, everbody says the way-back-when is over an' done with. Up there an' down here is all kinda folks tellin an' declamatin how it is. Just a-cucklin an' a-bleatin an' a-tellin us drasted souls whut to thank about this an' about that. Politics, money, religion. We got to thank whut *they* says we best be thankin an' whut we best be believin cause ain't nuthin but the best is the best. Natcherly. Ain't no reason at'oll fer no misdoubtin, hem-hawin, stutterin, or stammerin. The politics it runs in their veins an' if they was to be empty'd o' blood why then it'd run out into the tunnels dug unnerneath by meathungry worms but anyhow: politicians they is, natcheral politicians. Ain't no matter if the one's still a-livin an' the other stone dead. If you's a suit-wairin, fine-smellin, buff'd-up manfolk . . . naw, ain't no matter . . . aliv'd or dead . . . either way there'll be a theatrickal performance. An' money, man, the money it comes a-squirtin from outta their rear ends, they know exactly whut they got to do if they's wantin to git their guts an' the whole dadgum system inside o' theirselves a-crankin, them swaggerin pissants on the surface an' suit-wairin fellers down here in the unnerworld, just a-squirtin an' a-squirtin, up there an' down here they's just a-squirtin an' a-squirtin an' they's goozlin coffee an' squirtin gulpin consumin an' openin their mouths wide fer to be feedin on their own dewkie cause if they's able to *eat* money why they's able to *crap* money too, boy, if ye was wantin to go crappin then ye best be eatin an' ye best be drankin yer coffee barefoot both before an' after ye eat an' so I's a-thankin bout that late summer night an' I already done menshun'd them cows an' the concert they was havin . . . cows . . . poor ol' thangs . . . them cows who slid down the slopes smack dab into the Mare Cooter Canyon . . . slidin . . . bout four or five of 'em . . . each an' ever' one of 'em got their guts an' all a-crankin . . . but poor thangs . . . poor thangs. An' religion, man, religion . . .

The lady. The lady who was settin in the one recliner in my livin room back home . . .

She set an' set. That whole evenin. That whole night. My last evenin, the last night up on the surface . . .

She set there, sayin:

We need ritcherals. We need religion.

We? She say that? We?

She sure did.

O. That lady.

Money is religion an' religion is politics. A snip an' a snap an' a trippytriptrap.

It ain't a hunnerd percent whut she said. But anyways . . .

More. As 'twere woven in an' out. Mmhmm. Like as not ye'll git to hear the song, too. Song o' the Dead Feller. A right woeful ballit, down in the Mare Cooter Canyon that late summer night.

Yessir. You, too.

Or is it a song you still, after all these years . . . a song you still have inside ye somewhereabouts? You too? Just as much as I do?

Say whut, now?

I mean: Whut is it *you's* sayin you remember? Huh?

The Mare Cooter Canyon. Mare Cooter Canyon over by the Lunnerworld.

A gorge. One o' them big ol' gorges. Some call it a hollow, others a wood-hole, or maybe a jungal, mash'd betwixt a couple o' steep hogback volcanoes, because back when God had done finish'd makin the balloonblue earth an' most everthang was hummin along purty good an' all them dinos was a-walkin around rulin the planit it musta happen'd that there hill over by the Lunnerworld crack'd plum open an' the lava come a-bubblin up an' the smoke come a-billowin out an' boy, if that wutn't such a sight as ye never did see.

The canyon, whut later on would come to be call'd the Mare Cooter Canyon. That's where. Where the Dead Feller sang. Yessir, that late summer night when the whole shadowy hollow fill'd with song.

An' there was a plan behind it all. That's right. A quare good plan, too.

But it all went to sheeit an' Andy had to study up a new one.

This feller Andy.

Had hisself a flashlight, ol' Andy did. A bucket, too. An' in the bucket was a fistful o' gravel.

An' the shank o' the evenin come an' the night come so he brung out the flashlight an' he got out in front an' lit up the trail whiles carryin the bucket, you could hear the sound o' the gravel an' the flashlight was shinin brightly bright an' if the moon was out, standin there in all his glory in the late summer night sky . . . naw . . . cain't remember now . . . if the moon was out . . . the moon . . . but if he was out: whut d'ye reckon that feller the man in the moon was thankin bout this ittybitty light down in the Mare Cooter Canyon? Was he thankin that that there light, the light from ol' Andy's flashlight, done shook up them shadows who wutn't used to no other light but the light o' the moon? Course, there was one more light-makin contrapshun down there in Mare Cooter that night. Well, now, *two*, if you's countin the headlights on Pucky Paul's veehickle an' considerin 'em as *one* light tergither. The light comin from the flashlight an' two others: the veehickle headlights an' the lamplight from a cabin wender. Whut d'ye reckon the man in the moon was thankin to hisself?

But whether or not the man in the moon was keepin a close watch that late summer night . . . an' ol' Andy he'd had it all plann'd out an' know'd to a gnat's heel where to shut off the flashlight . . . anyways they was twigs an' sprigs an' blueberry bushes an' birch-stobs an' lingonberries an' spruces an' pines an' poplars an' hazles an' rocks an' all manner o' meaty mushrooms from penny-buns an' puffers to death-caps an' earth-balls an' they was a bog-hole too where they's muskeetoes an' mouses an' louses an' snappers an' adders an' snake-grass an' goblins an' sprites an' cattles an' cowboys.

Cowboys?

Durn straight. That's us boys. The cowboys.

An' by an' by we cowboys was able to hear the Song o' the Dead Feller. Fust the cow concert, then the Song o' the Dead Feller.

Me an' Andy.
An' ol' Pucky Paul.
An' ol' KurtSquirt an' ol' Rattlebones Roger.
An' that ol' Calf. The Calf.

> One late summer night, late summer night
> She couldn't resist, she couldn't fight.
> Found her a treasure, a purty sight
> One late summer night, late summer night . . .

But . . .
Yes?
The Calf? *The Calf*, did ye say?
'Swhut I said.
But . . .

He ain't like 'ta be right in the head. Durn'd if we ain't already done said so an' said it a-plenty. Folks come along fer to fix him up. We didn't see no lick o' him at'oll fer a spell. But then one day he come back. Spos'd to be fresh as a fiddle now. Livin in his own house an' makin on all by hisself.

We had us a little powwow up at the Diner. Discussin whut it was we should oughta do about it. This was around two or three o'clock in the afternoon an' the place was purty nair squinch'd full o' folk. Blatherin old folks, rambunkshus kids off school. Mighty popular, this here Diner. We had our usual spot by the wender. Lookin out over the town square an' the collossal transformator, that big ol' boxy thang they put smack in the middle o' the square.

We's settin there discussin. One o' us gits real ril'd up. Ain't no tellin whut a gol-dang'd fool like that'll git up to, says he. Says the secont feller, we might oughta wait a spell an' see. Wait a spell an' see? says the fust feller. Whut'n the hell? Till somethin was to happen? Then a thud feller says: I'll call the Sheriff. I'll call the Sheriff tomorrow. Ain't a bad ideer, says the secont feller.

The Calf. Yessir I do rickolect the one they call'd the Calf an' who never was know'd by no 'nuther name in all the world than the Calf. An' I recall how the tough kids chas'd him out o' the Tavern that late summer night. Sent him flyin, flappin an' flailin. An' I recall whut sorta hi-kaflutin speech-bubble ol' Andy blow'd up into the air. He was meanin to believe, ol' Andy was, that this here watersogg'd Calf done drindl'd down till he was no more'n a flea-siz'd streak a-hoppin an' a-dartin across a dustcover'd teevee screen. An' swoosh, man, says Andy. Swish swoosh.

That needle-thin ol' bugger Andy, he was standin there all wibbly-wobbly an' sweatin somethin awful an' smear'd in dewkie all over an' if you was to try to discern the indervidural puzzle pieces he was made up of you'd have yerself a heckuva hard time of it without you was innisherated as to the kind of assemblidge it was you was lookin at, whut with the bleach'd an' spik'd-up hairdo, ding'd-up steelrimm'd aviater glasses, pencil-moustaches, thick brassy necklace, brown leather jacket collar, an' then, unnerneath his wide miniskirt-lookin pocoloco sweater, pokin up from a couple o' busted leather adidasses, two tennissock'd pipecleanerlegs purty nair to squirmin theirselves clean out the bottom o' them locopoco britches.

Yep, ol' Andy he was standin there all wibbly-wobbly in the bus turn-out down yonder by the fork in the road in the wee hours o' the morn.

Swish swoosh.

He stagger'd a step fo'ward, this figgure who's havin to kinda lean up aginst the other bad sweatin, dewkie-smear'd, busted-up feller, an' he snorted an' he giggl'd, ol' Andy did.

He was one or two over the limit, like as not, on top o' bein pifflecated from some weird sheeit his pappie went an' sold to us kids fer smokin. But that ain't the reason fer how come his voice got all squeakified, ol' Andy. His voice hadn't gone thru no change yet, not one lil' pip, an' ever' time he open'd his lips, even stone sober, why, it was a loudmouth'd lady ye heard.

Swish swoosh swish, says ol' Andy. An' away he goed, that ol' watersogg'd Calf, that late summer night . . . wait, naw . . . naw, naw, naw . . . up on the dustcover'd teevee screen way up yonder.

Say whut now?

They chas'd him out, says ol' Andy. They chas'd him out an' he flew an' he flapp'd an' he flail'd till abracadabra he become a flea-siz'd streak. A-jumpin an' a-hoppin all over the dustcover'd teevee screen.

Teevee screen? Whut'n the hell teevee screen is you goin on about?

That *there*, says ol' Andy whiles kinda throwin his arm out to show me the teevee screen. Everthang. Everthang above us. Everthang. *That's* the teevee screen.

The sky? I says. You mean he done gone a-jumpin an' a-hoppin an' a-swooshin up off into heaven or somethin?

Plum fool, says ol' Andy. You ain't right in the head, boy. Heaven . . .

Okey. Okey, Andy.

Okey okey okey. Okey? Whut d'ye mean okey? Belongin to a gang o' thieves? Bein a space cretur? His planit . . . Oh yeah, his planit . . . Naw, you ain't a bit right in the head. But his planit . . . Ha ha . . . his planit.

The flea-siz'd streak got hisself gone but them tough kids done figgur'd out where ol' Calfy was headed an' they caught up with him out back behind the SportsMart an' it wutn't a bit true that ol' Andy hadn't flown out too.

Flown, flapp'd, an' flail'd. Ol' Andy he up an' flew out, too.

An' so now he's standin all wibbly-wobbly an' snortin an' gigglin in the bus turn-out all dewkie-smear'd an' bad sweatin an' the sun had just woke up an' he was fixin to explain whut *reelly* had happen'd last night an' so off he goed flappin his jaw before gittin the ideer to take a lil' walk on them pipecleanerhands o' hisn an' the jacket an' sweater sorta slid down over his face an' the thick brassy necklace clank'd up aginst his aviater glasses which natcherly after two-three seccuns had done landed smack on crackin asfalt an' that was when ye seen it: the streak you woulda never took fer a flea owin to the fact that it was bigger an' swole out more, ye'd sooner've took it fer a unburr'd chestnut, the streak, the brown streak on the seat of his locopoco britches, so nicely arrang'd as it was, smack dab in the middle of the rearview, an' it was somethin else other than the greenie-brown cowhockey he'd got smear'd on his britches, yep, somethin else . . . the streak . . . chestnutbrown an' matchin his leather jacket.

Sheeit.

He tripp'd an' he said Sheeit an' he took a noshun to lay there a spell just a-kickin an' complainin. Wutn't a lick o' laffin nor grinnin left in him now. Kickin an' complainin. Just a-kickin an' complainin.

Sheeit . . . dewkie . . . clart . . . cowhockey . . . sheeit . . . weird sheeit . . . money . . . shotgun . . . want muh shotgun . . . an' Helena . . . *Helena* . . .

Okey. Wantin his shotgun. An' his money too.

Okey. Okey.

But he'p him? He'p him git back up on his pipecleanerlegs agin? Supposin matterfactually it'd been *you* tergither with him in the wee hours o' the morn in the bus turn-out, you 'stidder me, that is . . . whut would you'da done? He'p him? Naw. You wutn't a-he'pt him. I up an' left him layin there a-kickin an' complainin, I did. Plag take it. I up an' left. Went home.

If he'd a-been livin some other time they'd a-burn'd him aliv'd. Sure as we's settin here . . . We done seen him, we have. Seen him git up to somethin he shouldn't oughtta have. Out in the woods. He likes bein by hisself an' they's a spot far off in the woods an' we done seen whut he gits hisself up to out there. Survaylance camera. One o' us done put up a survaylance camera up in one o' them tall pines. Pitcher quality ain't worth a flip but anyways . . . they'd a-burn'd him aliv'd.

Norrate fer ye. I sure will, here, where I's settin. In the unnerworld. Give ye a nice lil' norration about this an' about that. An' these chain-tooth voices way down inside the 'ol wore-out metal warsh-tub noggin o' mine, they sure git down to talkin. An' ol' Andy. I'll warrant he gits down to talkin, him too.

Talkin an' talkin but *sangin*? Naw, they ain't never been able to sang. Naw, never. I know whut I's talkin bout. Back when I's a lil' bitty gnome kid I got to sangin so purty in the cattle choir . . . I mean the *childerns' choir* . . . I know very well whut this is all about. 'Twas the Dead Feller sangin. A chaintooth voice. But that ain't no matter. He was sangin, that Dead Feller. The Dead Feller down in the overgrow'd Mare Cooter Canyon.

Maybe. I's thankin, as I set down here writin a lil' somethin ever' now an' then in betwixt all the import'nt work I got to do because they done tolt me whut a import'nt job I have now, I's thankin: *Maybe we gon' git to hear him sang some more, the Dead Feller*? Maybe.

> One late summer night, late summer night
> She couldn't resist, she couldn't fight
> She couldn't fight,
> That girl, that girl . . .

Here? Yep, here. Down here in my own lil' crannynook somewhereabouts in a mazy office landscape, as 'twere dug out an' hid away from all creturs great an' small, some few hunnerd foot below the surface o' the earth, man. It's here I's settin, thankin, writin. *Here.* In my own lil' crannynook. Down in the unnerworld.

Hullo hullo mighty please to meet ye welcome welcome just come on in now.

Spinnin chair. My own desk. It ain't too shabby. An' the Janitor's been real nice. Fetch'd me a beanbag chair, he did. A mintgreen beanbag chair from the good ol' days. So if I's wantin to stretch out the ol' man-husk why all I's got to do is git it over to the far co'ner of my lil' crannynook where the Janitor musta figgur'd was as good a spot as any fer safekeepin the mintgreen beanbag chair.

Right pleasin. Knowin that it's there. On the floor, unnerneath my crookedy back. Mintgreen beanbag chair.

An' I know I done already had the thought. That the man-husk is all stretch'd out an' the meckanickal barn gnome is a-sleepin an' a-snorin an' a-dreemin . . . dreemin that he's settin in a lil' crannynook somewhereabouts in a mazy office landscape an' inside o' that dreem a dreem about a late summer night an' inside o' that dreem a daydreem, that's right, a daydreem inside o' the late summer night's dreem inside o' the wore-out metal warsh-tub noggin inside the mazy office landscape down in the unnerworld.

Jumpin jehosephat. Cussidness an' devilment an' satanity. The thought, I done had the thought. Yeah? Whut says ye?

Ye says I was plum crazy, do ye? But it wutn't *me* who was plum crazy, naw, I'll be bound it wutn't me. I'll own they's a lot that's kooky bout me, but I ain't the one who was plum crazy. Nuh-uh. Plum crazy. Somebody else who was plum crazy.

But who?

Pshaw. The Dead Feller? Ol' Andy? The Calf? Or the feller they says done built hisself a boat down in the Mare Cooter Canyon, the feller they call'd the Prophet, the feller we was gon' pay a visit that late summer night, maybe it was *him* who was plum crazy? We was gon' pay him a visit. Have ourselves a lil' coffeeclatch. I remember it now. That was where we was headed. That's whut ol' Andy said we was fixin to do. That too. The coffeeclatch . . . An' I remember it now. Whut he said, the Prophet . . .

KillerHenry?

'Twas him they call'd the Prophet. They said he built hisself a boat down in the Mare Cooter Canyon. Said he was a-waitin on the rain. Waitin on the great flood, the big diluvy . . .

Naw, wutn't me who was plum crazy. Back when I's up on the surface . . . I was just yer ever'day meckanickal push-puppet man. Ordnary to a tee. An' it's right pleasin, knowin that they's a mintgreen beanbag chair on the floor unnerneath my crookedy back.

But how'd I end up in this here office landscape? Inside the labbarinth? Down in the unnerworld? How'd they git me to take a journey jaunt down here?

Ye see, I done read this pamflit, a pamflit with all these colorful drawin's, shiny an' fanty-sheeny. Menfolks an' wimmenfolks an' childerns an' lions an' sheepies an' papa cows wi' their springer hussies an' bunnyrabbits an' kangaroos an' geeraffs an' orangertans an' them cussid ol' llamas that'll spit in yer eye if ye lean in too close an' a blue allergater, too (why blue? Naw, ain't no tellin, an' I ain't the one to ast nuther, since the pamflit don't say nuthin bout how come the allergater's blue).

The lady, the lady over there in the one recliner. 'Twas *she* who give me the pamflit. 'Twas she who tolt me I's gon' start workin someplace where they produce the kinda doojiggers such as folks want to have an' she tolt me I's got to read that there pamflit ever' mornin.

Ever' mornin?

Ever' mornin. Read that there pamflit ever' mornin.

Alright. Been readin the pamflit ever' mornin an' when the fust mornin had done hatch'd forth the fust day, that's when I started workin here, in this here labbarinth. Took a journey jaunt down an' the fust day was a workday without so much as a peep o' sunlight.

Producin an' producin an' producin.

Down in the unnerworld the word is producin. Big producin.

Suit-wairin an' fine-smellin an' buff'd-up menfolks. Producin doojiggers. Genuwine-article doojiggers. Ittybitty digital doojiggers ye can gullup down yer gullick or shove up yer cornhole so's ye can feel all halesome an' peacified in yer soul.

Money. Earnin theirselves a gashful snort o' money. Sendin the doojiggers up to the surface so folks can buy 'em an' gullup 'em down or shove 'em up theirselves an' the money it warshes down like dewkie thru sewerpipes an' spatters out in the unnerworld an' the menfolks in their fancy costy suits git the water in their mouths an' they gawp an' they gawp. Doojiggers. Only the genuwine article fer folks. Ye know fer a fact how them humanfolks up on the surface gits awful stress'd whut with all the thangs they got to do an' cain't do even tho' they an' all the folks around 'em tolt 'em they got to do it. Stress an' potherashun. So much stress an' potherashun. From the mornin to the evenin. From the evenin to the mornin. Is you awoken or is you a-sleepin? Aliv'd or dead? Naw, naw, naw, it don't make no diff'rence nohow. Ain't no lack o' stress an' potherashun to go around anyhow.

But whut's a poor feller to do? Listen up:

Poor feller, he gon' gullup down a doojigger or shove it up hisself, he will, I'll be dod.

I know whut I's talkin about. Been readin the pamflit ever' mornin, I have. An' now I know whut I's talkin about.

The lady, that lady who give me the pamflit. She know'd whut was whut, she did. The doojiggers. She explain'd an' said how I's gon' be heal'd an' my soul becalm'd. That's right, me, too. Me. My soul. An' one fine day, the day after the last day in the time whut foller'd the way-back-when, that's when it'll git free from all stress an' git to wander, my soul, that is, it'll git to wander tergither with lions an' sheepies an' a blue allergater an' other very innerestin fennomena.

Gone. Git him gone. Gone gone gone.

Yuh-huh. We done reach'd a consensis about it. We was settin at the Diner all day yesterday. Talkin bout him. We reach'd a consensis. So now we know whut we got to do. We ain just gon' skeer him, we's gon' git him gone. Hocuspocus an' the moon'll come out.

The lady. That mystickal lady. Coal-black hair layin like a long-lost laurel wreeth all 'round her face, her face paler'n the palest corpse. Her eyes. That lady set her eyes on me, she stared at me an' her eyes was like the eyes my mama had. I seen it. Had them same eyes. Nose, jaw, mouth, chin . . . her face thin, long, stiff, paler'n the palest corpse. The pamflit. She give me the pamflit to read. Outta nowhere. Outta nowhere she was there in the darkness one evenin after I'd done curl'd up on the couch in my own livin room. Outta nowhere.

Tee-shirt an' joggin britches.

I's the kind o' gnome feller who lik'd wairin a tee-shirt an' joggin britches.

A black tee-shirt. I lik'd it because it was black. Maybe a spiffy-lookin graffic over the chest an' belly. Some kinda rock an' roll graffic from the way-back-when. A symbol o' some kind.

The joggin britches. Them's black too, my joggin britches. Glossy, able to withstand all manner o' splatterment.

Such a turrible slop-dozzler. Whuther I's drankin or eatin. Slobberin slobberin slobberin. But I always kep' me a wrung-out warsh-rag by the ol' coffee table, so before curlin myself up I'd use it to wipe up the slobberins an' soon enuff I's a-grinnin an' a-hummin an' them joggin britches was just as bright an' shiny as could be agin. I done drank an' et an' it sure as heck wutn't no moonshine in that jug I's drankin out of. Noway hosay. More'n likely some cheap sassprilluh. I pick'd up the jug . . . drank . . . sassprilluh . . . an' I et. Bustid open a big bag o' tater chips an' started noshin 'em down. Onion-flavor'd. Nom. An' I's slobberin slobberin slobberin. I took up the warshrag. An' when I's done wi' the warshrag I curl'd myself up. On the couch in my own livin room. An' there she was, man. Outta nowhere.

The lady. Her face. Shinin, her face was shinin. Shinin like a pale sharp moon in the darkness. Lady. That lady. Her.

It's right satisfactual to go an' set a spell at the Diner. It's bright an' halesome inside an' the coffee's good whuther ye take creem in it or not an' if ye'd like a bate to eat well just lookit all the choices ye got to choose from. Op'n-face sammiches. Cheeses hams weeners shrimps an' sallits . . . an' natcherly all the Danish kringle an' Norweegin custerd buns an' Napoleon cakes an' muffins ye could ast fer . . . I tell ye whut, boy. it sure is right satisfactual to go an' set a spell at the Diner. Bright an' halesome. An' we's part o' the regulars now.

Regulars, we is. All them choices to choose from. An' so much to talk about. Durn'd if they ain't lots to talk about. Durn'd if they ain't.

That late summer night. All them yesterdays ago. Yesterdays an' yesternights. I tried to fergit. Tried. But by an' by I ended up here. By an' by. The office landscape, the labbarinth. By an' by the unnerworld. I'd done drag'd wi' me the ol' rotted-out man-husk an' I drag'd him futher along after he got hisself stuck inside the ellavater, boy. Stuck.

That Janitor feller, him who done fetch'd me the mintgreen beanbag chair, one o' them old-fangl'd Janitors with his wool-cap cock'd to one side, his overall coat, an' a everlastin pair o' khaki britches . . . 'twas him who rescu'd me an' I drag'd the ol' man-husk wi' me . . . futher an' futher . . . slow an' easy . . . thru the tunnel . . . thru the tunnel . . .

Lawd a' mercy. Was it then, maybe, when I's stuck inside the ellavater . . . was *that* when it become so dadgum impossable to quit rememberin?

The right hand. The artifisshul right hand. It done scratch'd down a few names down on this here piece o' paper, the artifisshul right hand.

Pale an' sinewy artifisshul right hand. Lookit. Lookit that hand. Poor lil' booger. I feel a ittybitty bit bad fer it. A teenyweeny bit. Well, anyhow. The names. A few dumbassid names an' a chaintooth voice way down inside this 'ol wore-out metal warsh-tub noggin o' mine that says' ye got to read them names slow an' easy an' it says, the voice, that them names don't mean nuthin, nuthin at'oll . . .

Andy. Pucky Paul. KurtSquirt. Rattlebones Roger. An' that ol' Calf. The Dead Feller. An' ol' KillerHenry.

An' ol' Helena, Helena Bunnykins . . . had herself a purty nair meaningless name, too.

Fine. I remember names like that even tho' they ain't got no meanin to 'em. Names like that. An' lots more names besides. More? Yep. I was standin there, stuck in the ellavater. Naw, I *lay there* stuck in the ellavater. I lay there. Tucker'd out. Kaput. My nebbynose was pointin straight up an' I seen the rotted-out man-husk hoverin above me. Seen it mirrorwise. Tucker'd out. Kaput. My nebbynose pointin straight down. Say whut? Whut d'ye mean, say whut? Whut I mean to say is . . . *mirrors*. They'd done put up mirrors an' not just up on the ceilin nuther, nuh-uh, but all over the walls, the floorin: mirror mirror mirror. Well, I'll be switch'd. A mirror cabinet fer a ellavater. An' that's just whut the Janitor said. That was the fust thang out o' his mouth when he come an' rescue'd me:

Woah nelly, whut kind o'picklement you go an'git yerself into? Is you standin there stuck inside the mirror cabinet?

Lay. I should oughtta have tolt him I lay there stuck an' whut's more I's layin there a allfar'd long spell too an' where in the hell'd you done shuck'd off to anyhow? The husk. The rotted-out man-husk. Tucker'd out. Kaput. Hoverin above me. An' my soul. My soul was somewhere in there, too, fer sertin. Sweet jaysis. Cain't hardly believe it. That *you* was a-hoverin above me, I mean. Somewhere in there. You.

Maybe. Maybe *that* was when it become so dadgum impossable to quit rememberin? Ol' Andy an' ol' Pucky Paul an' ol' KurtSquirt an' ol' Rattlebones Roger. They was a-hoverin, them too.

That's whut I's thankin now, anyhow, settin here bout two-three days later. They was a-hoverin. Cowboys. Genuwine cowboys. That's whut we was. In the way-back-when.

So them cowboys was a-hoverin an' I recogniz'd 'em all, too, ol' Andy an' the rest of 'em. Ol' Andy, I know'd it was him dreckly. He hover'd up there right next to my man-husk lookin teeteeteetotally like hisself. Needle-thin as all-git-out. Spik'd-up hairdo, aviater glasses, pencil-moustaches, along with all them other crudcover'd puzzle pieces an' it wouldn't a-surpris'd me none if he had the chestnutbrown streak on the seat of his locopoco britches still.

I seen him. But didn't hear him, ye see. Or, naw, I did hear him. But not at fust. Look'd to me like he was noddin off, hoverin up there an' noddin off. Or maybe I's spos'd to reckon he was dead? Ol' Andy, ol'Andy dead? Huh.

I seen him. He hover'd up there next to the ol' man-husk an' I seen all of 'em all at once, recogniz'd ever' one of 'em, too. Ol' Pucky Paul an' ol' KurtSquirt an' ol' Rattlebones Roger. An' that ol' Calf.

Natcherly. I know I done already had the thought. Coulda been because I's a-sleepin. My man-husk didn't have to feel so lonesome up there because I was sleepin inside the mirror cabinet, just a-snorin an' a-dreemin an' that's how the ol' man-husk got hisself some company from them fellers just like that one time, one late summer night . . .

> They was jumpin an' hoppin
> An' trippin an' floppin'
> One night, one night,
> One late summer night . . .

Jumpin an' hoppin. Had to a-been. Naw, the Calf wutn't jumpin an' hoppin an' trippin an' floppin all by hisself, couldn't a-been, nuther.

Ol' Andy an' ol' Pucky Paul an' ol' KurtSquirt an' ol' Rattlebones Roger an' this feller, the feller that these chaintooth voices way down inside the 'ol wore-out metal warsh-tub noggin o' mine declare has got to be radick'ly diff'rent than the feller *I* declare he's got to be, that is, *me*, I declare he's got to be me, I declare an' declare an' keep on declarin it. But they . . . they declare he's got to be . . . well . . . all right . . .

Brr. I was a-sleepin an' I was a-dreemin an' that's all but if I was a-sleepin an' a-snorin an' a-dreemin too then wouldn't I have woke up agin by an' by? Or whut? Whut says ye? D'ye thank I coulda been a-sleepin an' a-dreemin withouten I e'er woke up agin?

The ellavater. Mirror cabinet. I lay, I look'd, an' this meckanickal barn gnome, native to Hadeland, settin here in his lil' crannynook . . . that feller who's a-thankin an' a-writin in betwixt all the import'nt work he gots to do . . . says he been awake this whole time.

Awake.

He'p. Hullo.

Cowboys was hoverin above his nebbynose. He lay there hopin somebody could hear him. He'p. Hullo.

But he wutn't functionin right, this feller from Gran. His longs was rattlin an' it was all he could do to barely bring out a holler fer somebody to come an' he'p him. Hullo.

Ol' Andy an' ol' Pucky Paul an' ol' KurtSquirt an' ol' Rattlebones Roger an' a fith creature an' yet another creature, man. They was all hoverin. They done stretch'd theirselves out an' was kinda sorta driftin in mid-air, face-down. Kinda sorta. Or kinda like they all got their own beanbag chair an' ol' Andy done slung it up over hisself like some big strong feller in a milk-churn-throwin contest but the beanbag chair didn't come down but stay'd hangin from some glassy dyaphram or some kinda funny-lookin see-thru stuff that somebody'd done flung betwixt heaven an' earth like some witch's cape an' so then Andy'd done foller'd after it an' the others had to do like he done an' slung their beanbag chairs up over theirselves so they's all stretch'd out an' hoverin like constellashuns on a map o' the celestyull sfeer with dee-tail'd drawins of how them constellashuns is spos'd to look in real life.

Hullo?

. . .

A sound. A lurch. The ellavater. Down. Last couple o' yards.

. . .

Yes?

. . .

Hullo, yes?

. . .

Woah nelly, whut kind o' picklement you go an' git yerself into? Is you standin there stuck inside the mirror cabinet?

The Janitor. That old-fangl'd jokin Janitor. Used to see him on the dustcover'd teevee screen back in the way-back-when. Full to bustin with all manner o' funny repartay. Spine stiff as a poke stalk. Pussle-gutted. Stove-up knees but still quick-footed. He know'd somethin wutn't right. He come on down.

Stuck? Yeah. Naw, I . . .

Up up up ye go now. Cain't lay down here all puny an'weak, not when they's a whole workday ahead o' us an' so on an' so futh. My hand, here. Up up up ye go now pardner.

Pardner? Naw, I . . .

I's just funnin wi' ye. Ye's able to git up now, ain't ye? My hand. Take aholt o' my hand now. Here ye done arrov'd. They's waitin on ye an' the Boss-Man . . . he ain't in the best o' moods. Ye's prob'ly fixin to git chew'd out but they ain't a whole lot o' grinnin down here nohow so it ain't no matter if the Boss-Man was to chew ye out. Ha ha. Ain't no matter. Come on, now. Up up up ye go.

Now. Up up up . . .

Lookee there, now. There ye go. Lookee here. My hand. Take aholt o' my hand, now. My hand. There ye go. Ahhhhhh rightrightright yesindeedy you's the new feller they said was a-comin . . . so that's you, all right. You the new feller. But . . . yer hand . . . it's cold as a tin can, buddy . . . whut kinda innvenshun is you spos'd to be anyhow? Gnome, troll, human, animal, or robot?

Pshaw. I thank I can say . . .

Space cretur?

Pshaw. I thank . . .

Ahhhhhh right. Rightrightright. Heydiddlediddle indeedily doo. Hullo hullo mighty please to meet ye welcome welcome just come on in now. This is where I putter an' potter. Back an' futh. Back an' futh. Lots to do I tell ye. Ever' minute somethin to do. A few days ago, just a few days ago . . . d'ye know whut happen'd? Naw, course ye don't. A few days ago, just a few days ago . . . I's putterin an' potterin an' the ellavater come along, that's right, the ellavater come like it come just now an' do ye know who was inside the mirror cabinet? Naw, course ye don't. It was the King. The King hisself. The old King. The old King hisself. He come fer to pay our menfolks a visit. An' I's the one wishin him welcome. So I git down on one knee an' I spread out my arms an' bow down real low an' says: *Ruh ruh ruh royall Muh muh ma just ee, wuh wuh wuh welcome.* An' the old vennerble King he gits somethin stuck in his throat, I tell ye, the old mole he takes to a-hackin an' a-hockin an' a-rattlin somethin pittiful, says: *Ih ihhh dyaagh*. An' I says: *Whut's that ye say? Ye done up an' died on us*? Ha ha. Ye unnerstand? Ha ha. Don't believe me? Ha ha. Let's go, huh?

Go? Okey . . .

Yer hat. Yer cowboy hat. Don't fergit that cowboy hat, now. Lookit. Here ye go.

A long corrider, a tunnel. Concrete. A handful o' ittybitty lights was dottin all along the walls plus the Janitor had done switch'd on a flashlight. His wool-cap was cock'd an' a hickory dickory dock. An' the old feller's spine reelly was stiff as a poke stalk, I'll swear to it. An' pussle-gutted he was too, fer real, man. An' his overall coat, I ain't foolin. With a lil' piruwett he was ready to go irregardless o' the swole-up knees an' was gone before I even had the chance to holler that they ain't no way in hell I's able keep up with him . . . swoosh, gone, awayward-ho, man. Not even a squeek from the rubbersoles o' his shoes. Awayward-ho. Him an' the flashlight.

Alrighty now. Arrov'd.

Ol' Janitor'd said I'd arrov'd.

Arrov'd . . . uh huh . . . at the *other* end of the tunnel . . . an' the voices way down inside the 'ol wore-out metal warsh-tub noggin o' mine take to talkin talkin talkin mostly sayin I best turn round now an' start draggin the ol' man-husk back to the ellavater an' mash the button on it. The up button. Up up up an' away. Weird ol' booger, that Janitor. Rescuin me, wishin me welcome, an' then gittin th' heck outta dodge. Fine. I'll git on all by myself. Operate my own self I will. Fo'ward. On I drag the ol' man-husk an' I ain't headed downways no more but straight ahead. I see the ittybitty lights dottin the walls all the way.

We's a gang whut meets ever' day, all year long. Them uppercrust folks done study'd us an' determin'd that we's the kinda gang ye'd name fer a solid brotherhood. An' them uppercrust folks know whut they's talkin bout.

Solid brotherhood. They stopp'd in one day when the birdsong was just gittin ratchited up agin after a few days o' thunderin an' rainin. Lil' birdies had been a-sangin all summer long . . . but it was only after a spell o' bad weather that it even occurr'd to us. How them lil' birdies wutn't sangin as much as they done wi' the sun out. But then it got nice agin an' them uppercrust folks they stopp'd in fer a chat.

They brung with 'em their cameras an' microfones fer to innerview us fer a show. Teevee an' all.

We's settin in the Diner. They come all in an' ast if we'd talk to 'em about politics an' suchlike. Aggracultural policy. Immigrayshun . . . An' they ast us if we had any commint on the hubbub in the board o' suppervisers. They done read some stuff in the local paper an' now they's wantin to know if we'd cyair to make commint.

One o' us fellers got kinda ril'd up an' started goin on bout aggracultural policy, immigrayshun, the hubbub in the board o' suppervisers, u.f.o.'s, an' space creturs.

But lookit the camera? Durn'd if he wouldn't. He kep' his eyes down at his coffee cup, kep' his eyes down like he's lookin fer somethin in it.

An' lo an' behold we was on teevee. Brotherhood. Solid brotherhood. Them uppercrust folks done study'd us an' seen fer theirselves, they did.

Gittin on all by myself. Operatin my own self. Like as not the only thang I can do. Just like I did before I stumbl'd into the ellavater too, back when I's still locater'd up on the surface.

The lady. The lady said I got to skedaddle off to work. I protested best I could, said:

Skedaddle? Ain't ye done seen whut I look like?

But by an' by I done like she said. Wi' the cowboy hat yank'd down over my top lid. Slow an' easy . . . down the road . . . up the slope . . . round the bend . . . thisaway an' thataway . . . slow an' easy . . . a wairy jaunt. I got on all by myself an' operated my own self an' I'll own it was me an' me alone who took this motoriz'd lawnmower without astin permishun, a rustid ol' red one with a driver seat an' a styairin wheel an' four misshelin tires, matter o' fact ye might mistake him fer a mini tractor or a.t.v. or one o' them motoriz'd wheelchairs.

Me. Me alone. Was *me*, buddy, me who took the lawnmower without astin permishun. Me.

The lawnmower. Park'd in the middle o' the yard in front of a ordnary twofloor house by the side of a narrer road or side-path I's draggin the ol' man-husk down an' it was clear as could be that the feller who'd done park'd there (the son, I figgur'd, the oldest son in the house) hadn't finish'd the job since they was still a good-siz'd patch o' grass pushin up wild an' tall in betwixt the palin an' the lawnmower, pushin up toward the onbeclouded clear blue sky up above my cowboy hat an' it bein a powerful fine mornin I took to whistlin as I push'd open the front gate an' so after I'd look'd around an' was satisfy'd they wutn't nary a soul in the house nor the carport nor no nuther place nuther I dragg'd 'em along wi' me, my legs that is, still a-whistlin an' feelin finer an' more 'lectrick than I'd done felt in a long time, more meckanickal, an' the one leg was wantin to burrow itself into the fresh-mow'd part o' the grass an' the other leg into the part o' the grass still growin wild an' tall an' the lawnmower stood red an' rustid right in front o' me an' they wutn't no way I's gon' turn back round now, that decision had done been made, boy, so I check'd the gastank an' it was purty nair full an' then lo an' behold I found me a gascan tied to the back o' the mower an' the gascan it was full, *full to the very rim* an' that just about beat all fer luck so I straddl'd wide as I could over the buggy an' shazam I's perch'd on the driver's seat an' it wutn't no trubble startin the motor an' I swerv'd over to the side-path an' after a minute or two at a nice an' easy speed I burrup'd out onto the main road I know'd I's spos'd to foller feelin mighty fine drivin a lawnmower an' it bein so nice out an' the cowboy hat yank'd down over my top lid an' it goed purty good the fust mile or two, I stopp'd an' fill'd the gastank before drivin on an' I's feelin purty good about everthang but later on, when the pickup come with brakes a-screechin an' a big ol' musslebound splutteratin fussyfied feller with a green trucker hat an' shiny sunglasses clumb out an' holler'd he's fixin to murder me, well, then I wutn't feelin too good no more, naw, wutn't feelin too good at'oll.

A wairy jaunt. This here musslebound Splutterfusserer he turn'd an' drove off. Left me kickin in the ditch where I could feel another dent had done been made in the ol' wore-out metal warsh-tub noggin. I cut out the kickin. Staggl'd back up on my feet. Found my cowboy hat. I had to git to where that lady in the recliner done tolt me I had to git to but now without no lawnmower to drive the rest o' the way.

The Splutterfusserer. He flung me down in the ditch an' trampl'd his sunglasses all to pieces after droppin 'em on crackin asfalt an' took to cussin like a tetchy ol' western Norweegin once he realiz'd whut it was crunchin unner them army boots which I could see he hadn't tied too good an' then he up an' hove the mower up on his pickup.

I lay there kickin in the ditch. He drove off. I cut out the kickin. I flung away a palmleaf-siz'd dandelion leaf that the ol' artifisshul right hand had done tore out o' the ground, only a seccun or two before I seen the whole ground was cover'd wi' dandelion leaves an' the dandelion leaves was all cover'd in exhaust dustins. Dandelion Ditch. Musslebound Splutterfusserer'd done flung me down into the Dandelion Ditch. I'd done been layin there a-kickin. I'd done cut out the kickin an' took up the wairy jaunt agin. Slow an' easy . . . down the road . . . up the slope . . . round the bend . . . thisaway an' thataway . . . slow an' easy . . .

An' then I caught sight o' a sign. The Logo. I caught sight o' the Logo. The pamflit. I'd done read the pamflit an' now I's catchin sight o' the Logo. That was the Logo, all right. I had to git to the ginormous buildin the arrer on the sign was pointin towards.

A castle. Some folks mighta nam'd that ginormous buildin fer a castle.

The castle. A outta-proporshun creemcusterd layercake castle. Like as not it'd been a hotel in the way-back-when with lots o' rooms an' numerus fasilities, a vast hotel such as folks from way over yonder who'd wander'd too far out on this side o' the 'tater field before it turn'd into a hotel woulda been spell-bound, posatively spell-bound to look at such a eksquizzit farmhouse, a farmhouse such as later would be built out an' made bigger an' more moderniz'd an' more eksquizzit (a hotel), mmhmm, the farmhouse on a big ol' farm, before the creemcusterd layercake become even more splendifferus wi' the addishun of a huge barn an' a huge meathouse on steddle stones an' the garden was mezmerizin too owin to them big ol' appletrees standin in the middle of it, a whole bunch o' big ol' appletrees with big red apples I seen hangin heavy an' shinin in the sun an' boy I tell ye whut, it was a big temptashun fer many a hongry push-puppet gnome-doll man to see them big ol' apples.

Lawd a mercy did I e'er git a hankerin fer a apple. A powerful hankerin. But it wutn't the time fer it, right then. I ain't no durn'd fool, nuther. So I leave off a-pilferin apples from my new employer an' fer all I know they's plenty o' apples fer the havin durin the lunch break since that they's a spesify'd place inside o' this here ginormous buildin fer gatherin an' talkin bout all manner o' topics consernin' creturs an' humans an' livin a stressfree life an' bein a good friend an' earnin a good sallery a real sallery a fur sallery. I'd done read the pamflit the lady give me an' soon . . . soon I'd be thankin an' thankin bout the late summer night . . .

In the garden so spayshus
They sang all tergither.
One an' fer all
Tergither, tergither . . .

An' then I arrov'd. They's talkin. Some few hunnerd foot below the surface o' the earth. Fellers was talkin an' jawin an' show'd me where I's gon' set. Stone-deef. I made like I couldn't hear nuthin at'oll.

Nuh-uh, nuthin at'oll. An' I ain't foolin, nuther: I's purty good at pertendin I's somethin other than whut I reelly is, man.

Playactin. I remember somebody tellin me one time Lawd knows how many years ago that I oughtta go to school fer it. Playactin. I'd done got thru tellin a tall tale an' put on one o' them looseykoftee sweaters an' him who was a-fixin to say somethin smart bout goin to school (a feller they ain't no room in this here norration fer to tell bout an' don't make no diff'rence nohow) took to rummagin around inside mama's closet fer more stuff an' he pull'd out this an' he pull'd out that an' it was awful fun, man. We's a-grinnin. We's a-laffin. Snortin. I made a funny face an' studied myself in the mirror, the mirror on the wall in mama's bedroom an' him who by now was goin on an' on bout goin to school fer playactin he sorta hunker'd down low on his hanches an' jump'd up onto the bed, in the mirror, behind my funnyface, jumpin up an' down, man. I grinn'd an' laff'd an' snorted an' couldn't hardly catch my breath an' took to coughin an' hackin like some ol' codger whose legs is ruin'd by the ol' arthur an' I's tryin, tryin to ast him to come over an' swollop me on the back when lo an' behold his britches split clean down the middle, boy. Them creemyeller corderoy britches o' hisn split clean down the middle an' boy if he didn't look just like a broody ol' goose whiles standin there in the middle o' mama's bed an' it was just like the goose had done froze up an' time come to a stand-still an' now they was a-bellerin into the right ear an' into the left ear one feller after the other took to a-bellerin an' I said whut an' I said say whut now an' everthang they done already said while they's a-bellerin, from A to Z, everthang they done said, they *kep 'on* sayin it over an' over agin.

Here, they said. Set down right here. In this here crannynook. Here. Yer own desk an' spinnin chair. Just set yerself right here.

Say whut?

Set down. Set yerself down, now.

> One an' fer all
> Tergither, tergither.
> One an' fer all . . .

Okey, so I set myself down. They talk'd an' talk'd, them suit-wairin menfolks. I set there prob'ly thankin that it was these chaintooth voices way down inside this 'ol wore-out metal warsh-tub noggin o' mine that was talkin an' talkin. Prob'ly I thunk so. Prob'ly wutn't quite believin that such fine-smellin folks as could write such purty words about lions an' sheepies could carry on so, bellerin an' commandin me like that.

Set down. Set yerself down, now.

I set myself down.

Git yerself up.

I got myself up. Nice an' slow.

Set yerself down.

I set myself down.

Git yerself up.

I got myself up.

Set yerself down.

I set myself down.

Yerself.

Myself.

Nice an' slow.

Turrible quality but anyways. They's one an' the same, this ghostly booger we seen on the survaylance camera an' that ol' sumbitch we been sayin since always-ago oughtta be sent back to the planit folks says he come from. Naw, they ain't no doubt about it. It's him, all right. Out at the spot far off in the woods where he likes to hang out whiles gittin up to somethin he shouldn't oughtta. Him. It's him. But just whut it is he's a-gittin up to in this here camera footige . . . naw they ain't . . . ain't no tellin but it's some kinda funny bizness, some kinda funny bizness he ain't spos'd to be gittin up to.

Lookit. That's his chest. Done took off his shirt an' jacket an' there he goes a-widdle-waddlin bare-chestid lookin like he done smear'd his paunch all over wi' dewkie.

Dewkie. Wouldn't a-surpris'd us none if it were his own dewkie nuther. Or else cowhockey. Maybe they's a couple o' fresh turds on the path he done he'p'd hisself to, bent hisself down an' had hisself a time smatherin all over hisself. Could also be paint or maybe markins from a sharpie. Naw, they ain't no tellin an' they ain't no knowin nuther.

But whutever it is he's a-gittin up to in this here footige, it ain't nuthin he spos'd to be gittin up to. That's fer damn sure. An' we who's a-watchin, we says all tergither: Whut'd we tell ye? Whut'd we tell ye? Send him back. Send him back.

Them voices. How many they is? Durn'd if I know. Cain't count 'em. Ain't no good with numbers an' cain't say as I e'er been nuther, or whut say you? Holy cow, cowboy, ye can thank fer yerself whut'd happen if somebody was to try an' make a rotted-out man-husk start countin numbers. Me? Screakin an' puffin an' pantin an' snufflin like a saddleback'd hoss as he tries to start countin only to stumble, stumble an' start countin all over agin only to stumble agin, countin stumblin countin. Talkin. They's talkin an' they's chewin on the thought I know I done already thunk: *Not a thang. Rotted-out man-shell dreemin dreemin dreemin . . .*

How many they is? Naw, cain't count 'em. But they's got to be enuff that a feller can talk about 'em in such a way as to bring some semblens o' order among all the chaos. Community. They's a whole community in here, inside the ol' wore-out metal warsh-tub noggin. Two- an' four- an' six- an' eight- an' thousan'-legg'd creturs an' houses both big an' small an' roads narrer an' wide an' all manner o' popular gatherin places. Yep. They done built theirselves a community, too, them voices. They built an' they arrov'd at a consensis. Whut's right an' whut's wrong. Community. Church. School. Sheriff's office. Credit union. An' one o' them big corperate banks, too. An' a town hall. An' a newspaper office. An' five-an'-dime stores an' a recreashun center an' a firestashun an' a hospital an' a courthouse an' a jail an' a castle. Sewers. Got them too. Huge pipes unner the earth. Sewers. An' unner the sewers is figgurs who ain't never seen no daylight an' cain't even see it in their wildest dreems nohow.

Lookit. Lookit, man. Lookit. Lookit his hand. Lookit it tremblin. Lookit. Lookit, man. Lookit.

Artifisshul right hand wi' the pencil stump gripp'd betwixt three dead fingers. A-tremblin an' a-bunglin an' a-scratchin down scrawny crookid gashly-lookin letters on this here paper that the rotted-out man-husk in his crannynook natcherly shoulda put thru the shredder the very fust day among the unnerworldly creturs an' they's fixin to be nuts an' bolts an' screws strew'd out all over the wax'd floor an' the whole right hand it clatters clean off an' the voices says that this ol' Hobblestiltskin done got tangled up in the late summer night, all tangled up in some yarn he like'ta just spun all by hisself.

Them. The voices. They says I got to fergit. Fergit, they says. Fergit. Best be fergittin.

Lawd only knows how long I done tried. Fer a long time, a long,

long time, I tried to fergit. Playactin. Shoulda took up playactin. Shoulda went to school fer it, I should. Playactin. Supremo playactin. Fergit. Fergit the late summer night an' fergit the one they call'd the Calf an' who never was know'd by no 'nuther name in all the world than the Calf, naw never . . .

But then I come here. Got permisshun to begin agin down here, begin workin an' earnin a honest day's dewkie, even tho' it was all over an' done with.

Here. In my crannynook down in the unnerworldly office landscape, the labbarinth.

The Calf. An' the girl, that girl . . .

> Found her a treasure, whut a purty sight
> One late summer night, late summer night
> She found a treasure
> A treasure, a treasure . . .

The Calf? Did you reelly say *the Calf*?

Yessir. The Calf. I seen him that late summer night. Fust I seen him . . . yeah-huh . . . an' then . . . an' then finally behind the Sports-Mart. I seen him kick off his benastied slippers, seen him wriggle outta his jacket an' his shirt too, an' I'll be dogg'd if he didn't wriggle outta his jeans too, man, a pair o' them stonewarsh'd scuff'd-up an' bedraggl'd bluejeans, ye see. He quiver'd. He quak'd. He was havin a fit.

But skeer'd? Skeer'd?

Naw, man. Wutn't a bit skeer'd. He was havin a fit. Havin hisself a big ol' fit.

An' he wutn't no flea-siz'd streak on no dustcover'd teevee screen nuther.

Naw, man. To hell with all that. To hell with whut ol' Andy

said. Sooner send up a poisanous gas-cloud toward that hi-kaflutin speech-bubble ol' Andy blow'd up into the air an' in some ways is still there today. Swish swoosh, said ol' Andy. *An' away he goed, this here watersogg'd Calf, in the late summer night . . . or naw . . . naw naw naw . . . on the dustcover'd teevee screen. Naw.*

The Calf. I seen him there behind the SportsMart, there, wi' this funny sort o' light a-glowin all around him like it do a space cretur who done took a wrong turn somewhere, an' it got real bright all of a sudden, a sight more bright than on yer ordnary moonlit late summer night. Ordnary? Pshaw. Dark but not pitch black. Ordnary moonlight. I thank. But the moon . . . if the moon was out? If the man in the moon was keepin a close watch? Ah. Lots o' thangs I done tried to fergit. Tried an' tried an' the only thang I's able to fergit . . . the moon . . . the man in the moon. The Calf. He's standin there, in the light, this space cretur in his kendalgreen unnerbritches that wouldn't hardly stay up no more an' one tennissock roll'd down to his heel an' the other sock lookin to me like a mongrel's tongue all dead an' shriveldy stickin outta the mouth o' his slip-on shoe.

> Mongreltongue mongreltongue
> Shrivelingalinga shrivelingalanga.
> Mongreltongue mongreltongue
> Ding dong dead.

More'n likely. That's whut they says. Says I *more'n likely* seen a lost space cretur wi' light all around him one late summer night. More'n likely. Don't make no diffrence. They says all kinda funny thangs, them voices . . . An' these suit-wairin menfolks they git down to all kind o' big doins down here in the office landscape an' they look a awful lot like them swaggerin pissants up on the surface too . . .

They says all kind o' funny thangs, these suit-wairin menfolks who look suspishushly like them swaggerin pissants up on the surface.

Smellin fine.

An' oncommonly buff'd up too, each an' ever' one of 'em. Oncommonly. Yessir, if you's aimin to strut around in one o' them nice fancy suits then ye best be exercisin, best be liftin the metal pole. Cain't git yer britches to fit ye, cain't git yer coat to fit ye lessun you been liftin the metal pole each an' ever' day. An' natcherly they's a place within the labbarinth where they make ye lift the metal pole each an' ever' day. Course I ain't in no kind o' keepin to lift nuthin like 'at, matter o' fact this here man-husk he's the exact ahpasit o' the kind o' man-husk whut goes a-liftin the metal pole each an' ever' day. My belly's all big an' round, swole-up, ye see, just as spongey an' squishy-squoshy as could be an' the system o' guts inside o' there ain't worth much of a flip nuther an' I ain't in no kind o' keepin to go liftin the metal pole noway nohow.

Praise the Lawd. I arrov'd. A wairy jaunt. Lawnmower. Musslebound Splutterfusserer. Creemcusterd layercake castle. Garden. Apples. Ellavater. I done dragg'd wi' me the ol' rotted-out man-husk through the tunnel. Janitor. He got hisself gone. Become shadow. An' I had to git on all by myself. Operate my own self. Brr. It took time. *It takes time.* To git there.

The menfolks. Four or five suit-wairin fine-smellin buff'd-up menfolks. I thank: *They's prob'ly waitin on me at the other end o' the tunnel.*

That lady'd done give the man-husk the low-down. I know'd they's somebody waitin on me. Waitin on this here man-husk an' whiles I's a-draggin him thru the tunnel . . . I's runnin awful late, I was, awful late, an' whiles I's a-draggin the rotted-out man-husk thru' the tunnel I kep' on a-thankin an' a-thankin: *They's waitin on me, them fellers, they's prob'ly waitin on me. But was they waitin on me that one time? Ol' Andy an' ol' Pucky Paul an' ol' KurtSquirt an' ol' Rattlebones Roger? Was they waitin on me?*

An' at the other end o' the tunnel they startid up wi' the barkin an' the jawin. All of a sudden. I squinch'd up because *bang*, when they startid up wi' up the barkin an' the jawin, why they was still invizable, ever' one of 'em. Woah nelly, now there's noise, now there's fixin to be a whuppin. Yessiree-bob. Brr. Bout four or five of 'em. Barkin an' barkin an' jawin an' jawin an' then they lit up their flashlights an' ever' one of 'em put it right up unner their chins makin funny faces an' then they wutn't invizable no more.

Arrov'd. *Now* I done arrov'd.

Whuppin? Naw, wutn't nobody gittin no whuppin. They kep' on barkin an' barkin an' jawin an' jawin an' bellerin an' bellerin an' made some more funny faces an' open'd the door an' turn'd off the flashlights an' flung 'em away donkdonkdonk down the tunnel an' took aholt o' my arm grippin it hard an' they dragg'd the man-husk off into the flickerin lamplight.

Office landscape. Such a pandemoniacal office landscape labbarinth.

Bingo. An' sometimes it do hurt a body to go operatin hisself.

Bout two-three days ago, all this. They dragg'd me in, a-bellerin an' bellerin. I set myself down where they said I's spos'd to be settin. There. *Here*. Here in the crannynook. Yessir. It ain't the fust time I been took aholt of an' took away, ye see, that ain't the kind o' thang ye fergit. They come on down to my mama's house an' took me, some mussleheads who said it was best thataway. I's screamin. I's screamin an' my mama's screamin an' my sister's screamin. We scream'd all tergither. But them mussleheads didn't take no heed. An' they was right. They didn't need to ast my mama whuther it was okey. The Law was on their side. They know'd whut they was a-doin. They come a couple o' weeks after ol' Andy an' me had done been down by the Sheriff. That Sheriff, his face was grey. Grey an' wrinkledy like some dang ol' durty warshrag someone done left on the kitchen counter all cover'd with greasy mugs an' bowls an' knives an' forks an' ladles an' he wanted to know, the Sheriff did, if we happen'd to hear anythang or see anythang but naw, we hadn't heard a thang nor seen no thang nuther.

An' the Calf?

Nope, not a thang, says ol' Andy.

Not a thang, says I.

An' whut about the cows, boys? Y'all seen anythang? Heard anythang?

Nuh-uh, says ol' Andy. Not a thang.

Not a thang.

So y'all don't know a thang bout who done broke into the cabin nuther, do y'all?

Nope. Don't know a thang. Not a thang. Nuh-uh.

My own desk, man. Got me one o' them spinnin chairs, too. Pencils. An' a pencil sharp'ner, a big ol' green one with a lil' crank ye turn on it, just like the one Miss Teacher had on up on the lectern in the way-back-when. I remember Miss Teacher. Her lectern. I's settin down here in the unnerworld a-thankin an' a-thankin bout a late summer night an' I rickolect Miss Teacher, her lectern, an' the green pencil sharp'ner with a lil' crank ye turn'd on it. But Miss Teacher . . . she wutn't there, man, down in the Mare Cooter Canyon . . . wutn't in the Tavern nuther, wutn't noplace at'oll . . . Well well. I remember the green pencil sharp'ner with a lil' crank ye turn'd on it. Paper. Pair o' sizzers.

I make like a stone-deef hillbilly. Hunch'd over an' crookid. I git down to workin. Sharp'nin the pencils. Cuttin the paper, shreddin the paper. Not a thang. *Y'all seen anythang? Heard anythang?* Nuh-uh. Not a thang. The cabin. Not a thang. Ain't neither of us know'd a thang. I's a-sharp'nin. I's a-clippin. I's a-shreddin. That's whut they done tolt me to do. Said:

Sharpen the pencils. Shred the paper. That's whut ye gon' do. An' coffee. Ye gon' git up once ever' hour an' crank up the coffeepot. The fellers who work down here have got to have bilin hot coffee an' ye gon' go round once ever' hour an' serve it to 'em.

Say whut?

Coffee. Serve 'em coffee.

Playactin. I ain't half bad at it. A stone-deef geezer, why I's a natcheral fer that part. Ho ho. Looseykoftee sweater an' all. Naw. Naw naw naw. A busseyroll shirt. A tatter'd busseyroll shirt with chaw-stains all down the front. Chaw, man. Real chaw, man. An' the streaks ain't flea-siz'd, the streaks all down the busseyroll is bigger, big as unburr'd chestnuts maybe, just like the streak on the seat o' ol' Andy's loco-poco britches. They's barkin, they's jawin, they's bellerin an' in the past few days they been sayin all kind o' funny thangs.

He's spinnin yarns.

That's whut they says.

He's a-dreemin. Gittin all tangled up.

That's whut they been tellin me. About how I been spinnin yarns. How I don't know the which from the other bout nuthin an' how I don't do nuthin but spin yarns. About how I's dreemin.

I'll be dadgum, I hear one of 'em say. Is you settin down here dreemin an' gittin all tangled up? Well well well I'll be dadgum. Is you settin here?

Say whut? says I. I says Say whut whenever somebody's talkin loud an' bossin me around an' the voices in my noggin they says:

Thang. Not a thang.

They says:

Thang. Not a thang. Dingle dangle lang.

The cows. Ho no, we didn't say a thang, ol' Andy an' me, about that tarnatious plan o' hisn: fer the cowboys to go rustlin the cows. Mare Cooter Canyon. The spot up on the hill. Ol' Andy's in front an' now the flashlight had to be switch'd off an' he had a fistful o' gravel in the bucket, ol' Andy. *Hyeeere lil' cowie cowie.* Not a thang, man. But a few hours before they chas'd the Calf out o' the Tavern . . . ol' Andy an' his cowboys was lurin the cows down into the Mare Cooter Canyon . . .

Phew.

They's talkin talkin talkin.

You's a-dreemin dreems, they says, the voices, them voices way down in this here noggin o' mine, they's a-whoopin an' wailin inside the metal warsh-tub noggin, since they cain't hardly be noplace else but inside the wore-out metal warsh-tub noggin, where the fuse-box is . . .

They done built theirselves a whole community too. So they got to stay up in there. They's there still.

Cables. All them cables. White, black, red cables. Fetch yerself a sharp knife, man, carve me up an' turn me inside out, see all them cables. My right arm an' right hand ain't the only thangs that's artifisshul, nuh-uh, the left hand's chock full o' cables too, just like the left arm an' the one leg an' the other leg an' the rear end an' the lil' whippersnapper an' the pussle-gut an' the chestchamber . . . Cablewires. Connector-pins. Systematic. Ever' cable spos'd to have its own connecshun in the fuse box. Spos'd to. Ye spos'd to leave 'em all alone, all them cables. Take aholt o' one an' squimmy him out? Better not better not better not. They done warn'd me plenty.

Analyz'd. Been analyz'd, I have, plenty. Ol' Domehead Doctor . . . he explain'd, analyz'd. Later on it was Miss Teacher, Mister Principal, the Preacher . . . an' then there was ol' Andy that late summer night. He had to analyze some, too. We was jumpin an' hoppin an' trippin an' floppin an' ol' Rattlebones Roger stumbl'd over the shotgun an' the metal warsh-tub noggin got ding'd an' it was after the cow concert had done ended an' we believ'd we's just about back at the veehickle agin when ol' Andy startid playin doctor an' tolt me to open my gap.

Open up, he says. Open up. Say ahhh. Open up.

It smelt like somethin burnt. Like a cross betwixt cowhockey an' somethin burnt tergither with blueberry an' wet woods an' ol' Andy was blindin me with his flashlight an' in the light he seen a skinny lil' skiver o' smoke come curlin up out o' my wide-open gap.

An' the lady, man. That lady over there in the one recliner . . .

Okey. So I got to thank about her, too. Thank about the lady, that lady over there in the one recliner. Past few days I been thankin an' thankin bout a late summer night I tried a long time to fergit . . . an' I got to thank about the past few days too. Here. Here where I's settin an' dreemin an' gittin all tangled up in some yarn I like'ta just spun all by myself.

They was jumpin an' hoppin
An' trippin an' floppin . . .

Say whut now? Spinnin yarns? Me? Just a-makin all this stuff up?

Ol' Andy. He turn'd his flashlight back on agin. It was down in the gorge, the wood-hole, down in the Mare Cooter Canyon over by the Lunnerworld. An' it was *after* ol' Pucky Paul had done stopp'd his veehickle an' took a good fistful o' KurtSquirt's hairlocks an' dragg'd him out so's this here yellerbellied troll o' the woods wouldn't go vommickin inside o' his veehickle an' this was *after* the lil' baby geeraff, ol' Rattlebones Roger, had done stumbl'd over the shotgun an' thangs was a-fixin to git real ugly but it was *before* the Song o' the Dead Feller, yes, *before* the Calf stood there in the light . . . *that* was when ol' Andy turn'd his flashlight back on agin.

Open up. Better open on up, now.

. . .

Lawd a mercy if ye ain't smokin like a two-dollar stove.

The Mare Cooter Canyon. How'd we git ourselves out there?

We was settin in ol' Andy's rumpus room. We'd done been settin an' drankin a spell an' ol' Andy he got to talkin bout ol' Helena an' ol' Pucky Paul wutn't havin none of it an' said ol' Andy was a plum fool who done gone an' stole money off his pappie an' so they's fixin to fuss at each other, ol' Andy an' ol' Pucky Paul, both of 'em actin saucy as a jaybird an' each tryin to outsass the other an' then ol' KurtSquirt, ol' Squirty hisself, he up an' open'd his beak an' stutter'd an' ast if we'd like to hear a limrick an' ol' Rattlebones Roger . . . naw he didn't say nary a word, ol' Rattlebones Roger, course he didn't . . . an' so . . . so we's settin there drankin an' after a while ol' Andy he gits up an' says:

Good good good. Let's git outta here, y'all. Let's go fer a ride.

The veehickle. Ol' Pucky's veehickle. He crank'd up the motor an' we shove off out o' there an' before we know'd it we's clear out o' sight o' the construcshun lot where ol' Andy was livin with his pappie an' which is also where fer a long time ye could go an' have a purty good view o' the u.f.o. traffic ever' night over the hillside, yep, up above the hills just south o' the construcshun lot, *that* was where the u.f.o.'s would go a-chippin around an' ol' Pucky Paul with his hands clutchin the styairin wheel he drove like a god. But did he believe in u.f.o.'s an' them u.f.o.-mens? Naw, ol' Pucky Paul didn't put no stock in it even after ol' Andy an' me an' some others had done tolt him all about it.

U.f.o.-mens? Naw, u.f.o.'s? Lie-tales an' flim-flammin an' hoss-sheeit an' bedevilry. Okey okey okey. Long as they ain't no denyin bout the Dead Feller runnin around in the woods. An' that ol' KillerHenry . . .

An' then . . . then they's fussin at each other agin. In the car. Fussin fussin fussin. Ol' Andy an' ol' Pucky Paul. The Boss-Man an' the Driver. Turrible speed. Blazin on fo'ward an' over an' down. Down down down. An' then . . . stop. We'd done arrov'd. The Mare Cooter Canyon.

Ol' Andy. He turn'd on his flashlight agin an' peer'd thru the thick lenses on them aviater glasses o' hisn, peek'd down into my wide-open gap an' seen a skinny lil' skiver o' smoke curlin up out o' there an' ol' Andy, he said it had to've been more'n seven cables that that meddlin robot-riffraff had done squimmy'd out, naw, more'n seven, fer sure. He shone the flashlight, peerin an' peekin an' talkin an' if he woulda come any nairer an' brush'd up aginst the tip o' my nose with his pencil-moustaches why then it'd a-catch'd fire, the moustaches. I tried to back up but they wutn't no place to back up to. I lay in the blueberry bush 'mong twigs an' sprigs an' suchlike as grow'd where the blueberries grow'd down in the Mare Cooter Canyon, man. Yes indeedy, I smelt somethin burnt an' I smelt cowhockey tergither with blueberry an' wet woods, I lay there wi' my gap wide open an' couldn't do nuthin but lay there wi' my wide-open gap maybe lookin like one o' them carniverish plants ye done seen in the movies where it's a histrionical horror-film set in the amazon an' ol' Andy kep' goin on about that meddlin robot-riffraff an' whut they done done to me an' I ain't fer surtin, as I's settin here, whuther ol' Pucky Paul an' ol' KurtSquirt an' ol' Rattlebones Roger know'd exackly whut it was ol' Andy was talkin about.

How in the hell is we spos'd to fix all this? Open wide. Open wide, now.

Ah ah ah.

Attaboy.

. . .

If that don't beat all.

. . .

How in the hell's this spos'd to work? How how how?

. . .

Open up. Come on now, wider.

I open'd up. Wider. Ol' Andy's flashlight was a-blindin me an' some kinda hard somethin began fiddlin with my teeth. A screwdriver. Ol' Andy had done tolt ol' Pucky Paul to fetch him a screwdriver an' whiles ol' Andy's settin there on his knees a-blindin me wi' the flashlight an' peekin down in my wide-open gap, ol' Pucky Paul was gon' go in an' squimmy out one o' them cables.

Whut d'ye reckon bout this'un here, Pucky? Whut say ye? Ye reckon we oughtta . . .

Hesh up, Andy. Hesh up. Doin my best here.

Open up. Come on now, wider. Yer teeth's in the way. An' looka there, smoke. Still smokin.

Reckon we better pull them teeth o' hisn. Squirty, ye got a pair o' pliers in yer pocket? Reckon . . .

Ah ah ah.

Quit yer complainin, now. Ye done heard whut ol' Pucky Paul said. We got to pull them teeth o' yourn.

Squirty, pliers.

Pliers? Ain't got no puh puh pliers, boys.

Troll o' the woods. Ye done heard whut ol' Pucky Paul said. Go fetch us some pliers.

Ah ah ah.

. . .

The lies keep comin one after the other. He talks an' talks, says he's gon' make up fer it all. But the lies is comin one after the other. Don't believe him. Don't believe him.

My teeth. The others didn't end up pullin 'em nohow. Nuthin come of that ideer an' praise the Lawd too an' I promise I'll tell you an' you alone whut happen'd *before* we ended up in the Mare Cooter Canyon, yes'n whut happen'd down in ol' Andy's rumpus room an' whut happen'd in Pucky Paul's veehickle an' after . . . afterwards . . . after we done come up out o' the Mare Cooter Canyon . . . *then* come the Tavern an' these toughies, them who was chasin the Calf, they chas'd him out an' he took to flyin an' flappin an' flailin an' screamin like a stuck pig before he come to a *dead stop* back behind SportsMart an' kick'd off his benastied slip-ons.

There. Behind the SportsMart. He come to a dead stop. They couldn't catch him agin. That's all just talk. Them sayin they caught him agin, that is. Naw. The Calf he come to a dead stop. He turn'd round. Waited on 'em . . .

That's whut happen'd.

Just like 'at?

Just like 'at.

So there's this collossal transformator standin smack dab in the middle o' the town square, right next to the platform they built supposidly so's they can have a decent outdoor stage. Durndest thang. Adoptin a resolushun bout puttin that transformator smack in the middle o' the square. Whutn' the hell we need a transformator smack in the middle o' the square fer? Tell me that. Smack dab in the middle o' the square? Durndest thang. A collossal transformator o' some sort. Big ol' boxy thang. Whut is it, pray tell? Whut kinda transformator is it? We sure wouldn't mind knowin.

Long time ago. The Calf. The late summer night. All them yesterdays ago. Yesterdays an' yesternights ago. A skyscrapin hourglass done emptied clean down to the bottom. Empty. It's all over an' mister meckanickal barn gnome is settin down here in his crannynook. Mmhmm rightrightright. Coulda been worse. Past few days. The meckanickal barn gnome's been sharp'nin the pencils an' shreddin the paper but he done took hisself a pencil stub an' took to writin down a name or two an' a few sinnences on some o' the paper he's spos'd to be a-shreddin. *Ol' Andy an' ol' Pucky Paul an' ol' KurtSquirt an' ol' Rattlebones Roger. Ol' Helena. The Dead Feller. Ol' KillerHenry. Lazarus. Sinnence A an' sinnence B an' another sinnence an' then another, man . . .*

Whut a strange late summer night. An' before it a strange afternoon, an' a strange evenin too.

That big ol' mapletree by the house where ol' Andy was livin with his pappie, 'twixt the front door an' the row o' mailboxes markin the outer edge o' the property, smack in the middle o' the yard: the mapletree, standin there a-bowin whiles ol' Rattlebones Roger an' me goed hunch'd over each carryin a beer tote, before stoppin an' wonderin whuther it wouldn't be better to go back an' find ourselves some other place to go a-drankin. But on we goed an' stoddl'd toward the front door, ol' Rattlebones Roger a step or two behind, beer bottles a-clinkin an' a-clankin an' the mapletree turn'd round an' foller'd us with his eyes as we walk'd, least that's whut I remember, I remember stoddlin toward the front door, hunch'd over an' nervous as all-git-out, ol' Rattlebones Roger's beers a-clinkin an' a-clankin an' my beers a-clankin an' a-clinkin too an' they's somethin, the mapletree or maybe somethin else, a-follerin us wi' their eyes as we stoddle'd on, I know'd they's eyes follerin me anyhow an' it wutn't ol' Rattlebones Roger's eyes nuther . . . naw, he wouldn't dare, wouldn't never a-dare'd it, ol' Rattlebones Roger.

Later. Spruces flyin by as ol' Pucky Paul's veehickle goed tearin on down the forest road an' soon enuff, man, soon enuff the veehickle was a-plungin down down down into the Mare Cooter Canyon an' I lean'd my metal warsh-tub noggin aginst the wender, an' we's squose tergither in the backseat cause ol' KurtSquirt took up all the room an' I seen the spruce trees a-flyin by. *An' maybe*, I thunk to myself, *maybe I's fixin to see the Dead Feller, just maybe, maybe them spruces flyin by is tryin, tryin best they can to reveal the Dead Feller?* KurtSquirt. He's a-moanin. He's a-wailin. Takin up too much room an' makin noises.

Later. Trees an' shrubs an' all them other thangs a-growin an' a-sproutin down in the Mare Cooter Canyon, woah nelly, a-growin, man, I tell ye the whole goddang place was overgrow'd with the bangest ol' bushes ye ever did see, an' course we shoulda had us some o' them vikingswordstiff knives such as ye see in the jungal where the 'rangatan lives considerable diff'rent than them characters they still call humans an' trolls an' gnomes, yep, by dod we shoulda had us some vikingswordstiff knives. Coulda smote our way thru, smote ourselves a path without bustin our guts overmuch an' found our way out to ol' KillerHenry's stable an' broke in an' seen fer ourselves whut it look'd like inside o' there. Green, green ever'where. A-growin an' a-sproutin. A-growin an' a-sproutin down in the Mare Cooter Canyon. *The girl, the girl.* An' ol' Pucky Paul done took on the job: the job carryin the shotgun, ol' Andy's shotgun.

An' then after. The Tavern. Afterward go to the Tavern. Cowboys gon' go to the Tavern. Everbody who gits down to drankin an' raisin cain gotta git on down to the Tavern. An' now more woods. More woods rollin on like a vast wrinkly rug coverin the hillside. An' the Tavern. The Tavern's on the other side o' the hill. Up. Up an' out o' the Mare Cooter Canyon. Git yerself outta here now. The Dead Feller. The girl. *Dead Feller's a-sangin so ye best be gittin yerself outta here right now dadgummit.* The woods. The spruces. It's thankin, that ol' warsh-tub noggin. Git yerself outta here. Right now. Dadgum. An' ol' Andy's a-whoopin an' stavin. *My money. My shotgun.* An' the years gallopin by. They's gallopin an' gallopin on by an' the warsh-tub noggin is tryin to fergit.

Knives. Shoulda had us some vikingswordstiff knives. Smote our way thru, we coulda. Smote an' smote an' smote our way thru.

Naw. Naw naw naw. He's tryin to fergit. But the years is done gallop'd by an' now he's a-settin there in a crannynook a-thankin an' a-thankin bout a late summer night. Thankin bout the Calf, somebody they call'd the Calf an' who never was know'd by no 'nuther name in all the world than the Calf, naw, never. He's a-writin. He says Say whut if one o' the menfolks was just here talkin loud an' bossin him around. It happen'd all of a sudden. He ain't functionin too good no more. He likes to believe that they believe he's the sorter feller who ain't worth a flip an' that they can just set him over in some crannynook at a desk next to the coffeepot without a whole lot o' backtalk an' now it done been decided: they's settin him there an' they's bossin him too. Now he gots to go sharp'nin the pencils an' shreddin the paper. A pencil sharp'ner an' a pair o' sizzers long as yer arm an' sharp as a tack, shazam, there they was waitin fer him. An' the coffee pot. There it is, right next to the desk an' it's your job, they says, it's *your* job to fiddle wi' the coffee pot an' go around servin the coffee.

Say whut now?

You. Your job.

Exackly. Happen'd all of a sudden. Just like that. Past few days. Time. Days, time. Done emptied out. Run out. That's all she wrote. An' the lady. All of a sudden in my livin room. Settin in the one recliner an' me layin on the couch. Mmhmm. Coulda been a-whiles layin there, watchin the teevee an' gittin aggervated on account o' all the dadblam'd foolishmint in the world. News. Currint happ'nins. Fer a long time I goed to bed early an' kinda sorta *had* to watch the teevee a spell 'stidder sleepin. The lady. Settin in the one recliner. A-lookin at me. Lookin at me, a touch o' fury in them eyes o' hern. How my mama look'd betimes. I remember. Remember my mama. Remember her eyes. Lookin at me wi' the same eyes as that wommon settin over there in the one recliner an' I hadn't the foggiest noshun how in the heck she got herself in, bein that the door was lock'd like always an' ye reckon I'da notic'd if she clumb in thru the wender.

Thru the wender. But whut kind o' wender would it had to have been in that case?

All the wenders in my house have got to be shut tight.

An' the blinds have got to be pull'd down. Just a teeny lil' crack at the bottom. So a teeny tiny skiver o' daylight can git in.

Ain't none o' these folks on the outside gon' git in. They know it, too, my sister an' her husbant an' their young'uns. Ain't no way they's a-comin in here. Ain't nobody comin in. Nobody.

My sister. She can rang the doorbell long as she wants to. I ain't anserin. An' that one time she an' her husbant made it their bizness to git inside my house, ye never seen such a ruckus as they was then.

The lock. They tried pickin the lock. Same as any ol' sneak-thief they tried pickin the dadblame lock. I scream'd. I scream'd wi' all the artifisshul screamin power my gurglin longs could scrape tergither but they kep' at it, my sister an' her husbant, they kep' at it an' the only thang I could do was git aholt o' the Sheriff. Dug my cellphone out o' the brown anorak I had hangin next to the front door an' heard how they's keepin at it out there, tryin to pick the dadblame lock, my sister an' her husbant. I's clean out o' breath. Longs was a-gurglin. I had to set down on the lil' rosepainted stool next to the front door an' with a heehawin jackassvoice I says:

Hullo this the Sheriff? Ye got to git down here, man. They's a break-in goin on. A break-in in broad daylight. They's tryin to git in here. Tryin to pick the lock, they is. Gang o' thieves, they is. They's two of 'em so ye better git down here an' take a man or two wi' ye.

An' they come all right. Strong couple o' fellers. In uniform. Come just a minute or two after my sister an' her husbant had done pick'd the lock. My sister an' her husbant trotted right on in, man. Fust my sister an' then her husbant an' they wutn't barkin but they was whoopin an' hollerin an' hneighin, hneighin like a couple ol' cumfluster'd hosses, they's rarin up an' kickin at me an' I's still settin there on my lil' rosepainted stool next to the front door, kickin at the ol' wore-out metal warsh-tub noggin o' mine, ye can imagine whut it musta been like fer me settin there, on my lil' rosepainted stool, waitin on thems that was comin in the name o' the Law.

Look, I says. Look. I pointed. They turn'd quick, my sister an' her husbant. The hosses turn'd quick an' the strong couple o' fellers was marchin on up. The po'leece was here.

All right all right whut's the trubble? says the one uniform an' my sister she tries to explain.

Yuh-huh yuh-huh, says the secont uniform. So they ain't no break-in here?

Nuh-uh nuh-uh, says I. That's exactly whut it is. It's a break-in. They done pick'd the lock. They done broke in here.

Yuh-huh yuh-huh.

Nuh-uh. Yuh-huh. An' my sister she's a-hneighin an' babblin away. I's settin there. I's settin there lookin up at her. Lookin up at her in profile. She's a-blushin somethin fierce. I didn't need to say nuthin. She done gone an' screw'd the pooch. The mare an' her husbant. They'd done screw'd the pooch an' they's a couple o' dellicate piles o' steamin fresh hoss-pucky on the linoleum floor next to my front door. My longs was a-gurglin. I's clean out o' breath an' I's a-gloatin an' a-gloatin an' a-gloatin.

Thief one an' thief two come to say howdy-do;
The colt an' the filly, a-boppity-boo.
Thief one an' thief two, tergither they hneigh
Hn-is this'n the hn-ouse where the ol' codger stay?
Thief one an' thief two, they git a reply:
Is ye lookin fer me? Hear ye by an' by.
Sure I's a codger, but I lay down the law,
Fer I eat me some hossmeat an' eat it up raw.
Thief one an' thief two the lock they do pick
An' then he's a-gobblin 'em on down his gullick.
Down the ol' codger's gullick, a-bippity-bop,
Till' his innards is bustin an' his bunghole say stop.
Thief one an' thief two come to say howdy-do;
The colt an' the filly, a-boppity-boo.

That time. But didn't somethin like that happen just a few days ago? Just a few days before the past few days, before the fust day, the day I arrov'd by an' by after a wairy jaunt an' set myself down by my desk, the desk next to the crannynook, right next to the coffee pot because of course I coulda been thankin an' thankin about thief one an' thief two an' I coulda been thankin that they musta had somethin to do with ol' KillerHenry down in the Canyon an' I coulda been thankin bout this mare ol' KillerHenry had done took such a likin to . . .

Oh yeah. I remember it now. Remember it was just a few days ago thief one an' thief two the lock they did pick.

The ol' codger. He pull'd one over on 'em, all right. Po'leece come an' thief one an' thief two had to git theirselves gone.

A few days prior to these past few days. They had it all plann'd out but the ol' codger pull'd one over on 'em. He gobbl'd down the whole dadblame scheme. Ha ha. Ever' bit an' grain.

An' ol' KillerHenry too, I know he was good at eatin, eatin up the best laid plans other folks had done cook'd up, never thankin they'd end up as chow fer the ol' codger's gullick. Ha ha.

An' that wommon? The lady? Whut kind o' plans had she been a-cookin? Whut was it she was a-aimin fer?

Talkin, she was. That lady was talkin bout me. Bout my life. *Yer life?* Yuh-huh. Had herself a neat lil' timeline an' everthang. Know'd all they was fer the knowin, she did.

I could hear her talkin. That wommon. Them eyes. Ah. Them eyes. Blind I sure as hell ain't an' anybody who stares at me is gon' catch learnin that I can stare right back. She stared. I stared. But in the fust place it was her talkin an' natcherly them chaintooth voices way down inside this ol' wore-out metal warsh-tub noggin o' mine, they was a-talkin too. They's both of 'em talkin, talkin an' talkin. That wommon an' them voices. I lay there. Hadn't snipp'd the ears off. Naw the ears was just as hale an' op'rashunal like always. Ain't nobody done said I oughtta snip them ears off o' me. Naw, that come later, in the time after, the time after a wairy jaunt, when I's sitcherated over in my crannynook by the coffee pot, it was *then*, I remember, someone done said I oughtta snip them ears off o' me.

Course he should oughta snip them ears off. Cain't hear nuthin with 'em nohow. Ain't no use keepin 'em, pair o' gnome ears like 'at.

Well fine enuff but that wommon? The lady? She didn't say nuthin bout them gnome ears o'mine. Nuthin. She talk'd an' talk'd. I lay there on the couch. Heard ever' word.

A job. Work. An' so on an' so futh. The lady give me a pamflit. A pamflit I's spos'd to go an' read. Read the pamflit each an' ever' mornin. Rememberize each an' ever' sinnence of it. *Apples. Is they gon' be apples now?* All the sinnences. Rememberize each an' ever sinnence by heart an' study the drawins' too. Menfolks an' wimmenfolks an' childerns an' lions an' sheepies an' lots o' other animals from the jungal an' the woods back home.

I got a job fer ye, says she, the wommon.

Amen.

I got a job fer ye. Read. Read an' learn. Read the pamflit ever' mornin before yer workshift.

Say whut now? A job? Work?

Mmhmm. A job. Work. Go on now, says she, the lady. Best be skedaddlin. Skedaddlin on down to work.

Skedaddle? Hain't ye done seen whut I look like?

Yep.

An' d'ye reckon I just gon' up an' skedaddle like some dang ol' Lazarus?

Yep.

You some kind o' enginair or somethin? I got all kinda looseygoosey cablewires inside me, I tell ye whut. Carve me up, look inside. Connect. Connect. Connect. The fust an' the secont ain't connected wi' the thud an' the fo'th an' I bet ye already knows it, since that ye knows all they is fer the knowin.

Yep.

Cain't skedaddle off nowhere. Sho' nuff I's one o' them self-operatin types but I cain't just up an' *skedaddle* off nowhere nohow.

I cain't, I cain't, says I, over an' over, but as ye prob'ly done realiz'd I up an' goed anyway, I drag'd the ol' rotted-out man-husk, by an' by I stoleborrow'd me a lawnmower, an' ye done heard all the rest.

All of it? Well. Whut I said bout the lawnmower . . . that was all just a yarn, ye see. They says I's real bad to spin yarns an' whut I said bout the lawnmower . . . *that* was just another o' my yarns, I'll own.

That ol' musslebound Splutterfusserer. He's drivin along in his pickup an' seen the meckanickal barn gnome wi' the cowboy hat yank'd down over his top lid draggin the ol' husk on down the big road an' he made up his mind to stop. The Splutterfusserer. He pull'd up to the side o' the main road an' turn'd on his blinkers an' clumb out the veehickle, walk'd over the yeller line an' he's standin right smack in front o' me talkin like he know'd me from before:

Ye best come along wi' me. Hop on in, now.

Hop on in? Me?

Now.

So I's settin there, right next to him. He's drivin an' talkin bout whut fine weather we's havin an' natcherly I's thankin whut a right lil' treat it was to go fer a ride in such a splendifferus veehickle an' seein as I hadn't nary an' ideer how much I should oughtta let on whiles settin aside o' him I ast him while we was cruisin on down the big hill if it was *him* that there lawnmower belong'd to . . . the one park'd in the grass . . . the lawnmower I's wantin to stealborrow an' it was *then* he come to a dead stop an' holler'd he's a-fixin to murder me.

Dandelion Ditch. Palmleaf-siz'd dandelion leaves all cover'd in exhaust dustins in the Dandelion Ditch.

Now ye know whut happen'd after. Now ye may as well broadcast fur an' wide that ye know all about it too. Talk. All that talkin. Ye done heard how they be a-talkin. Ye done unnerstood it. Whut all they said. They. All them there. Them voices. Them fellers. Them folks. An' all them other meckanickal gnomes. Yep. Them boogers with numerus cables branchin out unner their skin. Ivo Caprino-men. Yep. All them fairly ordnary barn gnomes, native to Hadeland. Yep. They's talkin all right. Talkin an' talkin. Yep. Yepyepyep. But okey. The lady. She know'd all they was fer the knowin. An' that ain't too shabby, that. To know all they is fer the knowin. She kep' sayin over an' over:

I know all they is fer the knowin.

Ain't too shabby. Point o' fact, I was mighty impress'd. Coal-black hair. Her face paler'n the palest corpse. Her eyes. Sharp moon in the darkness. I lay on my couch in my own livin room an' look'd at the moon, listnin, catchin on by an' by: whut the moon was thankin about this an' about that, about life, about me. The moon. Ain't too shabby. Mighty purty. This pale sharp moon that know'd all they was fer the knowin, sendin futh a pamflit in moonbeams an' tellin me I's gon' start workin someplace where they produce doojiggers fur all the flesh-an'-blood humans (aliv'd or dead) they can gullup down their gullick or shove on up their cornhole.

Humans. Odd-turn'd sort, they is. How is it they cut a compleetly diff'rent sort o' figgur than us meckanickal barn gnomes? Maybe the plans done been cook'd up a long time ago. Wouldn't a surpris'd me one bit. Ain't never been a bad ideer to go a-makin plans.

The Almighty. He cook'd up his own plans. An' ol' KillerHenry. He cook'd up some plans too. Durn'd if he didn't. Built hisself the boat. Waited on the rain. The great flood. The big diluvy. Said he done peer'd into the future. Said he done seen whut was to come. An' maybe that's how come they's so stress'd, them humans? They's short on time. Fur too short.

How come? My my. My my my. A job. Done got me a job. My my. Past few days. All of a sudden. An' the lady she said *we*, she said. She said *we stress'd-out humans* need ritcherals, we *stress'd-out humans* need religion, she said, ye see, the lady, the lady whut come home to me an' give me a pamflit she tolt me to study close an' carry fo'ward on into life. The lady said *we* an' purty soon I's like'ta thankin I's a human too. A real stress'd-out human. Be somethin else, wouldn't it. Real an' stress'd-out.

Ye should oughtta be happy, she said. Yer own desk an' so on an' so futh.

Hey you.

Yes?

You know it.

Say whut now?

You know it. All they is fer the knowin.

The Diner's a magical submarine. All ye got to do is step right on board an' find yerself a seat an' dive on down in the deep water just like them folks that's easy to fall a-broodin dive down deep into thangs they ain't able to fergit. Down. Down in the deep. Way down. An' the flashlight's turn'd on an' ain't nobody foolish enuff to turn it off while we's down in the deep. Nobody. It's bright an' halesome inside. An' the submarine's all magical-mystical. Where was it we dov'd down? Where is it we's a-goin? Where we gon' come back up? Lots to talk about. Durn'd if they ain't lots to talk about. The conversashun is a tremendious ocean . . . so all ye got to do is step right on board an' find yerself a seat.

Late summer night. That late summer night I done tried a long time to fergit . . .

Whut in the hell's goin on inside the ol' fuse box? *Apples. Big ol' appletrees.* How come this fairly ordnary barn gnome, native to Hadeland (goodwill, now, don't fergit that goodwill) done steer'd hisself into a mental condishun where they ain't no way to stop thankin bout somethin he done tried an' tried to fergit? *Apples. Et 'em up. Chew 'em good.* Ellavator. Mirrorwise inside the ellavator. Was *that* when it was?

Sharp moon in the darkness. It ain't each an' ever' night the moon talks to ye. Sees ye an' talks to ye too. But it'll prob'ly happen late one evenin. Whut I mean is . . . when ye least suspicion any danger . . . that's when it'll happen . . . that's when the moon'll come out. An' the late summer night? Anybody remember? Whuther the moon show'd hisself or not?

The feller they said's from another planit. He stood in the light. They was light all around him. Light comin out of him. That's whut we remember, anyhow. But does anybody remember whuther the moon show'd hisself or not?

Sharp. One o' them sharp moons. Kinda moon like the writers of fairy tale books an' funny pages know whut is. The moon. Keepin a close watch on us? Talkin? An' could it be the moonbeams was pointin, showin the way?

Ol' Andy he was so surtin. They's somethin he'd done got wise to. Somethin he'd decided we's gon' do. The shotgun. He said we better bring the shotgun. Ol' Pucky Paul drug the shotgun out from unner ol' Andy's bed an' brung it up the stairsteps an' put it in the trunk. Rest of us didn't thank nuthin of it at'oll. Wutn't the fust time ol' Andy see'd to it the shotgun was brung. An' they wutn't no use in puttin up no fuss. That shotgun was gon' be brung. But most always it stay'd in the trunk.

An' the flashlight, says Andy. The flashlight an' a bucket too.

One late summer night, late summer night
I couldn't resist, I couldn't fight
Found me a treasure, a purty sight
One late summer night, late summer night . . .

An' they says . . . they says . . . from the very fust day they been sayin that I's dreemin an' gittin tangled up in the yarns I's spinnin an' when I come around wi' the coffeepot, they's sayin the same thang all over agin, whut they done already said. Over an' over, agin an' agin. They got to keep sayin it over an' over, agin an' agin.

I'd been sharp'nin the pencils. I'd been shreddin the paper. Their coffee cups was empty. They holler'd an' holler'd but it wutn't long, natcherly, before they realiz'd it was a stone-deef feller they'd done been gifted.

Naw it wutn't no use to go a-hollerin an' one of 'em take to trampin tramptramptramp an' I's lettin on like I's just as stone-deef as they's takin me fer an' I flinch'd a little when he took to bellerin in my ear whiles crouchin with his knees all springy an' lookin prob'ly like some logbuster fixin to swing the ol' axe an' he kep' on a-bellerin an' a-bellerin an' later on it occurr'd to me that this feller's none other'n the Minister o' Justice in these parts an' he ain't no logbuster at'oll an' he give off a husky smell standin there in his bigboy britches just a-bellerin an' a-bellerin.

I reckon ye could say this ol' man-husk was smellin mighty husky too but it wutn't on account o' bein dipp'd in no perfume, naw.

Only thang this here rotted-out man-husk was dipp'd in was sweat. Genuwine feverfied manfolk sweat. Cowboy sweat.

I'd been a-layin there tossin an' turnin all night, after all. I lay on the couch wi' them voices goin on an' on an' on. I's tossin an' turnin an' winglin an' wrigglin. An' the sharp moon, that lady . . . hard to believe but . . . that lady still set there in the one recliner. I reckon'd it was about time fer her to git herself gone. Git on, says I. *Git on now. Best be gittin on.* But she kep' on lookin at me, she did. Lookin at me wi' them eyes o' hern. Just lookin an' lookin an' lookin whiles I's tossin an' turnin an' winglin an' wrigglin, th' rotted-out man-husk it wingl'd an' wriggl'd. I's sweatin. Sweatin somethin awful. Sweatin genuwine feverfied manfolk sweat. Cowboy sweat. Couldn't take off my clothes even if I'd a-tried. Tee-shirt joggin britches unnerbritches socks. She's settin there, that lady. Settin there lookin an' lookin an' lookin an' lookin at me. Couldn't put nuthin past her an' if I'd a-been younger an' if she'd a-been younger why I woulda ast her to come an' wingle an' wriggle tergither with me fer a spell, she coulda had the ol' husk toss'd an' turn'd herself but I ain't no good fer it no more an' truth be tolt I cain't rightly remember the last time I's layin tergither wi' no wommon.

So then come a wairy jaunt till I ended up down here in the unnerworld. Ass-bustin wairy. I's operatin myself an' just about bustid my ass doin it. An' the cowboy had done sweated some more.

An' he kep' up the bellerin, the Minister. The Minister o' Justice hisself was bellerin in my ear:

Ye better hot us up some coffee. Coffee.

I give a lil' flinch an' jump'd up a little in my spinnin chair. Yes-yesyes sir I's fixin to git 'er done I's gon' hot up the coffee an' git 'er done yesyesyes sir.

Yuh-huh, this'un's been spinnin his own yarns, I heard one feller say. A secont feller says: Been writin. *Writin on paper whut's meant fer the shredder.*

The rounds. I stood up an' doddle'd a few foot over to the coffee pot an' made the coffee an' when the coffee pot was full I straighted up whut was left o' my artifisshul back an' did another round servin pipin hot coffee an' could hear 'em talkin, they's talkin bout me. Dreemin. Spinnin yarns. Tangl'd up. Writin. Operatin hisself. More'n likely.

But I ain't gon' let 'em deny me. I's gon' keep on doin my own doins. I sharpen the pencils an' I shred the paper an' the sorta feller I's wantin to believe that they believe I is, I mean the type who ain't worth a plugg'd nickel an' who they can just set over in some crannynook at a desk next to the coffeepot without a whole lot o' backtalk, mmhmm, I reckon that feller's gon' keep on doin his own doins. That feller. Say whut?

All right then. I ain't gon' be deny'd.

Now, it ain't quite as easy to be the feller they call the Professor. A ol' hunchback I still ain't too sure whut sorta cretur he even is. Rabbit? Guinea pig? Water rat? Peart lil' booger he must a-been too in the way-back-when, no more an' no less'n anybody else. But now? If he ain't as ball'd-up an' lopper-jaw'd an' down-fac'd as I . . . shoot, whut is I spos'd to thank about him? That hunch o' hisn, the hump unnerneath his bluestrip'd 'nittid sweater, the hump he's doom'd to be a-luggin wheresoe'er he goes, of course them fellers just got to give him hell fer it an' that ain't all, they got to be a-pokin him an' pinchin him too. *Ow ow ow. Naw. Naw naw naw. Whut'd I do?* They give him hell about that hunch an' they be a-pokin him an' pinchin him an' he's a-whindlin an' whimperin all the while. *Whut'd I do? Whut'd I do? Naw naw naw. Naw. Ow ow ow.*

The Professor. Talk to him, show him some simpithy? Fer now I reckon I'll leave the simpithizin to somebody else whut cyairs to. I ain't innerested. Hell wi' that. To hell wi' this noshun o' *him an' me*, we two bein the odd ones out around these parts, me an' him . . . hell with all that, durn'd if I give a flip. They's givin him hell about his hunch, they's a-pokin him an' pinchin him an' ever' once in a while they want him to put on a lil' surkus rooteen.

Clownshow. We want us a clownshow. Come on, now, give us a clownshow, Professor, clownshow, now.

Naw naw naw. I won't.

Whut's that, ye won't? But ye got to.

Naw naw naw.

Lookie here. Give ye a wisp o' this here candy. But fust ye got to put on a clownshow.

Naw naw naw.

Burrup fer us. Swaller some air, give us a burrup an' flap them ears an' make that ol' hump go wibblywobbly unnerneath that sweater o' yourn.

I won't. Naw naw naw.

Goddammit, ye better.

Naw. Ow. Ow ow ow.

An' they sirkle around him an' take to a-pokin his hump an' pinchin him agin. The Professor he takes to whindlin an' whimperin an' protestatin an' even tho' I's settin at my desk an' ain't watchin the surkus rooteen on account o' the partishuns betwixt me an' the ring I know he's mortal ugly to look at, the Professor, with all these suit-wairin menfolks standin around him.

The Professor. Whut was it he was so schollar'd in? I don't know a thang about his life up on the surface but I hear whut all they says. (Stone-deef? Who me?) They say he done cheated, he done play-jeriz'd from other professors an' won fer hisself onrightful glory an' praise.

Ain't no tellin whuther whut they says is true or not.

Might as well let him alone fer my part anyhow.

They's talkin. Prob'ly been talkin since back before I got here. They know'd I was comin. The Boss-Man had done tolt 'em I's expected an' they'd prob'ly been talkin even *before* the Boss-Man got around to tellin 'em so. The Boss-Man. The Boss-Man in this here office. Directin everthang from behind his door where he sets in deep consentrashun. That's whut all boss-mens do. Goes without sayin. They ain't a bit like them folks who never hope fer nuthin more'n to be seen one day as ordnary folks thru an' thru or at the very least to be seen as them fairly ordnary barn gnomes, yes indeedy, seen as *meckanickal* thru an' thru or at the very least *fairly*, man, no foolin, buddy.

Boss-Man. Got his own room an' everthang. Own office. He been real smart about makin sure they's quiet worktime fer him an' the Secertary somewhere off inside the labbarinth. Storege closit. They prob'ly use a storege closit with a door ye can lock so they can go off an' do teamwork tergither. That's prob'ly where they's a-teamworkin, the Boss-Man an' the Secertary. I wonder if it was the door I pass'd by when I's a-draggin the ol' rotted-out man-husk thru the badly lighted tunnel after Lawd knows how long I done laid an' suffer'd whiles these fellers hover'd over this here wore-out metal warsh-tub noggin o' mine. They's a tiny lil' door there. It was lock'd. I shook on the doorknob. Naw, I *grabb'd* the doorknob. I knock'd on the door. Said hullo an' he'p me but didn't nobody anser.

Naw, I ain't e'er seen him, the Boss-Man. Dunno whut sort o' cretur he is, nuther.

An' the Janitor said the Boss-Man's gon' chew me out but so far I ain't heard no peep out of him, the Boss-Man. So far. Been about two-three days an' I ain't seen him.

Ain't seen the Secertary nuther. Dunno whuther the Secertary's a man or wommon or hermaferdite or . . . well . . .

I grabb'd the doorknob. Gentle. Grabb'd it just sorta gentle. Not hard. I's bein sivil-like. I knock'd. Hullo? says I, bein real cyairful since they might coulda been settin with all their earthly bodyparts right behind the door an' it might coulda jolted 'em real bad if somebody was to go shakin the doorknob an' bangin an' hollerin outta nowhere. The storege closit. Whut'n the hell did I know bout that storege closit? Narrer an' cramp'd inside, prob'ly. Ever' mornin the Boss-Man an' the Secertary cramm'd all their earthly bodyparts inside the storege closit an' stay'd there till time to go home. Stayin in there fer to run thangs in peace an' quiet behind the door. Goes without sayin that somebody whut's got to drag so to speak all his posseshuns thru the tunnel, somebody like yers truly, goes without sayin that somebody like yers truly, yer fairly ordnary meckanickal barn gnome, native to Hadeland, has got to remember to behave hisself an' not go standin by anybody's door like some dang ol' terr'rist.

Hullo?

Cyairful-like:

Hullo?

Sivil-like:

Hullo?

The days have gone by. These past few days. An' if the Boss-Man an' Secertary woulda come on down to my crannynook why we'd have ourselves a big ol' time an' before long they'd prob'ly manage to wring it out o' me: the truth, that is, the fact that I been thankin an' thankin these past few days bout a late summer night I tried an' tried a long time to fergit.

BOSS-MAN: Whut you thankin bout right now?

SECERTARY: Ye better tell us, now, whut you thankin bout, whut you been dillyin an' dallyin with.

ME: I's just a-settin here a-thankin an' a-writin . . . but everthang

I's a-thankin an' writin, everthang . . . naw . . . these chaintooth voices way down inside this ol' noggin o' mine . . . this wore-out metal warsh-tub noggin, ain't nuthin done happen'd, I's settin here dreemin an' gittin all tangled up in some yarn I prob'ly just spun all by myself but . . .

BOSS-MAN: But? Ain't no buttin around here, boy.

SECERTARY: Ain't no buttin, naw.

ME: Okey. I'll tell ye whut I's thankin bout, whut I been dillyin an' dallyin with.

BOSS-MAN: Good.

SECERTARY: Good good.

ME: Well . . .

> A late summer night, late summer night,
> A late summer night . . .

The Calf. The one they call'd the Calf an' who never was know'd by no 'nuther name in all the world than the Calf, naw not never nuthin else. He scream'd. He howl'd. He scream'd he's fixin to show each an' ever' one of 'em whut he's made of an' he yowl'd, the Calf, he scream'd an' he yowl'd.

Plum fool, I heard them tough kids holler. *He done gone tetch'd in the head. Lookit him lookit him. Pastywhite puddin ass. Roseberrysoup-ruddy hogface. Hyeeere Calfy hyeeere Calfy come on now Calfy.*

An' he scream'd an' scream'd some more, louder an' louder, yowl'd an' yowl'd. Them toughies tramp'd 'round him trampin their feet an' clappin their hands an' whoopin an' laffin an' snortin. Tramptramptramptramp, some six-seven of 'em, coulda been eight, coulda been nine. Toughies, tough kids, they's dancin, boys, dancin dance my lil' dollie as soon as the whole kit an' kaboodle was over an' done with, once the strongest toughie o' the bunch had done beat him half to death.

An' me, I's settin here, I's settin here a-thankin an' a-writin, right next to the coffeepot . . . I done made up my mind, if the Boss-Man an' the Secertary was to pay a visit to my crannynook fer a spell an' force me to talk, then I'll tell 'em bout the Calf an' I'll tell 'em how all that other stuff ain't easy fer me to thank about or write about . . . but the Calf . . . *him* I'll tell 'em about.

I'll tell 'em whut happen'd.

I'll tell 'em like it was. *Almost.*

I'll tell 'em how we didn't stick around at the Tavern.

Them toughies they chas'd him out an' flew after him an' was fixin to nab him an' we, ol' Andy an' ol' Pucky Paul an' ol' KurtSquirt an' ol' Rattlebones Roger an' me, we flew an' we flapp'd an' flail'd after them tough kids an' the thangs ol' Andy was rattlin off later on when the sun was comin up over that hill in the east, all that guff about how the ondescribabble watersogg'd figgure they's chasin just up an' become a flea-siz'd streak a-jumpin an' hoppin over some dustcover'd teevee screen . . . naw, like hell.

The Calf. They's tormintin him from the very fust day. *The fust day. The fust day o' the way-back-when?* I can remember seein him on his knees bendin down in a mudpuddle on the schoolyard an' how Mister Principal was tormintin him too. Mister Principal he snuck on over once he was absolutely surtin all the toughies had got their-selves gone an' give him a kick in the rear end an' beller'd at him to pull hisself back tergither an' git on back in the classroom an' now, after all them yesterdays, all them yesterdays an' yesternights, he lay there with his skull bustid an' his rear end expos'd back behind the SportsMart, the Calf did.

There. That's how I remember it.

Skull bustid. Rear end expos'd.

An' Mister Principal. That tempermint o' hisn. Sorter tempermint that was always outrunnin itself so if he wutn't roarin then he was a-laffin an' yellin hip hip hurra an' puttin on a happy face like he believ'd the young'uns oughtta do ever' year on constitushun day. Mister Principal. It wutn't that hard to read him. His mood. To read him an' try an' teeze out whuther he was loopy-mad or loopy-glad. Mister Principal. He didn't belong to that race whut durin the beginnin times breeded indervidurals ignorant of all knowins 'cept how to learn their desendints to keep well hid whut they (the desendints) had inside o' theirselves. Most o' the young'uns on the other hand they did belong to that race. They kep' well hid whut they had inside o' theirselves. That much I unnerstood. Most indervidurals was that way. Not the Calf. He didn't have nuthin to keep hid. Not a thang. In that way he an' Mister Principal was a lot alike. In that way. But they ain't no comparin the two of 'em nohow. Mister Principal an' the Calf they both come from two diff'rent planits. Mister Principal come from a planit where everbody's warrin aginst each other. The Calf come from a planit where they ain't no nasty-stankin ol' galoot tryin to git a rise outta the oddest lil' oddballs.

In. Back in the classroom.

The Calf didn't anser. Mister Principal give him another kick.

In. Back in the classroom.

Anser him? Anser that sorta nasty-stankin galoot? The Calf, on his knees in the mudpuddle. Was dreemin, maybe. Dreemin bout his home planit. Bout life on that planit. Bout the sorta space creturs whut go a-jumpin an' hoppin like flea-siz'd streaks on a dustcover'd teevee screen, a-jumpin an' hoppin so they wutn't no tellin where any one o' them space creturs was headed. The planit. A big ol' planit with rings all around it just like Satern an' it had a lot o' moons like they said Satern had too but beyond that, naw, they ain't no comparin 'em, since that they was a totally diff'rent atmosfeer on the planit the Calf come from. An' if you was to ast him, ast that ol' Calf, then after a spell ye might coulda heard a lil' story or two. A lil' ol' story bout his planit. Bout life on the planit. Bout the sorta space creturs whut go a-jumpin an' hoppin like flea-siz'd streaks on a dustcover'd teevee screen.

But how come he come down here in the fust place? They done found him deep in the woods. Fust they's thankin he must be one o' them chucky-dolls out o' some horrorfilm. Then they's thankin he must be dead. Dead? Naw, he wutn't dead. They put two an' two tergither. They'd all done observ'd u.f.o.'s before. An' one of 'em, right 'round the co'ner over here, done stumb'd over some motorscooter-lookin thang, 'cept it didn't have no wheels... an' then they's all in agreemint. They said a space ship done landed over in Tingelstad somewhere an'...

Naw, y'all can all believe whut all ye want to. That he done set hisself on a hoverbike an' tolt his parents that he's fixin to go out fer to do some botanickal investigashuns...

Believe whut all y'all want to. They says he took a wrong turn. They says he run out o' gas 'round the co'ner over here. They says he set off on foot. He goed an' goed, lookin an' lookin fer his space ship. An' that's when they found him. Horror an' tarnation... one o' them chucky-dolls out o' some horrorfilm deep in the labbarinth o' the woods.

In. Back in the classroom.

But anser? Naw, he didn't anser.

In. Back in the classroom. You hear me?

Naw.

I wouldn't a-gone back in, nuther. I'd a-krept unner the meathouse whut stood on steddle stones in the middle o' the schoolyard.

In.
Naw.
In.

But we's gon' play hushmouth, said ol' Andy many a year later. *We's gon' play hushmouth.*

The Calf.

O. I remember. I remember him layin there. Been thankin an' thankin bout it these past few days. Thankin bout lots o' other thangs too but if the Boss-Man an' the Secertary was to be astin me I's gon' tell 'em bout the incident back behind the SportsMart. Bout how he was a-layin there an' I's writin it all down. Writin down whut I remember. How I remember it. As I remember it, an' they's more to come, tellin ye. More to come but he'll prob'ly be down here dreckly. The Minister o' Justice. Gon' come bellerin into my ear that I best be hottin up some coffee an' then I's gon' have a sight o' trubble writin down whut I remember, whut I's thankin.

Hot up some coffee. Okey okey okey. Another round.

Ol' Hobblestiltskin wi' the coffeepot in his tremblin artifisshul right hand. Doddlin around, ol' Hobblestiltskin. Pourin coffee into all their nice porslin cups wi' the Logo on 'em whiles they's a-talkin. Talkin bout the ol' Hobblestiltskin:

. . . dreemin . . . tangl'd . . . spinnin yarns . . . writin . . .

But whut all he's a-dreemin about an' gittin tangl'd up in 'an spinnin yarns about an' writin down . . . they don't know nuthin about it. They know a-plenty but nuthin about that an' I's thankin about them. I remember them tough kids. I remember the Calf. An' if the Boss-Man an' the Secertary was to go astin . . . they gon' git to hear a little more.

No foolin?

No foolin.

Them tough kids. They's dancin an' whoopin. The strongest of 'em with them unnerbritches in his mouth. Another of 'em blowin his nose hard into a limpworn sock. But who was they an' how many? Some six-seven of 'em, eight, nine? An' who was that feller, the strongest o' the bunch? Naw, go an' ast the Calf? Ain't no use in astin the Calf, naw. The Calf. That feller, the strongest o' the bunch, had done beat him half to death an' when he could finally talk agin after layin Lawd only knows how long in a coma he had no ideer whut'd done happen'd an' ol' Andy went an' visited him in the hospital an' said he wutn't right in the head no more.

Ol' Andy. That needle-thin ol' bugger wi' the spik'd-up hairdo, aviater glasses, pencil-moustaches, an' thick brassy necklace.

Hell, man, said ol' Andy. *The Calf yeah ye know it the Calf yeah ye oughtta a-seen him ye oughtta a-heard him lay'd out in the hospital a-grinnin like a unplow'd girlie an' hell naw I didn't have no ideer whut to say to him or whut I's spos'd to thank naw whut in the hell's he thankin?*

A voice. One o' these chaintooth voices that ain't mine, it says, the voice says: *Goddamn ol' Calfy goddamn why'd ye have to go an' wriggle out o' them clothes back behind the SportsMart that late summer night come life or death?*

That voice. A voice whut's real easy to git me a-fantasizin about her, the wommon, the weepin wommon, a diff'rent wommon than the lady who was a-lookin an' lookin at me, lookin an' lookin wi' them eyes o' hern, the lady in the one recliner in my livin room, the lady, that lady, sharp moon in the darkness, naw that ain't the same one at'oll, this a diff'rent one, the weepin wommon, she's a-weepin an' a-wailin an' ol' Andy his voice was all squeakified an' if ye was to hear his voice on a tape recorder an' didn't know nuthin else bout them puzzle pieces o' hisn an' the sorta figgure he cut then ye might coulda insisted an' said it was a lady ye heard but this is a diff'rent one I's thankin of now, a radick'ly diff'rent sorta wommon an' she's a-weepin an' a-wailin an' a-weepin, sayin: *Why'd ye do it ol' Calfy come life or death why?*

Ol' Andy? Some believ'd he was a close confidaunt or anyhow a feller who in all the commoshun got to feelin like it was him an' not Pucky Paul (bein he was lay'd up after the car-crash) an' not KurtSquirt an' fer sure not ol' Rattlebones Roger who was gon' travel on over to Gorvik an' see fer hisself how the Calf was doin at the hospital after he (the Calf) could speak agin by an' by.

Some. Some folks believ'd that.

If only they'd a-know'd.

Ol' Andy he slamm'd his fist on the table an' knock'd over the dixiecup an' tolt me in no onsurtin terms to go an' hang myself an' scratch my goober, an' he said they ain't no way, ain't *no* way he's gon' anser that kinda plum fool question as to whuther he was hesistatin fer to go a-drivin up there, why he had hisself a drivin licence, by dod he's a grow'd-up man an' the very ideer some dad-blasted sonofabitch like *me* is gon' be the one to ast him if he'd been a-hesitatin, why it made him just as angry as all-git-out an' I could just as well go an' hang myself an' scratch my goober.

But I ast him. I remember astin him.

Water from the dixiecup run all over the table an' water dripp'd down all over the floor.

By dam ye can go hang yerself an' scratch yer goober.

Okey. That was his way o' talkin. One o' his fav'rit sayins. I know'd him. Remember this one time he said it to his pappie an' earn'd hisself a whuppin. Okey. The Calf.

He's layin here in that bed at the hospital just a-grinnin like all-git-out an' I tell ye he's dang demented he's ding-dong demented ye know not one peep out o' him ye know but I had to say somethin so I up an' tolt him how folks back in town thank its a sin an' a shame to let them kinda peckerwoods go runnin away gittin theirselves gone an' they wutn't nary a trace of 'em when that ol' warshwommon come an' found ye an' the po'leece come long after the ambulence personell had done left, ol' Andy said he said an' I's thankin it's a good thang he skipp'd over that one lil' deetail that both of us was there, two gumpshunless fellers who stood there an' seen ever' bit of it an' heard ever' bit of it.

Did we know anythang? Naw. Not a thang. Didn't know a thang. Not a thang. Dingle dangle lang.

Y'all seen anythang? Heard anythang?

We's gon' play hushmouth, said ol' Andy.

An' ol' Pucky Paul an' ol' KurtSquirt an' ol' Rattlebones Roger was a-noddin an' noddin prob'ly wantin to head home all three of 'em an' ol' Andy he said: *We's gon' play hushmouth bout this here an' we's gon' play hushmouth bout all that other stuff too. We done done more'n enuff, seein as we call'd fer the ambulence.*

We call'd fer the ambulence. Ol' Andy he said *we*. We call'd fer the ambulence.

Phone booth over by the bus term'nal. It was ol' Rattlebones Roger whut was rattlin over there fast as them bones could carry him. Natcherly. Natcherly it would be him, ol' Rattlebones Roger, that lil' ol' baby geeraff. He flew an' he flapp'd an' he flail'd off down the road in the ahpasit direcshun as them tough kids as they run off in a gaggle tergither toward the Creemery where some of 'em prob'ly had their veehickles park'd an' we, the rest of us, ol' Pucky Paul an' ol' KurtSquirt an' ol' Andy an' me, we prob'ly all of us reckon'd we knew where ol' Rattlebones Roger was headed an' whut sorta needcessities he had in his mind just then.

An' ol' Andy he's gainin on him. He wutn't no slow-poke nuther, ol' Andy. couldn't be no slow-poke, not with the sorta shagnasty he had fer a pappie an' the fact 'o his pappie havin to limp on account o' the jake-leg didn't make no diff'rence, nuh-uh, naw, fer ol' Andy's pappie, ye see, he had hisself one o' them magical brushbrooms an' a flyin carpet too, so they wutn't no use in tryin to git the jump on him, not on no wobbly pair o' legs anyhow an' he was gainin on him, ol' Andy was, gainin on ol' Rattlebones Roger, before he trotted right past him an' flung open the door to the phone booth an' fish'd around in the pocket o' his cowhockeysmear'd locopoco britches fer some loose change an' while he's a-fishin aroun' in there the bottom edge o' his wide miniskirt-lookin pocoloco sweater musta been drap'd over the pipecleanerstump he had fer a forearm an' then . . . an' then he's able to git thru to the ambulence.

Know'd the number by heart, ol' Andy did. So'd ol' Rattlebones Roger. That's how come he flew so fast, ol' Rattlebones Roger. The number, I reckon he musta said later, *was blinkin in just the right place inside o' his thankin-box*. Prob'ly. An' now he's fixin to call, call before it was too late but the feller who'd done already got thru . . . ol' Andy he said we'd done done more'n enuff, seein as we call'd fer the ambulence an' all.

We's gon' play hushmouth, said ol' Andy. Any o' us says somethin why then it'll be our turn. They know'd we was there. Course they know'd it an' they know who *I* is an' who *y'all* is an' who *we* is an' if they was to catch wind about all that other stuff, why it'd be the death of each an' ever' one o' us.

They, they, they know who we is.

Ol' KurtSquirt he took to snifflin an' weepin an' boohooin. Just a-weepin an' a-weepin. Wutn't no use tryin to stop him.

They n n know who we is.

Goddammit Squirty, cut the hell out. Goddammit.

Wutn't no use. Ol' KurtSquirt he wept an' sniffl'd an' wept an' his legs buckl'd an' the big ol' shaggy troll he melted an' lay like a big ol' piddlypuddle on the crackin asfalt.

Goddammit. Plum fool.

They, they, they n n know who we is. Ahhh they know who we is. They, they, they n n know…

An' we play'd hushmouth. I know'd none of us'd snitch. Ol' KurtSquirt he boohoo'd out ever' last drop he had inside that man-husk o' hisn an' we wip'd him up off the asfalt an' ol' Andy straighted his aviater glasses an' set to eyeballin him real mean with his eyes all red an' gashly, eyein him with a pair o' burnin hot coals in the long minutes betwixt the last dance in the late summer night darkness an' the slow but surtin traces of the wakin sun in the sky an' he hiss'd once more whut he done said once or twice already an' ol' Pucky Paul an' ol' KurtSquirt an' ol' Rattlebones Roger nodded an' nodded.

Okey?

Okey.

Okey.

Okey.

We done heard a little bout whut it was like livin on his planit. Wutn't no green space creturs there, naw. Them space creturs is so pastywhite ye could almost see straight thru 'em. An' they wutn't no need fer no laserguns or lightsabres there. Matterfactually they wutn't no need fer no armamints at'oll. But they's a lot o' woods on this planit an' fellers was always itchin fer to go a-shootin their bows an' arrers to try an' slay some o' the weird beests whut go a-roamin an' a-rummigin an' a-rootin around in them there woods. Or, they tried to git them beests to walk into varius traps they lay'd all about. He talk'd a little about that. Bout them traps o' theirn. An' he talk'd a little bout religion, customs, ritcherals. A good many folks was grain farmers an' before any of 'em could go a-harvestin they had to take off all their clothes an' dance the whole night thru an' lick on each other. Prob'ly good to git it done an' out o' the way. But his spaceship an' hoverbike? Naw, he didn't say nuthin bout no spaceship or hoverbike.

Long minutes. Slow but surtin traces o' the wakin sun. Phone booth. Bus term'nal. SportsMart. Behind the SportsMart. There he lay. The Calf. He coulda been dead. It might coulda been a dead body that ambulence was fixin to drive off with. Maybe.

The Dead Feller Calfy.

Dead Feller, ye say?

Dead Feller.

But . . .

The strongest toughie o' the bunch was featherin into him, the Calf was screamin an' yowlin an' the strongest toughie was featherin into him an' cuff'd him smack in the jaw an' the Calf he was reelin. Boff'd him agin an' the Calf he was wobblin. The strongest toughie's a-cuffin an' boffin him, kick'd him right in the cods an' the Calf he did tumble an' . . . an' then whut? Then a baseball bat. A louieville slugger. Louieville slugger? Yep. Out o' nowhere. That toughie. Strongest o' the bunch. Out o' nowhere his right arm had got double. All of a sudden. All of a sudden?

The sound. I remember the sound. I can hear the sound. *Whomp.* An' I see the wide leatherjacketed back o' that sasquatch-sonofabitch with his sluggerfied doublearm an' I see his bleach'd wolfwhite mullet go a-flappin thisaway an' flyin thataway in time wi' the whuppin. *Whomp.* An' his legs was so far apart it look'd to me like he's fixin to do a split clean down the middle. *Whomp.* An' him standin there with his legs far apart an' his bleach'd wolfwhite mullet an' his wide leatherjacketed back an' his sluggerfied doublearm, the sasquatch-sonofabitch: him standin there an' even tho' we cain't see his face . . . I's surtin he's a-smilin.

Surtin?

Well, maybe surtin ain't . . .

Well?

Aw hell naw, here they go agin demandin coffee an' now it's that feller wi' the wooden clogs comin on down. Clippity cloppin on down wi' them clogs o' hisn. Nairer an' nairer he comes an' soon he'll be appearin in my crannynook. I know he's dress'd up in one o' them fancy suits like all the other fellers an' perfum'd like all-git-out but he ain't exackly dry behind the ears yet an' ain't wairin no fancy shoes like them others an' now here he comes. Clippity cloppin on down. Nairer an' nairer he comes an' one o' them voices in my noggin done give him a name an' my artifisshul right hand scratches it down on the piece o' paper. The Kid. Naw: *Kid Clipclop*. An' I know his face is all pale, pale like a burial cloth somebody done hung up on a wall in a museeum behind glass where folks can go an' gawp at it an' fall to thankin bout how the Dead Feller couldn't a-just stay'd where he was but had to go bustin out o' his coffin an' diggin hisself a tunnel an' crawlin out an' set off runnin out o' the graveyard an' thru the woods an' course it wutn't until he was in the woods that he come to realize he didn't need no burial cloth no more an' when they's out a-lookin fer him, the Sheriff an' a bunch o' burlyhurlies from the shootin range, why he's already far above the hillsides an' the only thang they could find was that there burial cloth hangin from a pinetree branch an' they took it with 'em, give it to the museeum an' the newspaper come an' wrote about it, wrote about the burial cloth an' he's pale, Kid Clipclop, his face is all pale, pale as that burial cloth but I's a whole lot paler, pale as the lady settin there in the one recliner talkin bout my life an' givin me a pamflit,

I's dry behind my gnome ears an' I's pale as the sharp moon an' it's the moon the Dead Feller's headed towards whiles he's off an' runnin thru the late summer night an' now he done appear'd in my crannynook, Kid Clipclop.

He done drug out a long rope. Coil'd it up an' hook'd it around his right shoulder an' dadgum that lil' oddball sure looks like a bonafy'd cowboy a-wagglin on up the footpath. Cowboy hat an' cowboy boots. An' he's knock-knee'd like some dang ol' calf, this oddball with a rope. An' we done set ourselves along the footpath, at the edge o' the field, fer to be studyin his way o' walkin an' all his gear an' we cain't hardly he'p but laff an' give him hell fer they way he looks.

Where'd yer pony run off to? Yer pony? An' where ye goin wi' that rope? Gon' hang yerself?

Coffee. They's drankin coffee. Cussid lot o' coffee. An' then they's a-pissin. Pissin an' pissin. Off to the john they all run. Fellers in their fancy costy suits. Husky-smellin menfolks. Perfume-smellin. Off to the john they all run, it's a goddamn murrathon an' the door to the john where ye gots yer urinals an' a decent commode is sitcherated right next to the coffee pot. So each an' ever' one of 'em has done seen it. Seen whut I's gittin up to. Seen me settin an' writin when I's spos'd to be a-sharp'nin the pencils an' shreddin the paper. They's drankin a cussid lot o' coffee an' they run on past me an' they see whut I's gittin up to. They see it all right. An' it ain't too seldom I's got to run off to the john myself. Natcherly I do like everbody else when it come to chuggin down that coffee. O. Coffee. Mmm. They oughtn't to be lettin folks go a-chuggin down coffee all day an' maybe they believe its the doojiggers whut put all the pep back in a body but I know better. Coffee. The miracle cure is call'd coffee. Ye can go aroun' mimickin them swaggerin pissants from the commershuls, a-smilin an' a-barein all yer teefies. But the miracle cure is call'd coffee.

Oughtn't to be allow'd, I says. An' it ain't exackly optimal bein equipp'd with a artifisshul bladder nuther. Bout two-three cups is all it takes before the artifisshul bladder's full to bustin an' I's off to the john to sank my artifisshul whippersnapper down into the decent commode. That's how I been doin it. Ain't able to stand an' piss, naw. Artifisshul rear end. Fust I got to sitcherate the artifisshul rear end on the seat. It's a mighty fine artifisshul rear end. Goddang whut a fine rear end. Whittle'd from the rockhardest birchwood with a knot in it where they bor'd a hole, them who done restor'd me that is, an' believe it or not they's able to attach the rear end with glue an' so wi' this tecknalogickal marvel fer a rear end well sitcherated on the commode I's able to sank the limpsy whippersnapper nice an' slow down into the bowl. I ain't no good fer it no more. Like I done said I cain't rightly remember the last time I's layin tergither wi' no wommon. Lawd a mercy. Lawd a mercy if I ain't a ol' hag myself an' betwixt the legs o' this here hag they's a limpsy wriggleworm she got to sank down into the bowl fer to piss, boy. But the ol' hag she operates herself, she does.

Murderashun an' hellfire. Holy moly how it do be stankin in here. Hellfire an' murderashun. They keep on a-pissin an' pissin wairin their fancy costy suits an' earnin great gobs o' money an' eatin the money an' sousin theirselves all with perfume an' it's a loud-smellin perfume too but the perfume stank be mixin wi' the piss stank an' dewkie stank in here, that's right cause they's a-crappin, them fellers, I tell ye, they crap out money an' they's a-crappin purty dang nair as much as they's a-pissin an' by an' by it happen that I's got to run off an' crap too but I ain't ever been able to crap no money so fur. All this coffee don't do a stomick no good an' my artifisshul stomick's been botherin me a right smart since heck was a pup, fer many a year come to thank of it. Ain't no matter whut I put down my gullick (whuther it's food or drank or terbacky smoke or motoroil or other kinds o' oil whut protects aginst rust (the nuts an' bolts that is) an' on drumly days a few drops o' woodglue whut drips thru all the cracks in the woodworkins), it don't make a lick o' diff'rence. The artifisshul stomick it rombles an' I got to drag myself over to the john an' in a hurry too. Plenty o' times I done benastied myself in the britches. This grow'd-up gnome done benastied hisself a-plenty. But he operates hisself an' he ain't benasty'd hisself down in the unnerworld so fur.

O. Just thank. Thank if he could still go a-runnin. Run just like ol' Rattlebones Roger run, like ol' Andy run, like the Dead Feller run. Just thank.

Yes an' they's a bunch o' woods on this planit. Ye can go a-trampin an' trudgin fer weeks on end an' the only thang ye's a-trampin an' trudgin in . . . is woods.

Woods woods woods . . .

An' the trees is like the biggest trees on our own planit. Trees just like spruces an' pinetrees. An' the kind o' trees they got in English forests an' trees whut look like the trees in jungals.

Lots o' woods, boy. Ye can go a-trampin an' treadin o'er branches, limbs an' mosses.

An' it's prob'ly how come they's so pale, them space creturs we done seen a few specimins of. They's pale on account o' all the shade they is in the woods.

The big trees give off shade an' if ye's to go a-trampin an' a-trudgin thru the shadowy woods ye ain't gon' git no sunburn, exackly.

But come to thank of it a body could git mighty green from trampin an' trudgin in the woods. Green as the greenest o' trees. Green as the greenest o' shrubs. Green as the greenest mosses.

So how come ain't they all green theirselves, them dadblam'd space creturs?

The Dead Feller. Where'd he run off to? How come he couldn't a-stay'd where he was? Pshaw. Prob'ly just wantin to git the hell out o' there.

He'd done bustid out of the coffin an' he'd done tunnel'd thru th' earth. He done it, all right. Bustid hisself out. Dug his way thru. An' he done it wi' them riggermortis'd hands o' hisn. An' then? Then he run off thru the woods, fast as a hen a-peckin. The burial cloth, he didn't have no need fer it no more, so he wriggl'd out of it just like ol' Calfy wriggl'd out o' his jacket an' shirt. An' even tho' I got to hear him sangin, still I find myself a-wonderin:

Dead Feller, Dead Feller, where did ye go?

Thru the woods. Fast as a hen a-peckin. Yep. I remember I's runnin. I's runnin, I's flyin an' flappin an' flailin, I wutn't as quick as ol' Andy tho' I coulda gain'd on ol' Rattlebones Roger if I'd a-car'd to an' I remember how we run thru the woods, bunch o' ballhootin young'uns, fast as a hen a-peckin. Because the woods was a good hidin place, ye see. Colonize yer own square yard in the woods where ye can hide yerself an' just be there, be yerself.

We run. The young'uns. We young'uns off an' run like we's tetch'd in the head. An' that's exackly whut we was, we was tetch'd. Ballhootin young'uns. Tetch'd in the head. Said so. They all said so, Mister Principal an' Miss Teacher an' ol' Andy's pappie an' my mama an' my sister. Tetch'd in the head, they said. *Positivly tetch'd.* Ha ha. But if ye thank it's positivly onproblematical to go callin each an' ever' one o' us fer tetch'd why then ye best be rememberin that the one o' us don't favor the other any more'n you an' me favor each other. Barn gnome. Ye ain't no barn gnome, boy. Barn gnome. I's the barn gnome.

An' them times we's runnin thru the woods . . . the only gnome, the only *meckanickal* gnome runnin fast as a hen a-peckin, that was me, boy. Me.

Ol' Andy. He wutn't no barn gnome, boy. Wutn't meckanickal, nuther. Ol' Andy he liv'd in a house tergither with his pappie an' ye had to come pootin into a construcshun lot fer to find that house o' theirn. But his pappie . . . he was a gnome. Not no barn gnome. Wutn't meckanickal, nuther. Just a gnome. That dang ol' construcshun lot . . . Andy's world . . . an' if you was to ast me whut he look'd like, this needle-thin construcshun-lot cretur, if you was to ast me I'd tell ye whut I reelly thank: *A rat. Ol' Andy's a genuwine rat.*

An' ol' Pucky Paul? A gnawer too if they ever was one, maybe a beever, maybe a rabbit, maybe a cross betwixt a beever an' a rabbit, I don't know an' maybe it don't make no diff'rence no-how. But in the mirror, boy . . . when he was swayin over the ol' nebbynose . . . coulda swore he was as stiff an' funny-lookin as one o' them playmobil-figureens I remember him usin as ammuni-shun fer targit practice one evenin when school was out fer the summer with a slingshot he'd done bought hisself down at the five an' dime.

An' ol' KurtSquirt? That's a easy one. Troll o' the woods he was, the ginormous troll o' the woods with a head o' hair ye coulda used fer mattress fillins if Mister Principal an' Miss Teacher had a-took a pair o' sizzers to him an' gone a-clippyclipclippin over in the dunce's co'ner, but they never got to because that ol' troll o' the woods up an' melted thru their fingers an' they had to wipe him up an' throw him out an' later when he was off a-runnin thru the woods that matressfillin head o' hair was as hale as ever, boy.

An' ol' Rattlebones Roger? The oddball. Baby geeraff. Lil' chickee. Ribby ol' camel or wildabeest or deehidrayted ostrich.

Ain't no matter. Whut he was, was Rattlebones. An' he didn't, no he didn't, an' he didn't, no he didn't, no he didn't hardly ever say a thang, dangalang. Just along fer the ride, he was, ol' Rattlebones Roger. Tetch'd in the head like the rest of us. An' when he was a-hoverin up there . . . naw, whut was it he look'd like? A geeraff? A oddball'? Ain't no tellin an' it ain't no matter nuther.

Flyin. We was flyin an' flappin an' flailin thru the woods. Runnin. Ol' Andy an' ol' Pucky Paul an' ol' KurtSquirt an' ol' Rattlebones Roger an' me. In a hurry. *Thick woods. Ye was havin to clear a path now too. Try an' clear faster. Ow. Ow ow ow. Woods was thicker'n all-git-out. Darker'n all-git-out. Branches whippin ye in the face.* Dark. Awful dark. Or, coulda been broad daylight, I seem to rickolect it bein just after the fust day o' school . . . we run an' we's runnin in woods that wutn't the darkest of all woods an' they was some several of us young'uns, some fifteen-twenty ballhootin boys.

It wudn't the darkest of all woods.

Broad daylight. After the fust day o' school.

I remember it now.

A sunshinin day that I sorta imagine like a lamplight in the dark as I set here a-thankin an' a-writin. A magical lamplight in the late summer night dark.

Because it was on that very sunshinin day we come upon the Calf. Out there in the woods ginnin around wi' somethin. Gittin on up to somethin, Lawd only knows whut it was.

But he was up to somethin. Some kinda somethin.

A rope. The Calf had done tied hisself a rope around a big ol' pine-tree standin sorta all by herself in the middle of a loggin operashun. A long rope about chest-high with him standin there, the space cretur, standin there pullin it in a straight line, pullin the rope straight an' true betwixt the tree an' hisself an' then he took to a-babblin, babblin some kinda Arabic-soundin somethin . . .

La illa holla illo alla,
La illa holla illo alla,
La illa holla illo alla . . .

An' the fact that they was some fifteen-twenty boys . . . didn't bother him one bit an' he stood there a-yankin an' pullin the rope straight an' true just a-babblin an' a-babblin away. Ol' Calfy . . .

La illa holla illo alla,
La illa holla illo alla,
La illa holla illo alla . . .

An' ol' Andy took a noshun to go an' he'p him. He's wantin to go a-pullin on the rope too. Pull on the rope with them pipecleanerarms o' hisn. A-yankin an' a-babblin away . . .

La illa holla illo alla,
La illa holla illo alla,
La illa holla illo alla . . .

An' the Calf? Wutn't bother'd one bit. An' now ol' Andy's standin right smack in front o' him. Narrer back aginst the front o' his sweat-soak'd t-shirted pussle-gut. Ol' Andy was starin into the trunk o' the pinetree tergither wi' the Calf an' he took to sangin along, ol' Andy . . .

La illa holla illo alla,
La illa holla illo alla,
La illa holla illo alla . . .

But whut was it they's tryin to do? Ain't no tellin. I remember 'em standin here pullin the rope. Big ol' watersogg'd Calfy standin there an' standin in front o' the Calfy is ol' needle-thin Andy. They's yankin. They's babblin. I remember how they did babble. Lawd a mercy. A pinetree. Big ol' pinetree standin all by herself.

Ol' Andy's bleach'd spikey hairdo. Lookin like it was bristlin an' gittin spikier with ever' yank he took while he goed on a-yankin an' a-babblin an' if he wutn't yankin with ever' mite o' strength he had then it was enuff fer that his hair was sorta bein yank'd too, yank'd up toward the sky.

The Calf. He had a bleachy spikey hairdo just like ol' Andy's but on his noggin the spikes was lookin more like a bunch a flowers that'd done been completely demolish'd in a powerful ragin gully-whopper, the kinda gully-whopper the Prophet hisself, ol' KillerHenry, had been talkin about an' *we* was fixin to be talkin about, boy, by an' by, down in the Mare Cooter Canyon late one summer, an' he was plum red in the face, the Calf was, yankin an' pullin an' yankin an' babblin with all his strength an' even tho' I hadn't the foggiest noshun whut it was he's gittin up to I started havin a funny feelin while I's settin there on a stump starin wide-eye'd an' listnin: a feelin that they was some sorta plan behind it all, that the Calf had done thunk everthang out, that he'd done had hisself a ideer an' thankeriz'd an' cogitated an' spek'lated an' medatater'd on it from A to Z, thankeriz'd an' cogitated an' cook'd up a plan an' as fer the rest o' us who'd come a-runnin thru the woods, I's a-thankin whiles I's settin here: *Was we boys a part o' his plan all along? An' whut about ol' Andy gittin a noshun to up an' he'p ol' Calfy . . . was that all part o' the plan too? Whut was it or whut wasn't it that done push'd that lil' ol' thought-bubble into ol' Andy's noggin?*

They kep' on babblin. They kep' on yankin. I's settin on a stump. The other young'uns who'd come a-runnin they's settin on stumps too. Bunch of us. The others. A rabbit, a mouse, a roebuck, a moose, a weasel, a catamount, a bunny or beever, a ferrididdle, a geeraff, a zeebra, a lion, a troll o' the woods, a sheepie an' a gnome from Toten an' some peckerwood from who knows where an' a rattlebones an' a meckanickal barn gnome. The young'uns. The others who come a-runnin. Flyin, flappin, flailin. The others who come upon the Calf too.

An' a lil' witch. A lil' witch dress'd all in black. I remember the lil' witch girl. She's settin on a stump. Settin quiet all by herself studyin an' listnin when fifteen-twenty young'uns come a-runnin. Studyin the Calf while he yank'd an' pull'd, listnin to his babble. More'n likely part o' his plan too, the witch girl. Yes-huh. A funny feelin. A plan. A pinetree . . .

> La illa holla illo alla,
> La illa holla illo alla,
> La illa holla illo alla . . .

But the big ol' pinetree'd been standin here all by herself a long time an' hadn't never smil'd nor wav'd to no cretur whut had legs to run with, animals or humans or gnomes or space creturs or you name it. Never. Never in all the world. Because the big ol' pinetree was doin just fine standin all by herself without all them creturs an' hadn't never loosen'd her grip from the earth in the way-back-when because somebody else was wantin her to loosen her grip an' stretch on up. That pinetree . . .

> La illa holla illo alla,
> La illa holla illo alla,
> La illa holla illo alla . . .

Naw, smile? Wave? Naw, she don't cry nuther, nor scream nor howl nor clench no pineconefist an' go loose on no space cretur whut done tied hisself a rope 'round her trunk. Naw. Right there. She's standin right there. Pinetree's a-standin there an' that one feller, the one who done come out here before the Rat an' the other young'uns come a-runnin, this feller done tied hisself a rope 'round the pinetree an' he's a-pullin an' a-yankin that rope an' gittin he'p wi' the pullin from none other than that ol' Rat hisself an' they's babblin tergither an' the lil' witch girl she's settin on her stump, quiet, studyin . . .

La illa holla illo alla,
La illa holla illo alla,
La illa holla illo alla . . .

An' they was runnin an' runnin. Them young'uns come a-runnin. The Rat an' the others who was all tetch'd in the head. An' the Dead Feller. He run too. The Dead Feller. He'd done got away, got the heck out o' dodge, that Dead Feller.

Fer real?

Yep.

He'd done got the heck out o' dodge all right.

An' it was the moon the Dead Feller was headed toward once he set off runnin an' runnin' thru the late summer night an' it was another woods he was runnin thru now. Fast. Fast as a hen a-peckin. He's puffin an' pantin an' pushin hisself to the limit lookin fer all the world like a Amurrican outlaw like ye see in the movies who'd done bustid out 'o prison an' if he hadn't a-been dead already . . . well . . . might as well fill in the rest yerself. The moon. An' all of a sudden, boy . . . out o' nowhere come the other light. Wutn't comin from the night sky. Wutn't no stars out next to the moon. Wutn't no blinkin airplane nor a u.f.o. nor a spaceship nuther. Naw, it was a light down in a gorge, a hollow, a wood-hole, a canyon. Closer an' closer an' down the slopes an' ye come to realize it ain't the light from no car headlights but a light from a wender. A cabin wender. A parafin lamp in a cabin wender.

Yessir.

A magical lamplight in the late summer night dark.

That planit o' hisn . . . so infinnitly fur away an' still they's able to git him here all safe an' sound . . . But how come? How come they pick'd our planit out o' all the other ones? We cain't hardly figgure it. An' we done discuss'd it plenty. Back an' futh. How come? How come how come how come? Most o' the time we's unanimous. Been about two-three days since we's all last unanimous. We was discussin an' discussin an' after about a hour folks is fixin to git ril'd up but by an' by everbody says: We's unanimous.

Down here. To our planit. He was sent down here because they'd been powerful jealous o' us fer a long time. Them who sent him. They'd been powerful jealous a long time.

Hush. Such a eerie hush. Late summer night. Behind the Sports-Mart. O, such a eerie hush whut fell all of a sudden. An' we, ol' KurtSquirt an' ol' Rattlebones Roger an' ol' Pucky Paul an' ol' Andy an' me . . .

Naw, whut is I spos'd to say? That it was *now*, that very slap bang instant, we shoulda flung ourselves into the fray an' lit into them tough kids? The voice. The wommon who was weepin an' wailin, wailin an' weepin. Prob'ly thankin we oughtta go stickin our necks out. Thankin we oughtta do somethin. Weepin an' wailin an' weepin. An' we, we's spos'd to go flingin ourselves into the fray like a bunch o' whoopin an' stavin apes o' varius shapes an' sizes an' I's spos'd to grab onto the feller leadin the onslaut. The strongest o' them toughies. O how I shoulda grabb'd onto him an' yank'd hard on that bleach'd wolfwhite mullet o' hisn an' took to a-bitin him here an' bitin him there. Bitin bitin bitin. Flattenin him down into doin a split, clean down the everlovin middle. This whoopin an' stavin ape done flatten'd him. Him. The strongest o' them toughies. The feller leadin the onslaut. An' then . . .

Naw, whut is I spos'd to say? Hmm. They's dancin, dancin dance my lil' dollie, them toughies. C'mon boys, let's git the hell out o' here holler'd the strongest o' the bunch an' they run off in a gaggle tergither down toward the Creemery an' the sluggerfied doublearm was risin up so high an' these apes was a-starin wide-eye'd. The Calf lay there. An' Rattlebones Roger was rattlin on down fast as them bones could carry him. In the ahpasit direcshun.

The ambulence. Coulda swore I's hearin it. Way off yonder. I's roll'd up in a ball an' I coulda swore I's hearin the ambulence. But I know'd they wutn't no way I's hearin it.

Back home on the farm. Back home in my room. Home.

Whut was it I's tryin to fergit? Fergit dreckly?

Ol' Pucky Paul was drivin turrible fast cuttin curves all the way up an' we was lucky not to run into nobody an' the inside o' the veehickle smell'd o' beer an' cowhockey an' blood an' terbacky an' blueberries an' woods an' some weird sheeit an' I was the fust one who's havin to jump out o' the veehickle (down by the fork in the road, in the bus turn-out) an' that was how come ol' Andy's puzzle pieces got spill'd out.

Wutn't no other way. If I was to jump out then ol' Andy had to jump out before me, seein as this pertic'lar veehickle didn't have no back door, ye see, the door, the door I'd been beggin fer to be open'd an' I mean *beggin* . . . ol' Pucky Paul he stopp'd the veehickle in the bus turn-out, come to a dead stop there, but ol' Andy he just kep' on a-layin in the seat in front o' me an' the seccuns was tickin an' tockin on by an' it musta been some sort o' cross betwixt a threshin machine an' a alarm clock whut was makin our ears shake with all the tickin an' tockin an' I was *beggin an' prayin* . . . after more tickin an' more tockin I was beggin an' prayin . . . the door . . . that door Andy was callin his door an' it was *him* who lay there keepin me stuck where I was but ol' Pucky Paul he took the innishative, ye see, I's beggin . . . an' without so much as a pip he bounc'd like a red bouncy ball out o' that one door he an' he alone could open an' he bounc'd over the hood an' ol' Andy's door it open'd an' the Driver he got rid o' all them sweaty crudcover'd puzzle pieces once an' fer all, the bleach'd spikey hairdo, the ding'd-up steelrimm'd aviater glasses, the pencil-moustaches, an' the thick brassy necklace, yessir he got rid o' ever' one o' them puzzle pieces, one by one.

I didn't say no goodbye. Wutn't nobody sayin no goodbyes. Ol' Pucky Paul he bounc'd back in his veehickle an' stomp'd on the gas. Ol' Rattlebones Roger an' ol' KurtSquirt they's needin to git home too.

Ol' Andy he assembl'd hisself back tergither an' stood in the bus turn-out all wibbly-wobbly an' launch'd into his schpeel fer to explain whut *reelly* had done happen'd the past late summer night whut was now givin way to a risin sun.

Swish swoosh. The Calf, ye know . . . flea-siz'd streak . . . jumpin an' hoppin . . . teevee screen . . .

Like hell. I left. I's stagglin. Stagglin along the footpath. Stone drunk, natcherly. But bein I's stagglin so, whut with my legs not wantin to . . . O. My room. My room since I's a lil' boy. All manner o' cluttermint. I'd done piss'd. I'd done vommick'd at the edge o' the field but didn't none of 'em come up, the wires that is. I vommick'd normal, that is. Vommick'd till I's all empty'd o' vommick. Or so I thunk. I creel'd over onto my bed. Lay there. Breathin heavy. Stankin. Rear end sore. Sore ever'where. An' coulda swore I's hearin the ambulence.

In the veehickle, in the backseat, next to ol' Rattlebones Roger with his corpsepale face he's a sight fur sore eyes settin squose in betwixt ol' KurtSquirt an' me with his face pale as the burial cloth an' they wutn't no seatbelts in the backseat o' this here veehickle naw an' they ain't no tellin whut might coulda happen if we was to have a aksident sendin ol' Rattlebones Roger flyin flappin flailin thru the front wender, up up an' away . . . Beer. They's beer in a tote back here an' I's usin a empty chaw tin to jimmy open one bottle after the other, I's the backseat barkeep an' the Driver he's drankin too. We's smokin filter sigaretts, everbody's lookin down like ol' Rattlebones Roger, he said he couldn't stand no smoke. Goddammit goddammit goddammit, ol' Andy holler'd. Course he'd done had some o' the weird sheeit his pappie sold an' he kep' on repeatin his-self: *Hushmouth we's gon' play hushmouth goddammit goddammit goddammit.* An' ol' KurtSquirt he whimper'd, tryin to holt it in but soon enuff he's whimperin whimperin whimperin.

Dead stop. Tick tock. Ol' Andy out. I jump'd out too. Down by the fork in the road. Pedal to the floor an' the veehickle tore off. Ol' Andy all wibbly-wobbly, grinnin an' laffin. No more cussin from him now, naw. Instead he's gon' do some lecturizin an' explainin about the planit the Calf come from, that big ol' planit way off yonder an' ol' Andy he's sayin how the stars come out tonight before it got clouded over an' how he done seen the planit, he seen it all right, he's lookin up at the shinin stars back when we's well sitcherated at the spot up on the hill wi' the cattle layin there like old Edgipshun statues in the dark (but I wutn't able to see 'em, I's hidin behind a big ol' rock), it was *then* ol' Andy look'd up at the shinin stars an' seen the planit the Calf come from.

I's stagglin. Along the footpath. Stone drunk. Natcherly. An' yet they's somethin else, somethin else whut . . .

> She found a treasure, she found a treasure
> One late summer night, late summer night
> An' I an' I
> An' you an' you . . .
> We couldn't resist, we couldn't fight . . .

Whomp. Naw. Naw naw naw. Wutn't no use blamin the booze an' sayin I couldn't remember. She. The voice. The wommon whut was weepin an' wailin. She said it wutn't no use. *Whomp.* I was stagglin. Here I go a-stagglin. Ah. Piss. Got to piss. I fiddle wi' my belt buckle. Fiddle wi' the zipper. Ain't a bad little watercolor whut done seep'd into these undies. Undies? Hesh up bout them undies, now. Might could be dead, the Calf. Maybe. An' his unnerbritches . . . The strongest of them toughies had them unnerbritches in his mouth. He sure did . . . Or? Naw . . . But now I's gon' fish out the ol' whipper-snapper an' balence myself nice an' ellagint ellagint ellagint. Pissin at the edge o' the field. Phew.

Whomp. Ain't no use. Ain't no . . . an' ol' Andy, I know, he's just a-kickin an' complainin in the bus turn-out. I up an' left.

Now. Now it's comin. Now. An' I piss at the edge o' the field an' lose my balence an' fall smack into the wheat an' I know I done landed in my own vommick an' my own piss an' I roll around flat on my back, an' my chin, chest an' belly's all smear'd with more'n just cowhockey an' blueberries, yes, they's all smear'd with piss, with vommick, an' I thank: *Now. They's fixin to come up. All them wires.*

Heaven. The planit. Heaven? Naw . . . they ain't no massive teevee screen up there in the sky. Ha ha. Naw. Nobody. Nary a one. Ain't nary a one gon' git me to believe the sky's a bonafy'd *teevee screen.* But folks have believ'd many a thang an' still believe many a thang an' they says, folks they says . . . well whut is it they says, anyhow?

I remember Miss Teacher. How she talk'd about heaven.

My granny, too. She talk'd about heaven, sure enuff she did too.

An' the Preacher. Still run into him ever' once in a while. He goes around joggin an' joggin an' exersisin an' exersisin an' imaginin thankin he's gon' win a murrathon one day an' in the winter he puts on them skis o' hisn like some dang ol' birkie-biner an' goes a-pesterin us young'uns. *Hey howdy-do why hullo there ah hey you hey you hey you.* The Preacher. Pointin with one o' his poles, sayin: *Now now now y'all better git out them skis an' take a turn unner God's creashun open to all creturs great an' small unner the sky an' the moon an' the sun an' the clouds an'* . . . Do whut now? Whut in tarnashun is he goin on about? The Preacher. Our health-nut kangaroo preacherman. Cain't keep his ass still nor his tongue still nuther. *Why hullo there hey you hey you' hey you' why hullo there. An' if ye go runnin into him they ain't no gittin away from him fer a right spell. Hey hey hey hey you hey hey hey you you you you.*

An' ol' Andy, I know fer a fact, he dealt him durty. The Preacher. Even tho' he's a health-nut he still smokes a pipe an' this one time they's a big gatherin in the Preacher's home when ol' Andy was bein confirm'd an' ol' Andy he snuck into his office an' found whut he was a-lookin fer an' mix'd some other sheeit in with the terbacky an' bragg'd about it somethin fierce after he'd done tolt us whut he'd done got hisself up to, his eyes was a-sparklin an' he salervated an' lick'd his lips so the skin unner his nose was spick-an'-span where the pencil-moustaches was fixin to sprout an' he kep' up wi' the braggin sayin ol' Preacherman's fixin to find out whut bein a kangaroo feels like fer real wi' that fantastical blend I give him an' now he's a-doin his own doins down at the fork in the road, 'ol Andy is. He's a-doin his own doins too.

But how come? The sky, I mean? How come a poor feller layin on his back in a wheat field ain't allow'd to go starin up at nuthin else? The sky. Peep o' dawn. Late summer. All right. So I's drunk. An' I's starin up at the sky. The sky. Just a late summer mor'nin sky. Naw. The Calf. There. Behind the SportsMart. An' now I's layin here. Here. An' ol' Andy's doin his own doins down at the fork in the road. If I but turn the warsh-tub I see him. There. Down there. By dod he done got back on his feet agin. Back on his pipecleanerlegs. Just like he's dancin a ballay. Or maybe one o' them indian dances. Sun-dance, could be. Bout a hunnerd yards. Betwixt me an' him. I up an' left. I left him where he was in the bus turn-out an' a hunnerd yards along the footpath I tipp'd over an' lay there filosofizin. U.f.o. One o'them u.f.o.'s . . .

Ahhhhhh right. Up up up.

An' I got up. Stuck the ol' whippersnapper back in my britches an' toddl'd off on down the footpath. I's toddlin along. Knee sore. Rist sore. Rear end sore. Sore ever'where. Sore. An' the dent I got in the ol' warsh-tub noggin after I'd done roll'd on down like a rimreck'd bikewheel down the slopes o' the Mare Cooter Canyon . . . An' when we's clearin a path thru the woods . . . stiff an' sore an' plum beat. Was I bleedin? Coulda been. Coulda been a little blood runnin from my knee or my rist. Coulda been. I don't know. Don't know nuthin. I's fixin to protest, I is. He's fixin to git the whut-fer from me, he is. Who is? The Farmer, that's who, the Farmer whut owns all the land in these parts. Hey, Farmer, this here field o' yours is full o' stomblestones, ye hear. Ah naw. How come? How come ye ain't anserin?

I's doddlin along. Stomblestones. Field full o' stomblestones.

Farmer's off in a dreemland, where they ain't nobody callin his attenshun to me walkin an' talkin to him. Ow ow ow. So doggone sore. I's talkin. I's talkin to him. But he cain't hear me. Cain't hear. He ain't here. Not now he ain't. Used to seein him out early but not this early. Me an' ol' Andy's the only ones out this early.

I'd done got up. I'd done doddl'd on down the footpath. I doddl'd the last few yards. An' I didn't turn round no more fer to lookit whut ol' Andy's gittin up to.

Naw. Ain't turnin round now.

Doddlin along.

Ow.

One o' my shoes. Tatter'd velcro runnin shoe. Somethin stuck on the bottom of it. Somethin I's expectin to come in handy.

Dadblame it. Ow.

Driveway. Up the driveway. The yard. Granny's house. Cowshed. Barn. The meathouse. Carport. My mama's house. An' her veehickle. The veehickle she let me borrow if I ast nice. Her veehickle's park'd outside o' the carport, whut always meant my sister'd done come home fust an' park'd there before mama could. Strict, my sister was. Ever' bit like our mama. Squareheaded folks, the both of 'em. Not meckanickal. Squareheaded. Just squareheaded. Me, on the other hand. Meckanickal. An' in a few hours I's fixin to git chew'd out, so I thunk. So I said. *Listen here, Farmer... in a few hours I's fixin to git chew'd out.*

O. If only one of 'em done left out the key. My mama. My sister. One of 'em. Ow. Knee. Rist. Stomblestones. Full o' stomblestones. Field full o' stomblestones. Ahhhhhh right. Dreemland? He'll be wakin by an' by, that Farmer. That ol' boar my mama's always fussin an' fightin with. He'll be wakin soon, I reckon. Wakin up an' lomberin out o' his sty feelin tickl'd to death that he's still a-livin an' inside the john he gits to feelin even more tickl'd. He swings hisself, the piggybear he swings hisself up an' flops his blobbery ol' ass down on the commode lettin loose everthang that done been pressin aginst his hanches durin the wonderful, extra speshul late summer night. Everthang. Ow. But if he's ever so tickl'd . . . money, crappin money . . . naw, don't be talkin bout no money now . . . an' he bellers, that ol' boar, bellerin like a bellcow headed fer the slauterhouse. An' my mama? My sister? The key?

Naw, lookie here, now. Lookie here. One of 'em remember'd to lay out the key an' now they done drunk up all the coffee an' now I's plum empty too, ain't a drop left in my cup an' that kid wi' the clogs . . . Naw, whut was his name, pray tell? His name. His christian name, not no name some voice in my head done nam'd him. I plum forgot. Or maybe he never did menshun whut his name was till now, Kid Clipclop? Prob'ly fixin to come clipcloppin on down the wax'd floor an' still believin, just like everbody else does, that he's stone-deef, that there coffeemakin gnomedoll man . . .

Coffee. Another round. Serve it up.

Back home on the farm. Back home in my room. I coulda swore I heard the ambulence an' I's roll'd up in a ball like a hedgehog. Lawd whut a stank. Vommick, piss. Dewkie. Cowhockey. Blueberries. Woods. Woods? *But the woods smell good. The woods smell good.*

I'd done took off them tatter'd velcro runnin shoes an' my eyes like'ta bust outta my skull when I seen whut'd been hid all them hours unnerneath the sole o' one of 'em.

Woaaaah nelly.

An' I took off all my clothes an' put 'em all in a plastic bag an' shove 'em down into the dresserdrawer whut was already overstuff'd wi' durty unnerbritches an' figgur'd I'd prob'ly have to dig me a hole down by the Rand-fyord an' light the bag an' all its nastyness afire. Ain't no way my mama's gon' stumble across this here, nuh-uh, nor my sister nuther. Yucko. Prob'ly shoulda been cleanin myself up. A shower now woulda been right satisfactual but if I's to go an' turn on the fawcet they's both of' em gon' be jumpin outta bed an' runnin over to the door poundin on it demandin to know whut'n the hell I's gittin up to in the middle o' the night since that they could both hear pipes a-squeakin an' now that the water's a-tricklin an' floodin all over the floor they thank I done doz'd off in there or else black'd out when the bilin hot water hit the man-husk an' they thank I's bein bil'd aliv'd an' they thank I's fixin to short-surcit yes because if you was to go an' warsh yer 'lectric toaster with the plug in the sockit then ye best be readin the instrukshun manual fust an' be cyairful as all-git-out an' they's demandin to hear tell, hear tell hear tell hear tell, my mama, my sister, my mama in her pink nightgown an' my sister in her pink tee-shirt an' pink pannies an' both of 'em with their permanints stickin straight up an' side-ter-side an' front-ter-back an' they ain't no way I's gon' risk that kind o' potherashun I tell ye whut.

Hedgehog. Roll'd up in a ball on the bedspread. Nekkid. I's stankin. It's all hush'd an' I could swear I's hearin the ambulence.

Ol' Andy. It was ol' Andy who made the phone call. He's tremblin an' he's shakin an' he's havin to repeat hisself over an' over agin. Talkin fast, talkin everwhichaway. Slubberin an' slobberin. Ziggin an' zaggin from one topic to the other. Wutn't makin a lick o' sense an' kep' on havin to repeat hisself over an' over agin an' ol' Pucky Paul's tryin to he'p him but by this time ol' Andy's utterly an' completely mommix'd an' said *dammit Pucky goddammit hang yerself scratch yer goober* an' they ain't no tellin whut the poor feller on the other end's able to anser after that kind o' sassin. Maybe the feller'd been thru some kind o' trainin module fer that sorta thang. More'n likely. Ol' Andy took to cussin some more an' shov'd ol' Pucky out o' the way an' kep' havin to repeat hisself over an' over agin.

Ol' Andy ol' Andy . . .

Rain'd somethin powerful all night long. Didn't none of us git no sleep. So everbody got theirselves up an' made coffee an' turn'd on the computer. By dod. Everbody was on there. No foolin, wutn't nobody able to sleep.

Naw, none of us. Everbody. The whole gang.

Ain't nobody sleepin . . . so now we's here . . . an' we can write commints an' then commints on the commints an' we's espesh'ly commintin on the sorta thang the newspaper's done posted up on their website.

They's some folks whut believe they's gon' be acheevin somethin in this world. Effectin change. An' it's them folks we's gon' grab aholt of an' shake 'em with all we's worth. They ain't gon' just go around actin like their britches is so much bigger'n everbody else's. Hell wi' that.

An' ye cain't have no debate withouten a little temperture, after all . . .

Rain'd somethin powerful all night long. Didn't nobody git no sleep. An' didn't nobody need no sleep nuther. They was too much to write, too much commintin to do.

Solid brotherhood . . . solid brotherhood . . .

. . . an' a chaintooth voice said I'd better pull myself tergither an' I clos'd my eyes an' seen the sluggerfied doublearm risin up high, I didn't want to hear the cattle a-lowin, didn't want to hear the Dead Feller sangin an' a wommon's voice said I'd better pull myself tergither an' ol' Andy he's talkin fast talkin everwhichaway, I wutn't talkin too much an' ol' Rattlebones Roger wutn't talkin too much (naw espesh'ly not him) an' ol' KurtSquirt wutn't talkin too much nuther, ol' Andy he's talkin an' ol' Pucky Paul he's talkin but nowhere nair as much as ol' Andy's talkin.

Ol' Andy ol' Andy . . .

A few hours before they chas'd ol' Calfy out o' the Tavern, yep, a few hours before them toughies set after him . . . there, down in Andy's rumpus room, there we sat, the whole gang . . . an' ol' Andy he was settin there a-talkin an' talkin an' boozin an' jabberin an' Pucky Paul he was talkin too, talkin an' boozin but not nowhere nair as much as ol' Andy.

Helena, says ol' Andy. If I ain't as cadgy fer Helena as could be.

Helena? says Pucky Paul. Naw, fergit it.

Shet yer mouth, says ol' Andy. Helena, man. Them bubbies. Them some mighty fine bubbies. Big ol' bubbies. An' them poutin lips. Coulda been in movies, she could.

Helena? Naw fergit it. Helena. Like you ever seen her nekkid.

Shet it. Go hang yerself. Ol' Helena. She's the one fer me, fellers. She's the one. Bubbies. Poutin lips.

Don't fergit that tush. If they's anythang big on her, it's that tushie.

Shet it, Pucky. Just you shet it. Scratch yer goober. Like *you* done seen her nekkid. Ye see, ol' Helena she done tolt me. Last Sa'erday she tolt me I's gon' to git to nibble them bubbies. Sure as I's settin here she said it fellas, only . . . it woulda cost me some money an' I didn't have none an' didn't git to.

Money? How much how much?

Five thousan', she said.

Five thousan'?

Yep. *Five* thousan'.

Five *thousan'* kroners just fer to nibble her bubbies? Just fer *nibblin* an' not no more?

Ehh I mean it coulda . . . gone some-a-wheres . . . but just you shet yer mouth, Pucky. Shet it. Ye can slip on a chicken turd fer all

I cyair. Helena done said whut I said. Five thousan' kroners an' I done got me the money.

Stole. Stole it from yer pappie.

Shet it, Pucky. You shet it up right now.

He's the brain, he is. Ain't no doubt about it. Electrick. Wholly electrified brain that sets off a-cracklin when black clouds is a-gatherin in the sky.

Yer old-timey radio with its cracklin noise. Thems that remember could swear to it, they'd swear that his cracklin mimicks the crackin in yer old-timey radio . . .

Oh, thems was the days. The radio. Like a magnet, the radio. Just thank o' the sound comin dreckly from the loudspeaker, maybe a voice . . . then more voices speakin tergither . . . music . . . o, the radio . . . An' sometimes he too set off a-cracklin . . . an' now the cracklin from this here electrified brain . . . naw, ain't no doubt about it. He's the brain, he is.

Helena. I know'd who that was. My sister done learn'd me a thang or two about her. An' I'd done seen her, seen how Helena grow'd out o' the push o' folk an' become vizable an' stood there flauntin herself. How she grow'd out o' the push o' folk in the Tavern. Many a time I'd seen her. Many a time in the Tavern. An' my sister done tolt me a thang or two. Helena. Bubbies. Lips. Tushie. Ol' Andy an' ol' Pucky Paul sat there a-fussin at each other. Ol' Andy, he was doin the most talkin an' boozin but ol' Pucky wutn't too fur behind whiles ol' KurtSquirt sat a-squirmin an' squirmin an' couldn't hardly set still an' after they'd been fussin back an' futh a spell he took to stutterin an' ast if we'd like to hear a limrick. A limrick, Squirty? Well come on, then.

A buxom young lady from Skreia
S s strode up the hill so spry, yah.
Th th then come a laddie
In the pants of his daddy
But the daddy's the one who did ride 'er.

Uh huh? So . . . th th then *come* a laddie. Yeah?

But ol' Andy, he wutn't laughin at'oll, just said, dreckly: She ain't from Skreia.

Course. Course H H Helena is, said KurtSquirt an' then it got real hush'd.

Weird. Weird how hush'd it got down there in Andy's rumpus room.

The alarm clock. Alarm clock's whut made it so weird an' hush'd. Tickin away. Alarm clock tickin. A tickin sort o' hush. Yep. Sort o' hush such as only a tickin alarm clock can conjure futh. I set there a-waitin. Waitin on Andy to say somethin, do somethin. Waitin. An' like as not ol' Rattlebones Roger was havin the same thought as me: *Five thousan' kroners I pay it soon as I git me the chance if she was to tell me I could nibble them bubbies so long as I plonk down the cash just you see me pay it soon as I scrape up the money*. An' just like that the whippersnapper took to rarin an' struttin up unnerneath my fly an' the pants of his daddy was tight an' I set up, real slow, set up nice an' slow in the beanbag chair where I'd been a-lyin purty nair a hour an' lean'd fo'ward, nice an' slow, just like nuthin outta the ordin'ry, like nuthin like nuthin like nuthin like pinga-linga-not-a-thing-a . . .

Helena. Ol' Helena she grow'd. Out o' the push o' folk. Become vizable. Standin there. Flauntin herself. Helena. I seen her. I seen her all right. I seen her. Now. There. In Andy's rumpus room. Helena. Ol' Helena. Grow'd. She grow'd. Grow'd. An' the whippersnapper strutted up unnerneath my fly. An' Rattlebones Roger made a sound. Just one ittybitty sound from deep down in his gullick. A cough.

This one time, 'round about the same time they had the Shopping Center's grand openin hullabaloo, after a wonderly long summer (full o' skinnies dippin in the sunwarm'd lake), that was when ol' Rattlebones Roger got hisself run over by a veehickle an' was layin there in the ditch, leg broke an' a-hollerin fer someone to he'p him.

Was out bikin. A-bikin an' a-bikin . . .

That bike. A black-varnish'd, Apache-brand bicycle with no less'n three moped mirrors mounted on the handlebar, two to the left side, one to the right, an' on the long black leather highback seat he'd done hung hisself a foxtail an' on the end of the foxtail with its soft creamspatter hue there was feathers, chickenfeathers, so's to make the foxtail seem even longer than it was an' it sure was a sight to behold, ol' Rattlebones Roger, when he come flyin on down at full speed with his foxtail a-flappin an' a feather crown on his head, a right handsome headdress he'd done made hisself usin a ordnary woven sweatband (such as ye see on them longhair'd menfolks playin tennis, the bank give it to him in recognisshin fer him turnin in his piggy bank), feathers, chickenfeathers, plus a couple more feathers he'd done clipp'd from a swan whut lay dead unner the dock down by the shootin range an' he tied feathers to the sweatband an' rubb'd paint on his face, a ginuwine warpaint it was an' off he went a-bikin, ol' Rattlebones Roger, ribby as a lil' newborn baby geeraff he went bikin down the main road an' the baby geeraff was a-wobblin thisaway an' thataway before a veehickle come a-ballhootin from the other direcshun just as Roger come a-wobblin into a sharp bend where the veehickle an' black-varnish'd Apache bicycle collided sendin ol' Rattlebones Roger a-flyin an' flappin an' flailin through the air like some skeer'd lil' chickie an' tergither with headdress an' foxtail he flew up an' flail'd down landin flat in the ditch where now he lay with his leg broke, hollerin fer someone to he'p him.

A angel. A angel they said it was done grab'd aholt o' him, an' sav'd him.

A broke leg. An' that, they said, *that* was diddly compar'd to whut *coulda* occurr'd, they said.

The veehickle. Ballhootin from the other direcshun. Smack into the bend. An' he wobbl'd. They said he wobbl'd. They know'd he wobbl'd. Fur sure he was just as shackl'ty an' unheedful as could be, this here geeraff this skeer'd lil' chickie this Indian this pikepole this rattlebones. He wobbl'd. Unsteady. Unheedin. He wobbl'd. He crash'd. An' a angel, they said. A angel had grab'd aholt o' him. A angel had jump'd up from his cloud an' spread them wings an' pointed his neb straight to the earth an' grab'd aholt o' him just in time fer the crash. Just in time, they said. A angel. Feathers. Angel feathers an' chickenfeathers an' two more feathers clipp'd from a swan. Ol' Rattlebones Roger lay there in a heap o' feathers. Lay there with his leg broke an' hollerin fer he'p after a angel had done grab'd aholt o' him an' sav'd him.

Say whut? A angel? Ain't no easy thang to reckon, sure as I's settin here it ain't.

Ain't nary a trace o' no angel here. I's sure of it.

Maybe they done been here once before but it musta been a long whiles ago, so long that thems that is here now, them fellers dress'd up in their fancy suits an' ties, smellin fine an' liftin the metal pole ever' day, ain't never heard tell of when the angel come fer to visit. Naw, they ain't never heard tell. Naw, where ought they t'ave heard such a tale anyhow?

They ain't nobody who can tell it nohow, nobody, not one livin soul.

But the veehickle? The Driver? Same ol' tune. Ol' Rattlebones Roger flew up an' flail'd down an' the veehickle it purr'd off in the other direcshun swoosh an' was gone. That there yellowbellied Driver. Takin off so. The Driver they call'd yellow. A sin an' a shame, they said. They wrote to the newspaper an' they read it ever' day an' kep' on talkin. Know'd all about it. From beginnin to end. Bout Rattlebones Roger an' his wobblin. Bout his flyin an' flappin an' flailin through the air. Bout how the angel jump'd off his cloud. Bout the veehickle purrin off in the other direcshun. They held the Shopping Center's grand openin hullabaloo an' 'twas 'round bout that time ol' Rattlebones Roger got hisself run over by a veehickle an' was layin there in the ditch, leg broke an' a-hollerin fer someone to he'p him.

Ol' Rattlebones hollerin? Say whut? I coulda swore, as I's a-settin there in ol' Andy's rumpus room that evenin, that I never once done heard no hollerin out o' ol' Rattlebones Roger. But soon . . . Naw ol' Rattlebones, he just wutn't the sort to open his jaw too much. Kep' it shut. Dadgum if he didn't. He kep' it shut. But they said he lay there in the ditch with a broke leg, that ol' Indian. He holler'd fer he'p. Angel done sav'd him. He holler'd fer he'p. They said. They said quite a bit. Wrote to the newspaper, said a whole lot more. I read that there newspaper. I can remember readin the newspaper just after the crash. The Sheriff sent out a a.p.b. fer the Driver an' anyone else who coulda been settin in the veehickle with him. Nobody know'd if the Driver was by hisself at the time. Supposin the veehickle was pack'd full o' folk? The Sheriff'd like to have a word with them that seen or heard somethin, if they was anyone that seen or heard somethin, but ain't nobody seen nor heard nuthin. Wutn't nobody who did. They said. An' they know'd whut all there was fer the knowin anyhow. My mama. My sister. The Farmer. Mister Principal. Miss Teacher. The Preacher. Andy's pappie. An' ol' Andy kep' on talkin an' talkin. Tolt us all over an' over agin whut his pappie'd done said an' he lick'd his lips, ol' Andy. His eyes was a-glist'nin an' his nose was a-drippin an' he lick'd his lips. Lips was dry. Sore. Maybe his lips was easy to git sore an' dry, an' now, bout two-three years after Rattlebones Roger lay in the ditch with a broke leg a-hollerin fer he'p, now, in ol' Andy's rumpus room . . . I seen his lips was dry. Plump ol' lips. Lickin them lips. An' jabberin about ol' Helena. That Helena. She grow'd. Out o' the push o' folk she grow'd. He lick'd his lips an' his tongue got the pencil-moustaches all drippy wet . . . lickin an' a-lickin . . . an' the words they come up from some-a-wheres an' he plum fergot all about the drankin (boozin the most o' all o' us he was) an' maybe that was whut made his lips dry an' the ol' whippersnapper took to a-struttin up under the fly o' my britches an' ol' Andy kep' on talkin an' talkin, just as cadgy as a frustrater'd ol' tomcat he was. The rat. Helena. Ol' Helena. O that Helena. She grow'd an' I's a-thankin: *I'll pay it I'll pay it I'll pay it.*

Naw, man, says ol' Pucky Paul. Fergit it. Fergit it? says ol' Andy. Look man, ye done forgot all about the drankin, says Pucky Paul. Ye done fergot all about the drankin. Shet it, says ol' Andy. Shet it, says he with the drippy moustaches. Hey man, cheers, Andy. Fergit about that Helena, now. She ain't no good an' you know it. Cheers, man. Shet it. Go hang yerself. Now, Andy. Hang yerself. Cheers, buddy. Yeah, boy. Cheers, buddy. Cheers. Go hang yerself.

Money. Ol' Pucky Paul says Ol' Andy done stole money from his pappie. Five thousan' kroners. S'whut she said, ol' Helena. Five thousan' kroners. Five thousan'. I's settin in ol' Andy's rumpus room with the whippersnapper struttin up unner my britches an' I's thankin bout them five thousan' kroners ol' Andy done stole. He done stole it. Ol' Pucky Paul says ol' Andy done stole money from his pappie. Says Pucky Paul. Ol' Andy. Money. I's a-settin an' a-thankin. O that Helena. Five thousan' kroners. S'whut she said. Five thousan' kroners fer to nibble them bubbies an' like as not a lil' extra natcherly. Like as not. O that Helena. She. I know it. I know how ol' Helena. Know how she. How she. An' my sister done said it an' my mama done said it too. They know it. Know whut kind o' thangs Helena gits herself up to. They know. I know. They. They. An' all these cadgy cumfluster'd tomcats. They know whut ol' Helena gits up to. Money. Lawd a mercy. Ol' Andy got hisself some money. Ol' Andy says he done got hisself some money. Ol' Pucky Paul says Ol' Andy done stole money from his pappie. An' Ol' Andy's pappie ain't worth much of a flip anyhow. My mama says he ain't nuthin but a shagnasty. Best keep fur away from his kind. Says she. My mama. She mislikes that I's a-spendin so much time in Ol' Andy's comp'ny an' I done tolt her it ain't ol' Andy I's a-runnin tergither with ever' weekend an' I done tolt her it's me an' ol' KurtSquirt an' Rattlebones Roger, why we's as thick as three to a bed but my sister says if that ain't the bangest story she ever did hear fer she done seen me at the Tavern. She done seen ol' Andy too. Ol' Andy an' me at the Tavern. Ol' Andy an' me an' ol' KurtSquirt an' ol' Rattlebones Roger an' ol' Pucky Paul.

Ol' Paul, huh? Him too, huh? my mama says.

Yuh-huh, ol' Pucky Paul too, my sister says.

I tell ye. If I ain't a-fixin to smack her right upside the head. That she-gossip, my sister. A-talkin an' a-gossipin an' a-talkin. An' on they go a-talkin an' a-gossipin. Money.

Is you done stole from yer pappie?

Well hullo. Ol' KurtSquirt opens his beak agin. Says KurtSquirt:

Money? Stole from yer pappie? *Yer p p pappie?*

Shet it, Squirty. Shet it. Ye hear me?

I hear ye.

An' ol' KurtSquirt he shet his beak back up an' didn't talk no more. Not about that, anyhow. I believ'd he was a-fixin to offer another o' his limricks, since that he got such a powerful ticklement out of writin em, scriblin down all manner o' limricks such as the newspaper likes to print up. That there limrick contest. They was invitin limricks the whole summer long so folks was a-sendin 'em in an' the newspaper printin up whole pages of 'em front an' back an' ol' KurtSquirt he took to a-tremblin all over an' he felt in hisself the innsperashun fer to try his hand at limricks an' he stutter'd sayin he's gon' write some an' he's aimin to win that there limrick contest, so he got hisself one o' them newspapermens' notepads an' a fountain pen, that troll o' the woods, an' he set hisself to writin an' writin an' out it come a-squirtin an' he send it in an' I dunno whut they was a-thankin at that there newspaper but anyway there was one helluva ruckus when they went an' printed that one limrick, the only one he manag'd to git printed, *the only one*, why it got folks so aggervated that they ain't no telling how many up an' wrote a letter to the Editor an' call'd up the Editor too fer to keep up the complainin over the phone.

Callin an' complainin.

S'whut my mama said. *Callin up the Editor.* S'whut my mama said, yowlin an' carryin on, protestin. Naw, she call him too? Ain't no telling. She was yowlin an' carryin on an' my sister she read it up out loud:

> A dude in the john out in Roa
> Hook'd a catch with his curlicue boa.
> Thru' the doney-gal's thicket
> In the stew he did stick it.
> –*Did ye' likey the bait?* –Hohoho-ha!

She read it out loud, my sister. An' whut I was spos'd to do then, I didn't know which nor whuther. Felt sorta chaw'd up, tell the truth. Just like it was *me* who done wrote that there limrick an' was settin there havin to answer fer it, like it was my fault, my fault, ever' bit of it, but didn't know which nor whuther whut to do, dadgummit, that dadgum ol' KurtSquirt, that dadgum ol' beaky poet who set hisself to writin an' writin an' ever' bit of his writin was my fault, that dadgum beaky ol' poet an' now, in ol' Andy's rumpus room, I thought he was a-fixin to offer another o' his limricks but naw, he kep' that ol' beak o' his shet an' wouldn't say no more, not one more word about it. *Woah.* Ol' Andy holler'd, he got up an' stood straddlin over ol' Rattlebones Roger layin all stretch'd out, he teeter'd, he totter'd, he just about tippl'd right over, ol' Andy, he straighted hisself up an' holler'd, holler'd loud as a cumflutter'd ol' hag o'er the barnyard, the Farmer's ol' lady a-hootin an' a-hollerin while she flies thisaway an' thataway in her heavy boots, the ol' hag, a-hootin an' a-hollerin, Lawd only knows whut it is she set herself a-hollerin fer, but round an' round she goes a-flyin an' a-flappin an' a-hootin an' a-hollerin, that ol' hag, pointin her neb straight up to the sky an' they was this one time she didn't have a thread on her other than that there pair o' heavy boots but didn't nobody make anser all the same an' ol' Andy holler'd just like that ol' hag down in the rumpus room, they was somethin he was wantin to do, somethin else he's wantin to do an' he took to hollerin an' dancin dance my lil' dollie.

We's known each other since always-ago. As fur back as we can rickollect, we been runnin tergither. Mmhmm . . .

Ain't no tellin all we done seen an' heard tergither. A-jauntin around an' a-layin out in the sun an' a-gallavantin with the girlies too.

But mostways we been hangin round here. An' it's tollerble well satisfactual, too. Satisfactual to be hangin round here. Powerful satisfactual.

The Diner. Tollerble good times down at the Diner, I mean to say. Cain't say it often enuff. Just the other day one o'us pip'd up an' said: Fellers, I's powerful obleeg'd fer all the fellershippin we got us here at the Diner. Powerful obleeg'd. Why whut would we'd a-done if we wutn't comin tergither here ever' so often?

Hell, whut would we'd a-done?

An' just like that a tear done fell from his eye. He meant ever' word whut he said. Almost religious-like, it felt.

They all said so. Said ol' Andy shoulda had him a mama.

Ain't no good, they said, seein as ol' Andy grow'd up all mama-bereft with his pappie. An' his pappie. The jake-leg . . . Naw, he's a shagnasty, said my mama. A shagnasty, they said an' course they was right. The jake-leg. Wound up in the pen back when ol'Andy's just a lil' boy. An' them years she was tergither with his pappie . . . wutn't no good herself, nuh-uh. You shoulda seen her, said my mama. Shoulda seen her, they said. Cussid ol' strut-fart, she was. Struttin around on them hi-heels, triptrap triptrap trippytrippytraptrap. In them costy garbs an' with a thick layer o' paint on her mug. Like as not a Indian herself. Warpaint. Ugh ugh. Dusky she was too. Like as not she come from some kinda wanderin folk. An' them newfangl'd hairdos o' hern. Shoulda coulda seen her, you should. His pappie. A shagnasty if they ever was one but poor feller. Endin up with that hussy, the durn'd fool. It's how come he turn'd into a shagnasty. Couldn't never put the yoke on that ol' hag o' hisn. Little lady. Strut-fart. Wutn't never no satisfyin her. Hair-do. Face-paint. Costy garbs an' hi-heels. An' ain't nuthin but the finest nylons would do fer her, nuh-uh. An' San Tropay. She just had to go to San Tropay. San Tropay. So off they flew to San Tropay. An' then he wound up in the pen. They come an' got him one evenin. Said he was smack drunk. Smack drunk an' fightyfied.

A knock-fight in the livin room. Said they'd been a knock-fight in the livin room.

Ol' Andy don't remember one lick of it. Lil' baby boy just barely out o' his dippies an' a tub o' guts fer a kiddie he was, too, ol' butterball, not a bit like this here needle-thin spikey-hair'd feller . . .

I done seen it, the pitcher he won't let his pappie have hangin on the wall. The family pitcher whut was took around the time of the knock-fight in the livin room. The livin room where that family pitcher hung on the wall. *Woah.* That livin room. Right above us. Where his pappie got hisself laid smack on the floor. Where his mama fell faintified an' donk'd her head on the shelf. Donkdonk. Up there. Right above us.

Good, says ol' Andy. Good. He was finish'd lettin out his *woah* an' he says: Good. Good good good.

Do whut now? Whut's good?

This here, Pucky. This here. All this right here.

This beer you mean? Durn straight the beer's good.

Come along, Pucky. Y'all come on too. Let's git outta here, y'all.

An' we got ourselves outta there. Up the stairsteps an' outta ol' Andy's rumpus room an' out into the hallway. Up, up, an' up. Beer crate an' beer totes. Up up up.

Come on, now. The shotgun. Gotta bring that shotgun. Bonesy, go git the shotgun. Bonesy. Bonesy? All right, Pucky, you go git my shotgun. My shotgun. An' the flashlight an' a bucket too.

Last man out. Me, that is. I turn'd slap around. Halfways up the stairsteps. Thankin I done fergot somethin. My billfold. Whiles I's a-settin there leanin fo'ward in the beanbag chair an' the whippersnapper rarin up under my fly I sorta had to extracate my billfold from outta my back pocket. Ain't much comfort with a billfold press'd up on one o' yer hanches whut with the whippersnapper a-rarin up too so I took it out an' set it down on the table.

My name. Ol' Andy hollers down the stairsteps, hollers my name. Git on up, ye hear? he hollers. Whut in the hell is you dilly-dallyin fer?

My billfold, I yell. I done left my billfold down here.

Well okey.

My name. Once more. Pucky Paul this time.

My sunglasses. You see my sunglasses?

It's late in the evenin, I holler. Ain't long before night-time.

I tell ye I need 'em.

How bout you, Squirty? I holler. You fergit somethin too?

Naw.

An' whut about you, Bonesy?

(Ain't no anser.)

My billfold. I set it down on the table. I know I did.

My name. Ol' Andy. Ol' Andy keeps a-hollerin an' hollerin my name.

Found it, I holler. I done found it. Layin on the rug. Musta fell somehow.

Okey then.

But them sunglasses. Whut you done do with yer sunglasses, Pucky?

The hell I know. Look fer 'em.

Idiot.

Okey.

Okey. I's a-lookin, I holler. I's a-lookin. Wait up, ye hear.

Okey-doke. We'll set out in the car. Latch the door, will ye, hollers ol' Andy down the stairsteps. Key's in the door so you take 'er an' hang 'er up on the hook in the carport.

Okey.

The hook. The hook. Hook'd a catch with his curlicue boa. Idiot idiot idiot idiot. Ain't nobody down in Andy's rumpus room but me. Me. Surrounded by empty beer bottles an' all manner o' cluttermint an' it's purty nair nightfall now, late summer night. Clean the place up? Ol' Andy clean up? Go hang yerself, he done said. Whut I says goes, he said. It's his rumpus room. Ol' Andy's rumpus room. Bedroom up on the fust floor belongs to his pappie an' ol' Andy ain't allow'd to go in there. Sometimes his pappie'll manage to drag some ol' nag or other inside an' wants to be let alone fer a spell an' ol' Andy (if he's at home) has to stay down in the rumpus room with a couple o' nudie mags an' mastrabate hisself beerbottleempty an' then I spy them sunglasses but naw these is ol' Andy's sunglasses so I's got to keep on a-lookin an' the fellers is a-settin up there in the veehickle an' ain't nobody hollerin down the stairsteps now, ain't nobody hollerin my name, naw.

Music up on his planit ain't the kind o' music we's used to. Our music goes up an' down an' back an' futh. An' ye can dance to it. But his music? Ain't no dancin to it at'oll, it don't go up an' down, nor back an' futh nuther. His music's like a spiral, a goddang ol' spiral, it goes down an' down an' round an' round an' ye's like' ta git all woozy woozy woozy...

Empties. Mugs. Cups. Half-et bags o' tater chips. Terbacky pouches an' rollin paper an' I dunno whut in tarnation plus stacks an' stacks o' nudie mags he's collectin an' won't borrow out to nobody an' if we's wantin to peek in 'em when we come over then we got to be mighty cyairful, ol' Pucky Paul an' ol' KurtSquirt an' ol' Rattlebones Roger an' me. Dadgummit. Where in the hell is them dang ol' sunglasses? Ain't long before night-time but he's just got to have 'em, ol' Pucky.

Waitin. They's a-waitin. They's settin up there in the veehickle a-waitin on me. Cuttin up an' horseyin around gittin drunk as a skunk. An' I's by myself down in ol' Andy's rumpus room. Ain't ever been down here by myself before. All alone in ol' Andy's rumpus room. Just me. Nobody else. I keep on a-lookin fer them cussid sunglasses belongin to ol' Pucky Paul. Idiot cain't be bother'd to look fer 'em hisself an' it's a right favor fer me to go lookin fer 'em.

The rumpus room. Just like always. Empty beer bottles an' all manner o' cluttermint. An' nudie mags. Yessir. Sure enuff. Yep. An' yet. An' yet somethin do feel mighty quare. But whut? Naw but whut? It's me bein down here by myself. That's whut's quare. Right quare fer it to be just me an' me alone. Down in the rumpus room all by myself.

That alarm clock o' hisn. Somewhereabouts in this here rumpus room there's a alarm clock. He sleeps down here, after all, in a bed so narrer it's all he can do to not to fall clean out by staplin hisself to the burlap wall coverins an' I hear that alarm clock tickin away. Yessir. Sure enuff. Yep. Quare. Shh. Hush'd. An' then . . .

I find it.

It ain't no pair o' sunglasses. It ain't the sunglasses belongin to ol' Pucky Paul I done found me. Naw I done found me somethin else entairly. Somethin ol' Andy had set in his pocket an' musta believ'd was safe an' secure but naw, man, ain't never been too smart to leave a big wad o' cash in yer pocket, spesh'ly when it come to the kind o' big bills yer buddy says ye done stole from yer pappie.

Tick tock. Money. Helena. It's *me* an' not *ol' Andy* who's a-fixin to pay ol' Helena tonight. Alarm clock. Tickin. Money. That money. Neatly roll'd an' done up with a rubber band an' the whippersnapper takes to rarin up agin under my fly. I bend right over an' since that my britches is tight it do hurt a right smart to bend over whut with the whippersnapper a-rarin up so an' I pick up them bills an' the alarm clock keeps on a-tickin an' I feel that roll o' bills in my clammy artifisshul right hand an' I feel a avalanch go thru me an' my knees begin to give out but I got to hide them bills lickedy-split so I take off one o' my velcro runnin shoes an' I's all woozy an' I swallow an' sets them bills down unnerneath the shoe sole in a hurry an' puts the shoe back on. Helena. Me. Not ol' Andy. Me.

Later. I lock'd the door behind me an' hung the key on the hook in the carport an' now I's settin in the backseat an' the driver, ol' Pucky Paul, inquir'd as to the whereabouts o' his sunglasses, I said they wutn't no findin 'em in all that cluttermint an' ol' Andy said I was a pansie an' ol' Pucky Paul give a grunt. Shitass. Shitass one an' shitass two. I says, mutterin'. The hell you say? says ol' Andy. Nuthin, says I. But they heard it. Course they did. I aim'd it so. One an' two. Shitass. Shitass. An' shitass one had done shove his seat so fur back that they wutn't no dadblame room fer my legs at'oll an' they wutn't no dadblame room fur a beer tote back here nuther, I pipe up but ain't nobody listnin, ol' Andy got to have hisself a lot o' room, says he, an' he says he got to stretch his legs out an' set slaunchways since that he was so cadgy an' if he was cadgy then they ain't no dang way fer him to set normal in no carseat, he had to stretch his legs out an' set slaunchways fer otherwise it hurted him so at the root o' the ol' tallywhacker, says he, right there, at the root, woah how it hurted, woah woah woah, cuttin up now, the blatherskite, havin hisself a good ol' time now an' says he's a-fixin to whip out the ol' tallywhacker an' give him a extra good wringin, a few good twists thisaway an' thataway an' don't be alarm'd, now, ye hear, if the squirtins, *the squirtins*, ol' Squirty, land up on the ceilin o' this here veehickle.

Nuh-uh-uh you better not jack yerself off in my veehickle ye can jack all ye want once we git there but ain't no jackin in my veehickle ye hear.

Naw? Stop this here veehickle, Pucky. Stop in the nairest bus turn-out ye come to an' I'll git 'er done an' over with.

Dawgsquat, Andy. Dawgsquat. I's spo'sed to stop? You tellin me to stop?

Stop, Pucky. I got to I got to.

Dawgsquat dawgsquat dawgsquat.

Got to got to got to. Now now now.

Ah ah ah, says KurtSquirt in the backseat an' ol' Rattlebones Roger who's settin betwixt ol' Squirty an' me takes to a-flingin his arms thisaway an' thataway an' I give him a piece o' my elbow but my elbow didn't biff him that good an' he kep' up the flailin an' I tolt him cut it out an' ol' Pucky Paul holler'd cut it out. Yea cu cu cut it out, ol' Squirty demanded an' kep' on carryin on. An' he cut it out, ol' Rattlebones Roger. Fer a minute or two.

Got to got to, ol' Andy he kep' at it. I got to I got to.

An' ol' KurtSquirt kep' on carryin on: Ah ah ah.

The gang. The gang's on its way down into the late summer night. Gang o' cowboys, man. Boozin gang. Carouisin gang. Andy's gang.

Andy's gang? Yep. That's us, man. Here we is. The gang. The boys. Ain't nobody mistakin who's a-comin on down the road. It's us.

The Driver. He sure likes a-drivin that there veehickle, he sure loves a-drivin it, an' even tho' it ain't been too long since he got his licence it don't stop him from drivin like a god, that ol' Driver. *Like a god.* Ain't no mistakin when that Driver come drivin like a god an' right next to him is the Boss-Man, that cadgy ol' booger who'd done grow'd up on a construkshun site, an' now he take to flappin his jaw an' puttin on airs an' puffin hisself up sayin that he naw *he* ain't no countryfied yokel why *he* is somethin else, somethin else altergither. An' now that lil' pipecleanerpipsqueak done shove his seat back an' the seat is lean'd all the way back. The Boss-Man. But this here veehickle belongs to the Driver an' in the Driver's veehickle cain't ol' Boss-Man just do whutever he wants to. Whip out the ol' tallywhacker? Give him a extra good wringin? Nuh-uh, boy. Boss-Man's the Boss-Man but the Driver's the Driver an' this here veehickle it belongs to the Driver an' in the veehickle the Boss-Man ain't the one decidin the letter o' the law. The Boss-Man he gits to tell the Driver when to set hisself behind the wheel, start up the motor, an' drive. But *then* it's the Driver who's decidin whut's whut. The Boss-Man knows it. *He knows it.* But he ain't fixin to let up nohow. Cain't let 'em fergit, the Driver an' them fellers in the backseat, cain't let 'em fergit that the Driver ain't the Boss-Man, the Boss-Man is *him*, but naw, in the veehickle it's the Driver decidin. That's how it's spos'd to be an' them fellers in the backseat better not say nuthin. Nuthin.

Squose. Them fellers is squose tergither mighty tight in the backseat. One of 'em, one o' them backseat kids, the one they call'd KurtSquirt since he was so easy to fall a-snifflin an' a-blubberin an' squirtin them tears out, has got broad shoulders, that broad-shoulder'd ol' KurtSquirt, tall an' broad-shoulder'd he is. An' the feller in the middle, ol' Rattlebones Roger, it ain't the shoulders, naw, but the legs on him, the legs on that ol' beanpole, like on one o' them geeraffs or ostreches, that silly ol' coot, hangin on, hangin on at ever' curve. An' here, here we have the last feller: squose in real tight, skwunch'd in real tight, so maybe that last feller oughtta've set hisself back in the trunk, it ain't like he ain't ever rode in there before, he's right consentable to it, matterfactually, don't bother him none, lyin back there in the trunk of the veehickle next to the beer crate so's he can carry ol' Andy's shotgun but now he's a-settin here, squose in, skwunch'd in, scrumpl'd up, cattycorner'd. Lookit this here noggin o' his. This here metal warsh-tub fer a noggin.

Like'ta git ding'd up, that ol' warsh-tub. Fer the feller in the middle, the geeraff, done took to a-flailin with his arms real bad an' a-donkin the warsh-tub donkdonkdonk up aginst the wender.

Lickedy-split. Ol' Driver drivin like a god an' it's a devilish sort o' light them round headlights is castin over the humpy stumblin road an' into the woods. Lickedylickedylickedy-split an' danktadankta-dank clean over a cattle grate. Fer sure night done fell but it's yet a while till the place'll fill up an' thangs git to poppin. The Tavern. Fixin to be a thunderstorm inside the Tavern. *Thunderin n' lightnin, boys. Thunderin n' lightnin.* The gang. Andy's gang. Got to find us somethin to do in the meantime. Somethin or other. Driver's a-drivin. Over the humpy stumblin road. Thru the woods. An' the Boss-Man livin it up an' puttin on airs an' puffin hisself up. Cowboys got to find somethin to do. Woods. Woods outside o' the wender. Dark woods flyin on by. A warsh-tub noggin squintin with his eyes an' the dark woods outside a car wender flyin by, flyin by.

> Swish swoosh.
> Into the woods an'
> Swoosh swish.
> See the Dead One?
> The feller who is
> Dead an' walkin?
> Or is that the
> Sheep a-flockin?

Naw, man. Ain't no sheep out there. Ain't no Dead Feller, nuther. Nuh-uh. No way it coulda been him. Ain't no catchin sight o' the Dead Feller. They done look'd an' look'd fer him, the Sheriff an' them burlyhurlies from the shootin range, but could they find him?

Ain't no way. They come a-lookin high an' peerin low, trampin thisaway an' stampin thataway on down thru the woods, an' didn't find nuthin 'cept his burialcloth hung from a pinetree branch. I reckon it was none other'n the same pinetree the Calf tied his rope around. I remember how ol' Calfy stood there givin the rope a few good yanks. He stood there a-yankin an' a-babblin. I set myself down on a stump. Watchin. Listnin. Dead Feller. They wrote all about the Dead Feller in the newspaper. Printin up whole pages front an' back an' people took to a-readin an' readin an' talkin an' talkin an' purty soon the whole town was all a-buzz about it. Pitchers. I done seen pitchers. Grainy ol' pitchers from times o' old when the menfolk drank like oversiz'd pieplants in the peltin rain an' jacks an' queens an' kings an' all them other cards in the deck rais'd hell an' the menfolks drank an' gambl'd away their farms an' kep' up the drankin an' in them ol'-timey pitchers the Sheriff has got a spiffin hat an' moustaches, some real walrus moustaches, man, not some dang ol' durty warshrag-whiskers an' all them burlyhurlies from the shootin range have cowboy hats an' moustaches just like the Sheriff. The Calf. The pinetree. Giant pinetree standin all by itself. Yankin an' yankin. Yankin that rope. Yankin an' babblin. Watchin, listnin. Me an' them other boys who come a-runnin an' that lil' witch girl, too. We watch'd. We listn'd. An' the Boss-Man, ol' Andy, it was *him* who'd done decided we's gon' out lookin fer the Dead Feller. Now he stood there a-yankin an' a-pullin too. Ol' Andy. The Calf an' ol' Andy. The Calf an' the Rat. Whut'n the world was they gittin up to? The hell was all this fer? I lean'd my noggin up aginst the wender. The car wender. The woods. Them dark woods flew by. Had to git ourselves somethin to do in the meantime. Ain't no use gittin there early. Them kind o' folks who git to the Tavern early, they ain't never sat too well with us. Egg-suckin kind o' folks. Soon as they done watchin their kid-shows on teevee they git to thankin how powerful nice it'd be to have a beer at the Tavern an' shoot some pool an' fling a dart or two an' have theirselves a nice agreeable evenin hours an' hours before the partyin begins fer real. Sheeit, them kind o' folks, said ol' Andy. Them kind o' folks. Thems the kind o' folks who git gone like steam from a bilin kettle just as soon as the ponytail'd feller behind the bar ratchits up the music. Sheeit, them kind o' folks, said ol' Andy in the rumpus room an' so we's havin to find ourselves somethin to do an' we's a-settin down there drankin an' ol' Andy kep' up the talkin about ol' Helena an' it got to be late in the evenin an' he said we better go drivin a little whiles, the Boss-Man.

But where? said ol' Pucky Paul.

Just ye wait, said ol' Andy. Ye'll see.

I got to know where we's a-goin.

Why'nt ye take a guess.

Over to ol' Helena's? Is you gone tetch'd in the head?

Go hang yerself.

I ain't drivin to ol' Helena's.

Plum fool.

You's the plum fool.

I's the one decidin where we's a-goin.

Cut it out.

Me?

Yeah you.

I's the one decidin.

Cut it out.

Cut it out? Me? Shotgun. Gotta bring my shotgun. Go git my shotgun. You, Rattley. She's right unner my bed . . . Rattley . . . Rattley?

Naw, I is. I's gon' carry that there shotgun. Outta the way, Rattley.

Fine, Pucky. You do it instead o' ol' Rattlebones Roger. Fine . . . An' bring the flashlight an' a bucket too.

Wender. Car wender. Outside the wender. *Swish swoosh.* Naw. Didn't see him. Dead Feller. Didn't see nary a trace o' the moonglowy Dead Feller in the swishin an' swooshin outside the wender. Not one sheep nuther. But where'd that idea come from about the Dead Feller still runnin thru them woods? Coulda been because . . . because . . . because . . .

Religion, man. Whut fer? When ye thank o' the space cretur comin down here fer to live . . . like that alone don't beat all. But fer him to be bringin along his religion, too . . . naw, Lawd a mercy . . .

Better safe than sorry. S'why we done put up this here survaylance camera. Bought it off some feller who said he done bought it off some Rushian feller. Then we mounted it high up in a pinetree. A pinetree far off in the woods.

That's where that one space cretur gits up to somethin he ain't spos'd to be gittin up to. Some kind o' religious somethin'-or-other.

I lean'd my noggin aginst the wender. Ol' Rattlebones Roger'd done let up flingin his arms a bit. Ol' KurtSquirt set hisself a-hummin an' it was one o' them popular tunes he humm'd, a song to neck somebody to or else put ye in mind of a lady, a tigerstrip'd purrbred kitten with long redpainted claws fer nails who'll come a-sneakin up on ye, some sneaky ol' puss from Amurrica who'll deal death to ye, natcherly. Boss-Man took to a-wrigglin in his seat. He wriggl'd an' talk'd an' talk'd. An' whut was he a-goin on about? *Don't know an' don't cyair.* An' the Driver was gittin mighty aggervated . . . ye can just about imagine . . .

Me?

You. Nobody else. You. Nobody. Dead. Dead Feller. *Swoosh swish.*

Say whut?

You. Nobody but you. S'you I's a-talking to.

Say whut?

Coffee. Hot us up some more coffee. I's thirsty. Everbody's thirsty so git that coffee hottin now, ye hear. More coffee. More coffee. Everbody's thirsty. Folks is thirsty.

Say whut now?

Coffee.

Okey. Okey, I says. I's fixin to go hot up some more coffee. I git up nice an' slow an' if he but know'd, Kid Clipclop. If he but know'd. Pencils. Paper. He knows I done started usin the pencil. He sees the paper. Sees handwritins. He knows I's a-workin on somethin else other than whut they done tolt me to do down here. Down here. I's down here. Down here's where they done put me. Here. In the unnerworld. He knows it. Kid Clipclop. Prob'ly ain't too bad a feller. An' he's a-writin down sinnences too. Thankin an' writin an' producin all manner o' doojiggers. He got hisself a humongus screen in his booth. Ever' one of 'em's done got theirselves a humongus screen. Partishuns an' innervidual booths an' a humongus screen an' ever' one of 'em a-thankin an' a-thankin an' writin an' writin bout how green it'll be up on the surface. Green. Fust folks have got to git peacified in their souls, then it'll be green up on the surface. Everthang gon' git green like a sugarsnap, like broc'li, like unripen'd bananners, like 'tater leaves on a midsummer day, like a moldy ol' slice o' gouda, like a palmleaf-siz'd dandelion leaf rins'd clean of exhaust dustins, like ol' Calfy's kendalgreen unnerbritches. Green. Soon as all them doojiggers is finish'd doin their jobs. Doojiggers ye can gullup down yer gullick or shove up yer cornhole. Green over the whole surface soon as all them doojiggers is done their jobs but miracles . . . *that's* where the coffee come in an' them fellers down here be drankin it an' takin turns zippin off to the commode fer to piss an' if they ain't a-pissin money they's sure to be a-crappin it. *Okey*. He says *okey*, Kid Clipclop. I git up. Nice an' slow. Woah, nelly. This plum rotted man-husk. O if he but know'd.

Coffee.

Black coffee.

Black.

Fine.

The transformator smack in the middle o' the town square. We done read in the newspaper bout how someone done tried an' make destroyment on that there transformator. Took a axe to it, leavin deep gasshes all over. An' folks is curious. Take to specklatin an' wonderin whut kind o' rampageous innervidual coulda done it. An' we had to go see an' judge fer ourselves too. Standin there studyin the gasshes. We took to a-guessin an' a-guessin.

'Twere the space cretur's doin, says one o' us fellers. They got to go an' make destroyment, them creturs.

An' the other feller says, Naw man, ye best be believin . . . But if I's to guess, I'da thunk he was actin alone . . . the one, ye see . . . the one who done done this.

Mmhmm. That lady. That lady in my livin room back home. That lady who done give me the pamflit. Her eyes. Touch o' fury in 'em. An' her bein dress'd like it was winter. Nair as I remember. Dress'd fer winter on a late summer night. But didn't have no cap on. Her hair. Black hair. An' Lawd only knows how she done got in, that lady. I lay'd on the couch. I prob'ly been sleepin after watchin the teevee, news, currint happ'nins, fell to sleepin an' havin some funny dreem or other. Yep. I'd prob'ly done fell to sleepin an' havin some funny dreem or other an' sweatin somethin fierce. I dreem'd. I woke up. I's surtin I woke up. Surtin I lay'd on the couch an' seen that ol' hussy. Settin in the recliner. Open'd her mouth, said my name an' I prob'ly seem'd purty confus'd an' I know fer a fact that this was whut she said:

Long time no see. Don't ye recognize me?

Say whut? says I. Naw, says I, don't believe I do.

Naw?

Naw, should I oughtta've? Should I oughtta've recogniz'd ye?

Naw.

Naw?

Ain't no matter, says she, the lady. Ain't no matter.

An' her eyes. Touch o' fury in them eyes. Naw. Didn't recognize her. Should I oughtta've? Naw. Ain't no matter. That lady. Uh-huh. Mighty purty. Gotta admit. Maybe like somebody I'd done seen before, in the way-back-when. Somebody I'd done notic'd before. Some wommon I lik'd bein able to look at. A real lady. Mighty purty. But who? But who? My mama. It's true, she sometimes had a touch o' fury in the eyes too an' my mama was mighty purty. Cain't but allow it. My sister. Mighty purty too. Yet an' still. It wutn't my mama she look'd like, that lady. Wutn't my sister nuther. She look'd like . . . naw.

Naw?

Naw.

A pamflit. She give me a pamflit. Says I's spos'd to read it. Read that there pamflit ever' mornin, says she. Ever' mornin before ye skedaddle off to work, says she. *Skedaddle?* says I. Skedaddle, says she. It look to you like this here man-husk's fixin to up an' *skedaddle* off to work? says I. Skedaddle, says she. Dadgum, says I, this here man-husk, this rotted man-husk, the hell you thankin? Lawd a mercy. I's one o' them self-runnin models but you reelly reckon these artifisshul achey legs is gon' up an' skedaddle off to work ever' mornin? Read it, says she. *Read the pamflit*, says she.

The pamflit?

Read the pamflit. Read him. Only a couple miles to go the fust day.

Okey.

So I took to a-readin. Fust mornin. I woke up a couple minutes before seven. An' the clock kep' a-tickin. A-tickin an' a-tockin, that there threshin machine. But then I thank the thought. I thank: *Pamflit. Read the pamflit.* Slow-pokin. Course I's awful slow-pokin, havin to wake up like that, but she wutn't funnin, that lady. She shook me an' said I got to git up now fer real. Now, she says, it's mornin. Say whut? It's mornin? I thank to myself: *Pamflit. Read the pamflit.* The clock. That lady. Wutn't even seven o'clock. I's awful slow gittin up but when ye got to ye got to an' she'd been settin in the recliner the whole livvylong night. A-watchin me. The lady. Fine lady. Pale shimmery moon straight from the fairy tale, the funny pages. When's last time somebody'd set up watchin me the whole night? An' they was two of 'em. Pale shimmery moon didn't come by hisself. Man in the moon. He come along too. I wake up. Eyes. Shakin me. Eyes. I thank: *Pamflit. Read the pamflit.*

Nice an' slow, nice an' slow. I read it slower'n I's used to. *This here . . . this here's a trifle much, an' that's accountin fer all I done read an' seen on the internet. Doojiggers. Jungal. Dinosauruses. Surface is gon' be green. Woah. Woah, there. Woah, boy. Woah, nelly. Woah, now. To he'p an' to comfort. To he'p an' to comfort an' to he'p me but . . . but can it all be true . . . is this here all true?*

Ever' bit of it, says she, the lady. It's all true.

I reckon'd it so.

An' now it's yer turn. Up. Git up off that couch, now . . .

Up, up, up . . .

An' I got up off the couch. Plum rotted man-husk. Hobblestiltskin.

He got up off the couch. He got up. One mornin, the fust mornin in a new calendar epock he gits up off the couch an' as soon as he done done whut needs to git done in the bathroom (hackin, hockin, pissin, shittin, moanin) he drags hisself into the kitchen with a pamflit in his hand he manag'd to read before he got hisself up.

The lady, the wommon whut was settin there all of a sudden in his livin room. Astin him if he recogniz'd her but naw he couldn't recognize her.

Wutn't ringin no bells. No bells a-ringin. Dingalingalingin. Just the clock whut was tickin, a-tockin an' a-tickin. Her name? She say whut her name was? Naw. Okey. Prob'ly nice enuff, that lady. Watch'd over him, she did. Her an' the man in the moon. Sayin: *We's watchin over ye, we is.*

Then he fell asleep. Slept all night (I thank so anyhow) but the plum rotted man-husk was a-tossin an' turnin an' sweat was a-pourin an' his clothes got all soak'd thru an' he's havin weird dreems an' the mornin come an' he woke up to the lady a-touslin his hair, his sweaty black mophead o' hair all ting'd with grey an' this here noggin o' hisn, tellin ye . . . A warsh-tub fer a noggin, a wore-out metal warsh-tub. Lookit. Lookit the dent in his forehead. Dented-up nose o' hisn. Had to've bustid his nose somewhere, this here feller. Whut happen'd? Pshaw. A fist-scrape? Fallin down drunk? A car wreck? Yeh-huh, maybe it was *him* who come a-bikin an' a-wobblin an' the veehickle come bang into the sharp curve an' off he goed a-flyin an' a-flappin an' a-flailin thru the air an' a angel grabb'd aholt o' him till he landed flat in the ditch an' he scream'd screamin in a heap o' feathers with a broke leg an' bustid nose? *Him*. Maybe. Was it *him?* An' these black bushy eyebrows, these smoky eyes, this whompy-jaw'd cranksided puckermouth, this clump fer a chin an' the neck, the neck all thin an' spindly, it's a wonder how in the heck a neck like'at could even hold up a metal warsh-tub noggin an' then we come to these juttin shoulders an' this flat chestcage, the lady she tells him to wriggle out o' that soak'd-thru black tee-shirt with the rock an' roll graffic an' show off that flat chestcage o' hisn but he says they ain't no way he's gon' do that nuh-uh ain't no stranger gon' go examinin this here swole-up dispeptick stomick, ain't nobody, says he, why it's bad enuff havin his arms all nekkid, them artifisshul arms thin an' sinewy with ten stubby lil' fingers, grubby lil' stubby grubby fingers an' nails all gnaw'd down to the bare nubs an' yet here ye go tellin me to take off my soak'd-thru joggin britches an' my soak'd-thru unnerbritches so's ye can he'p yerself to the view o' the ol' whippersnapper an' my rear end too but ye might as well slip on a chicken turd fer I ain't gon' go flingin off my clothes an' these legs is ever' bit as thin an' sinewy an' artifisshul as the arms, these achey legs an' feet an' toes: never in all the world, never ever in all the world is you gon' git to lookin at these feet an' them toes, I ain't about to go takin off my socks nuther. I's tremblin. I's shakin. I'd done come up off the couch. I'd done read the pamflit an' I'd done been to the bathroom an' in the kitchen an' now I's standin here in my livin room. My own tiny lil' livin room, boy. I's tremblin. I's shakin. Lady's lookin at me. The lady in the one recliner. Lookin at me with a touch o' fury in them eyes o' hern. Whut more I's spos'd to say, I'd no ideer. More? the lady she said. *Ain't obleeg'd to say no more.* Naw? *Naw.* Yes?

An' the man in the moon . . . the man in the moon in my livin room . . . he was there all right. In my livin room. My room my room my room. There all right. He'd done come on in . . .

> A dead-sick feller from Hadeland,
> Had done had too much reefer beforehand.
> He was shakin an' shiverin,
> There was quakin an' quiverin.
> Now he does all the best whut he can, man.

Reefer? Go hang yerself. I don't smoke no reefer. I mostly just smoke store-boughten bug-dust but ol' Andy he smok'd reefer, I remember. Ol' Andy an' ol' Pucky Paul. Ol' Pucky Paul he smok'd reefer too.

Ol' Andy's pappie's the one who procur'd all the reefer. His pappie, with the jake-leg. Procurin an' sellin that weird sheeit. His livelihood. How he made his livin. How he got hisself arrested when ol' Andy's just a lil' boy.

His mama, ol' Andy's mama, the strut-fart. She was the accounant. Counted the money an' spent the money while the pappie's procurin an' sellin an' sellin an' procurin.

Woah nelly. Whew doggies. Bound to go wrong. Bound to go all wrong, that lil' hustle. The pappie wound up in the pen an' the mama took off an' folks started talkin. Turrible sitcherashun. Have ye done heard. Whut a shagnasty. Whut a hussy. Shagnasty. Hussy. Turrible sitcherashun. Have ye done heard. Lawd I never. A goddamn shame. A goddamn cussid shame. The hell she run off to? That ol' hussy, the strut-fart? How come they never throw'd her in the pen? Tell me that. Poor feller. That poor feller. Goin an' marryin a hussy like 'at. Poor kid. That poor kid. That boy o' theirn. Whut happen to the kid? Foster home. Prob'ly a foster home. The boy. Who'll take him in? Ain't nobody gon' take him in. Naw, foster home? Prob'ly his grandma an' grandpa'll take him in. Will they? An' he'll have to go live with his pappie after. Turrible. Turrible sitcherashun.

A gnome who had kinfolk in Toten
Heard tell that the weed was in fashion.
He bustid his ass
Buyin all the world's grass.
Then he shot hisself. In the foot, man.

Babblin. Cain't take all the babblin. I'd no ideer whut more I's spos'd to say. But I stood there a-babblin anyway. The lady in the one recliner heard everthang I's sayin. Heard all my babblin. Heard these chaintooth voices way down inside this ol' wore-out metal warsh-tub noggin o' mine. The pamflit. I'd done read the pamflit an' I's standin there babblin an' the voices was babblin an' I couldn't take all the babblin an' the lady she put the quietus on it, sayin:

Hey, now. Ye's fixin to be late, now. Best be gittin on, now.

Do whut now?

The job. They's waitin on ye.

They?

They's waitin. Folks is waitin.

On me?

Anorak, says she. Shoes.

Okey.

Best be gittin on. Git on, now.

Hat, I says. Cowboy hat. Lazarus's cowboy hat.

I got on, all right. I give in an' got on. Okey. She an' she alone was in command. Command over me. (But I's operatin myself. Accordin to the manual I's one o' them self-operatin types.) Her eyes. Them eyes o' hern wi' the touch o' fury in 'em, an' the pamflit she give me. Ever' word, ever' sinnence was true an' it was a-clangin, whut I'd done read that is, clangin an' clatterin somethin powerful inside o' my wore-out metal warsh-tub noggin an' them voices they sang tergither in one refrain after the other. By dod it was a blessin I'd done had the thought to go yankin my cowboy hat down over my top lid. A trifle too tight, that there cowboy hat. I got to yank it down if I's wantin it to stay put but if I yank it down then it stays put an' I's a cowboy an' the hat it's there so my head don't go explodin on me. Cause it's a explosion them voices is goin on an' on about.

One helluva explosion. On an' on they go an' one day it'll all blow up but fer now I's safe. I yank the cowboy hat down over my top lid. I's a cowboy. Some other day. My head it'll go explodin some other day. Some other day. Some other. This here day, it's the fust day.

Somebody once said, exactly who I cain't remember, but somebody said: *If ye's up to yer neck in dewkie, ain't nuthin ye can do but start sangin.*

This here neck o' mine's all thin an' spindly an' if I stand up straight then I's up to the neck in dewkie but start sangin?

An' they's nuthin else to do? Start sangin? Me?

I done sung me a right piece in my day. Done sung hymns an' a lot o' other cultural versificashuns. My sangin was so purty. That's whut they said. That I's sangin so purty an' that's how come they said I oughtta be in the childern's choir. The childern's choir at church. Didn't make no diff'rence, me bein a meckanickal barn gnome an' all. I's sangin so purty an' it was writ up on a star that' I's gon' be sangin in the childern's choir at church. Course my mama said it was all a crock o' hooey an' of course my sister had to go a-tyrranizin me with her blaggardy blather but my ol' granny she said oh how nice it was fer me to be sangin in the childern's choir at church. I's sangin. Me an' a bunch o' other devout childerns stood sangin in front o' the church. We's sangin. I's sangin with all the breath in my gullick but I cain't say as I's standin up to my neck in no dewkie back then, naw. Cain't say I was, naw.

Choir. I's sangin in a choir. A meckanickal barn gnome whut sang in a childern's choir at church.

Alrighty-ho. Now I's a cowboy. Dewkie, cowboy's got to go a-wadin through it most always. Yessir, if he ain't *a-standin* in the dewkie then he's sure as hell *wadin thru* it an' now I's a-wadin thru it. Wadin thru the dewkie. Slow an' easy. Yep. I thank it was a nice day, onbeclouded, comfterble temperture, I's wistlin, feelin more elecktrick than I'd done felt in a long time. Yep. But I's wadin thru dewkie, slow an' easy, on an' on, up an' over an' on agin, round the bend an' down, down an' up agin an' there it was, the husk had arrov'd. Took quite a while, I'll own. Took a right bit o' time even tho' I got me a ride along the way. The musselbound Splutterfusserer. He came along, he did, in his pickup. The long ride down that hill. Tried to murder me. I cain't figgure out how in the heck he didn't end up stompin me flat. Cain't figgure it out. Flat. That's how it is with a lot o' thangs. Cain't figgure thangs out, that is. An' time . . . took a right bit o' time . . . but then again whut *don't* take time? *Nuthin. Ain't nuthin don't take time*. I'd done read that. An' the lady she'd done said it too. An' the musselbound Splutterfusserer he said it too, in his own way I mean. Hop on in, now, he said. Keep on crawlin like'at an' ye won't be arrov'd till dark. Hop on in, now, he said.

Hop? Me? Dark, ye says?

Dewkie.

Standin in dewkie. Wadin in dewkie. Slippin an' slidin thru dewkie. I remember it was dark an' we was slipslidin thru dewkie, we cowboys was slipslidin an' the feller there who was me was rollin on down like a rimreck'd bikewheel endin smack at the bottom o' the Mare Cooter Canyon with all the others.

But it wutn't dreckly after the ol' musselbound Splutterfusserer had done tried to kill me, naw it wutn't *then* I's rememberin the thang bout standin up to yer neck in dewkie an' slippin an' slidin an' rollin in dewkie, an' it wutn't when I's layin there in the Dandelion Ditch, it wutn't *then* I's thankin bout dewkie an' cowboys an' the Mare Cooter Canyon, naw *that* come later an' prob'ly it was when the ellavater's stuck a good long while an' the gnome whut was trapp'd inside couldn't he'p but remember an' he might coulda took to sangin, maybe just to hisself, sangin, back in the childern's choir at church agin . . .

We done tried an' tried to git to know him. Ast him if he's wantin to play kickball, maybe a round or two o' poker, go skiin, trade stickers . . . We done tried an' tried. But he didn't want nuthin to do with any of it. Ain't nuthin whut we tried was good enuff. Nuthin . . . so we give up. An' from then on ain't none o' us wantin to be friends with him. From then on, that's just how it was.

Almost arrov'd. Ain't no misdoubtin about it. The man-husk was gittin close. Soon.

The Logo was shinin at me on a sign down by the driveway an' unnerneath the Logo was a thick black arrer pointin the way. There. Thataway. Right yonder. Follow the arrer. Go on now. The Logo. The arrer. Go on. I dragg'd myself on, me an' the whole shebang shebang shebang. The clangin an' clatterin in my noggin an' the voices whut was sangin tergither, sangin one refrain after the other *an' a-heydiddlediddle an' dance to yer pardner an' say hey man an' a hopdiddlydoo an' a bamp in the bamp in the bamp she-wamp she-wamp herp in the derp up yer wazoo wazoo dingdong an' a once an' a once an' a once upon a time a feller goin to Saint Ives met a man with seven wives an' all the wives had seven knives to skin the sacks off seven cats sayin heeere kitty kitty it's Sheer Thursday snippy snipp snip but the knives they was dull an' the balls they was slipp'ry an' the tomcats was a-leapin head over tails.*

Yes?

The loudspeaker.

My name. I tolt 'em whut I's nam'd.

A sound . . .

. . . an' the gate open'd up.

Hullo?

Resepshun.

Hullo? Anybody there?

Hush'd.

Eerily hush'd.

The sangin had done finish'd an' the voices give me a break but I don't believe I's thankin bout the Dead Feller just then.

. . .

Hullo?

. . .

Hullo?

. . .

Anybody there?

. . .

It's me.

. . .

Hullo?

. . .

Okey. Trustin my instincts. Findin the way with neither map nor compass. Instinct itself. I reckon I'll find the way. If they's anythang I's been capable of in this here life it's findin the way. Cowboy. A bonafy'd cowboy, that's me boy an' I'll warrant the fellers who's waitin fer me somewhere off in this ginormous buildin prob'ly know it already. Why the lady she said it too: *You's a bonafy'd cowboy*. She sat there in the one recliner lookin at him sayin she know'd the meckanickal barn gnome's a bonafy'd cowboy. This here meckanickal barn gnome, ye see. Trustin his instincts. Findin the way. Operatin hisself. He was wadin thru dewkie an' now he's draggin that plum rotted man-husk an' dadgum whut a ginormous buildin this is. That Logo shinin at him on a sign down by the driveway, it wutn't lyin, that's fer goddamn sure. Big doins. That's whut they's thankin up an' workin out down here, it's whut he read about in the pamflit the lady give him an' natcherly they's gon' thank it up an' work it out an' be produsin an' produsin them doojiggers in such a ginormous buildin as this. Castle. Some folks'd maybe say this ginormous buildin reminds 'em of a castle. Maybe. Maybe we'd go a-thankin this or a-thankin that. A creemcusterd layercake. The Dead Feller. Maybe *he'd* be a-thankin it, the Dead Feller. Thankin the ginormous buildin reminds him of a castle an' maybe it was *here* he done hid hisself, the Dead Feller. Here. In the castle. The creemcusterd layercake castle. The hotel. The farmhouse. Yeomens an' kings an' queens. O yes. The cowboy done look'd fer the Dead Feller an' it'd be a right satisfacshun to go a-lookin fer him agin. *Hullo?* Ain't nobody. Nobody in resepshun. Ain't nobody poppin up from behind no sheeny countertop fer to anser. *Hullo?*

Nobody.

The Logo. The Logo shinin at him on a sign down by the driveway, now it's shinin at him from o'er the sheeny countertop.

A arrer. A new arrer. A new sign. At the resepshun desk.

There. Follow the arrer. Go on, now.

Ellavater. Take the ellavater.

Up?

Down.

Take the ellavater down.

. . .

Is you sure?

Down.

Instinct. Trust that instinct. Find the way.

Okey.

The cowboy. Zippin on down. In the ellavator. Kind o' ellavator ye can cram lippin full o' folks. Mmhmm, cram it lippin full. Down.

Down down down. Folks. Lippin full o' folks. Lookit. They's mirrors in here. Walls, ceilin, floor. Mirrors on these slidin doors, too. If that don't beat all. They had to go an' install slidin doors on the inside o' the ellavator itself. Slidin doors with mirrors. Wutn't enuff havin the usual sort o' slidin door at ever' floor where the ellavator's stoppin, nuh-uh, they had to have theirselves slidin doors with mirrors, here, inside the ellavator itself. Folks. Lippin full o' folks. The mirrors is lippin full o' cowboys. Hunnerds o' cowboys zippin down in the ellavator. All the cowboys is zippin on down. Lookit.

But how fur down is they goin, reelly? We ain't fussin bout bein short o' time. Ain't no reason to be a-fussin. Fer ye see, time done kinda sorta stood still. Time. *Kinda sorta*. Kinda sorta stood still. Now. Now an' back before whut we's callin now an' whut we says is fixin to come. Everthang's done been flung into this here mirror cabinet fer a ellavater an' if you's misdoubtin the truth of it all why just open them eyelids o' yourn an' take a lil' gander around. Lookit.

I's lookin, all right. I's lookin all around.

Whut is it ye see, now?

The cowboys. All them cowboys. They's zippin on down.

They's zippin on down but time's kinda sorta standin still. Happen'd all of a sudden. Seems like she's standin still.

She?

Durn straight. She.

But where? I cain't see her.

Exackly. Time. Seems like she's standin still an' everthang whut done been flung in here, yeah, it's everthang that takes time.

Do whut now?

Ye done said it yerself: *Whut don't take time?*

Nuthin.

Exackly. Everthang. *Takes* time. Not to menshun, makes time kinda sorta stand still.

Exackly? I said I been readin an' the lady she said so . . .

The lady.

. . . an' she wutn't standin there, nuther, she's settin there, in the one recliner . . .

All night.

All night.

The whole livvylong late summer night.

Down down down. Ever' one o' us an' all the cowboys was zippin on down an' I look'd around an' I's hearin how them voices was talkin an' I look'd an' look'd around an' I took it all in, everthang, *everthang* that'd done been flung into this here mirror cabinet fer a ellavator. An' I tell ye I know it. I know how some says I was dreemin.

But time was kinda sorta seemin to stand still an' maybe that's why it seem'd so goddang'd long, that ellavator ride. Wutn't no itty-bitty swoosh from the fust floor down to the basemint. We's zippin on down an' we seen ourselves in the mirrors, listn'd to whut them voices was sayin. An' I tell ye I know it. How some o' them voices says I was dreemin. But that ain't no matter. It's *whut* I remember an' *how* I's rememberin it, that's whut counts. Countin numbers, cain't do it. But I know whut counts. It look'd to me like ol' Andy's a-noddin off an' maybe I's spos'd to reckon he was dead but naw, he's prob'ly havin hisself as good a time as ever, hoverin up there mirrorwise in the ellavator. His voice among the chorus o' talkers. Just pretend-sleepin, was all, an' I heard his voice among the chorus o' talkers an' he's talkin loud an' time's kinda sorta standin still an' course I wutn't misdoubtin fer even one seccun that it was a nasty lil' plan he'd done hatch'd, one helluva nasty plan. The cowboys. Squose. Squose tergither in the backseat. I's hearin 'em talk an' I look'd around, round an' round I look'd before my eyes come to a dead stop an' the backseat kids become vizable. Sqwunch'd all tergither they was an' one of 'em lean'd his metal warsh-tub noggin up aginst the wender. The mirror. Wender. Car wender. Lookit. Lookit there. Down. Down a long long long hill. The hole. Down the hole. Right on down. Down the wood-hole.

Ah ah ah.

Ol' KurtSquirt started up agin.

Ah ah ah.

Cut it out, Squirty, says ol' Pucky Paul. Cut it out.

Ye's drivin t t too fast.

Too fast? says ol' Pucky Paul. Whut'n the hell you talkin bout, fast. This ain't nowhere nair fast. Just wait an' see, I'll show ye fast.

Naw. Naw naw naw.

This here's a reg'lar speed, say ol' Pucky Paul. This ain't no faster'n whut's reg'lar.

Naw.

Cadgy so cadgy so dadblam'd cadgy I cain't hardly stand it no more, ol' Andy kep' at it.

Well all right but I ain't stoppin an' I'll be goll-durn'd if ye's gon' be jackin in my veehickle ye hear.

Hey, Squirty. Whut say you we try an' flood this here veehickle betwixt the two o' us? Let's flood this sucker. How bout it, you an' me?

Naw.

Aw, come on, Squirty. Come on.

Naw. Naw naw naw.

KurtSquirt. Ol' Squirty. Squirty Kurt. Kurt Squirtin Kurtie who come to thank of it I seem to remember anserin to names like ol' Sob-n-Blubber an' ol' Bawl-Baby, cause that was always the problem with him: always stutterin an' stammerin an' strugglin to keep the saltwater from bustin futh an' soon enuff he was sobbin an' blubberin an' bawlin. Like a baby. Like a slobberin lil' baby. Hard to figgure. Feller like him. Big ol' booger, bigger'n ol' Andy an' ol' Pucky Paul an' me put tergither. Tall. Beak where ye ought ter've found a nose an' a mouth. Ginormous locks o' hair. Broad-shoulder'd. He'd a-been a funny sort o' gorilla if he'd a-been born a ape. He'd a-been a funny sort o' polar b'ar if he'd a-been born a b'ar. Frumpy, clumsy, but not a bit like th' sorta ondescribabble watersogg'd figgure ol' Calfy was. An' his best friend . . . was none other'n ol' Rattlebones Roger. Ol' Sob-n-Blubber an' ol' Rattlebones Roger . . . them two, them two . . .

I remember them two. Won't never fergit 'em. The one tall an' broad-shoulder'd. The other tall an' skinny. Two big letters, a tall V an' a tall I comin on down side by side lookin like a twoheaded troll an' the troll it tower'd over everbody else an' the one head it may've been sportin a homemade feather headdress.

V an' I.

Two capitle letters.

Comin on down.

Or maybe sqwunched tight tergither in a veehickle, a twoheaded troll who's havin to set in the backseat.

Now. *Now an' back before whut we's callin now an' whut we says is fixin to come.* Twoheaded troll on the road goin down to the wood-hole.

Naw. Naw naw naw.

Aw, come on, Squirty. Come on.

Naw.

Whut about you, Bonesy? Rattley? Is they any squirtins inside o' you?

Naw.

I's talkin to Rattley, Squirty. I's talkin to ol' Rattly now.

. . .

Bonesy?

. . .

Hullo?

. . .

Earth to Bonesy. Dead. Is you dead, Bonesy? Dead?

. . .

Okey. Okey okey okey. Drive on, Pucky. Drive on. Seem like we's standin still here. Dead still.

Stop.

Go hang yerself, Squirty. Go hang yerself.

Now now . . . I's gon' . . . go go go hang. Stop.

. . .

Stop? Ye's astin me whuther the ellavater ever come to a stop? Course it did. You know good an' well, buddy. The ellavater it stopp'd an' it stopp'd abruptedly an' I tombl'd over an' all the cowboys took a tomble an' fell down with a splat too. Woah. Abrupted sudden stop. Woah nelly. Flung. Flung back from the wallmirror I's leanin the plum rotted man-husk aginst an' smack into the slidin doormirrors an' I's layin there on the floormirror maybe moanin a little an' seen all the rest of 'em hoverin up above. Now now . . . I's gon' . . . go go go hang. Stop.

This the bottom? Is I come all the way down?

Stood up. Tried to stand up. couldn't stand up.

All the way down? Is I?

Naw.

Naw?

. . .

But I staggl'd back up on my feet agin an' after the utmostest struggle I's luckly able to lift my arm an' mash the button in all the way with my fist but the slidin door it wutn't budge. Naw. Naw naw naw. The ellavator. It's stuck. This goddamn ellavator's stuck. An' me. I's stuck in it. *In this mirror cabinet fer a ellavater*. Ha ha ha. I's stuck. I's stuck in the ellavater, man. I lay myself down an' I's gon' study the mirror in the ceilin fer a spell. Ha ha ha. I's stuck here. Stuck, man. Ain't like I ain't been stuck before. I remember how they shut me in some sorta claustrofobick room like this'un. Wutn't no mirror cabinet fer a ellavater but still. They shut me in an' the room was claustrofobick an' they tolt me to set a spell an' just be *me*. An' I didn't have no ideer whut to say. Ol' Andy he came fer to visit. This woulda been dreckly after he'd done been at the hospital fer to see fer hisself how the Calf was gittin on. The Calf. Dang demented. Ding-dong demented. Dingalingalingadingdong demented. The strongest toughie'd done feather'd into him an' beat him half to death an' now, some time after, he's awake agin an' he's dang demented, man, that ol' watersogg'd Calfy, man.

Calfy Calfy, watersogg'd Calfy.

He don't remember nuthin. Nuthin at'oll.

An' when I'd done heard Andy's schpeel I mighta said somethin too:

Is you sure?

Nuthin. He don't remember nuthin.

La illa holla illo alla,
La illa holla illo alla,
La illa holla illo alla . . .

But had ol' Andy been hesistatin fer to go a-drivin up there? Go hang yerself, he said. Go hang yerself an' scratch yer goober.

He got his own religion, he does. His own. An' from the nashunal an' city gov'mint come riches an' splendiferusness out o' thin air like ye wouldn't hardly believe. When all's said an' done it's a blessin he ain't too innerested in politics. Supposin he had been . . . Whut would he'd a-done? Join tergither wi' the soshalists? Ho boy. We'd be havin ourselves a time, then. We'd sure have ourselves a time, boy.

His own religion . . . If that ain't the durndest.

The Calf. The late summer night. They shut me in an' I didn't wanna be thankin bout no Calf. Didn't wanna be thankin bout no late summer night. Fergit. I's tryin to fergit an' fer a long time I believ'd they's nuthin to it, fergittin. *Nuthin to it.* Squimmy him out. The right cable. Take aholt o' the right cable an' squimmy him out. Simple. Long as I's able to take aholt of him, the cable. The right cable. Numerus cables branchin out unnerneath my skin an' all thru my flesh. Numerus. White, black, red cables. Some long, some short. Ever' one with its own connecshun to the fuse box in the warsh-tub noggin like they'd done explain'd to me. Connecshun, contextua-lizashun. Agin an' agin they explain'd it.

The fust time. Five or six years old. Childern's choir. Religious. I lay there in my bed all fev'rish openin my mouth wide starin up into eyeglasses big as supperplates wrapp'd tight round the domed head of a doctor my mama'd done summon'd futh out o' thin air. A doctor's domehead so round an' polish'd an' fine an' givin off a rarefy'd smell an' I's havin to open my mouth wide starin up into them eyeglasses big as supperplates.

Cables. Ol' Domehead Doctor was goin on about them cables. On an' on, explainin.

Lookit. Lookit here, he said. Lookit.

I look'd, all right. Seen my own jaw mirror'd in the glasses. Mouth open wide.

Lookit. Cables. Numerus cables. White, black, red cables. Lookit. Lookit here.

A finger. All of a sudden he stuck out a long, thin finger. Ol' Domehead Doctor. A long, thin finger an' in the eyeglasses it become a yeller snake such as ye see folks holdin up on the teevee. A yeller snake somewhere off in the jungal or behind the wall-glass of a aquarium at the zoo an' the folks down at the teevee stashun they film a natureshow an' lookit, man, lookit how the snake he's windin on down the wide-open gap. Aaaah. I's gurglin aaaah an' ol' Domehead Doctor he says: *We's gon' just take a look at one o' them cables o' yourn.*

Aaaah.

Open up, says my mama. Open up. She's leanin fo'ward, peekin over ol' Domehead Doctor so she can foller along.

Aaaah.

Attaboy.

Lookit. Lookit here.

An' the yeller snake in the eyeglasses done become a claw an' the claw by dod it done took holt o' one o' the cables, a red one, man, naw, did ye ever see . . .

An' my mama she's starin . . .

An' ol' Domehead Doctor he's talkin . . .

An' my mouth's wide open an' I's gurglin aaaah an' I's starin up into them eyeglasses big as supperplates.

The cable. Red cable. The claw it took holt o' one o' the cables unner my skin in my flesh an' sorta pull'd on it a little. Ol' Domehead Doctor. He pull'd it an' ast if it hurt at'oll.

Aaaah.

There there.

Nuthin to it. Squimmy the cable out. The right cable. Ol' Domehead Doctor. He'd done took aholt o' one o' the cables an' nair as I can remember now settin here creakin in my crannynook he made quick work of it. Sqwip goed the yeller snake down into my wide-open gap an' sqwup come the claw up wi' the red cable. An' when I's shut inside that room I's tryin to sqwup up the right cable too. Sqwup sqwup sqwup it up. O. Couldn't be nuthin to it so I took to sqwippin too, gaggin an' heavin all the while. Fergit. I's wantin to fergit. Sqwippin. Gaggin an' heavin. Tryin. O. O o o. There. Got him. I's openin my mouth wide as it'll go. I's squippin a finger on down an' gaggin an' heavin an' the finger whut was a yeller snake whut was a claw done finally grab holt o' the one cable I thank has got to be the right cable.

There we go.

O.

Out.

. . .

Squimmy it on out.

. . .

Out.

. . .

Ow. Dyaagh.

. . .

Dyaagh? Whut's that ye say, dead? Is you up an' dyaagh-dyaagh-died on us?

. . .

Birdsong. Once y'all done heard the birdsong out in the woods one late summer mornin then they ain't no need fer to go a-listnin to no shrieky sangin chantoosies no more, the kind o' screamin shrieky chantoosiesingers such as ye hear sangin as they go struttin an' smackin an' schmoozin an' strippin an' stealin away all yer presshus time. Birdsong. The birdsong out in the woods one late summer mornin when they'd done already been sangin fer a couple o' moons, o them warblers, cain't nuthin stop 'em 'cept fer bad weather. Chirpin an' sangin. Been practisin an' practisin, An' whut ye's hearin is perfecshunated birdsong. Yep, out in the woods one late summer mornin hearin perfecshunated birdsong an' ye best give thanks to yer lucky stars fer gittin to hear them meckanickal musical birds sangin.

So how come this here chantoosie's got to go actin the superstar sangin that screamin shrieky chantoosiesangin out here on the town square?

In the newspaper, it was. Bout her comin here fer a concert. From out o' town. From Honerfoss, matter o' fact. They done set a stage up an' all. Right next to the transformator.

So I guess we's gon' git to hear her sangin. Since they ain't no way we's gon' shirk our meetin at the Diner on account o' no chantoosie sangin right outside in the town square.

Ol' Andy. Was him who come on down with his potherashun. Him who come a-visitin an' goin on an' on about the Calf. I'd done purty nair forgot. Purty nair forgot all about the Calf. I'd done squimmy'd out the right cable (so I believ'd) an' purty nair forgot everthang an' then here he come teeter-totterin back an' futh on a wood chair in front o' me with a dixiecup full o' water on the lil' table betwixt us just a-talkin an' a-talkin an' a-talkin, ol' Andy.

I, he said. The Calf, he said. Dang demented, he said. That other stuff, he said. That other . . .

. . . a-thankin an' a-writin, right next to the coffeepot . . . don't wanna thank about it, nor write about it, all that other stuff . . .

Whut was I spos'd to say? Footloose an' fancy-free, he was,

ol' Andy. Wutn't *him* they'd done drug out, drove off with, shut inside.

His pappie, who had the jake-leg. He'd done been in the pen fer a spell an' ol' Andy he know'd well whut it was like bein the shagnasty's boy. Lookit him. That there's the shagnasty's boy. Ye know it. They pointed at him, whisperin bout his pappie, whisperin his pappie's name an' pointin, sayin one day he's sure to wind up in the pen hisself, ol' Andy. If not the pen then the nuthouse or as some folks was sayin: kidnapp'd by them u.f.o.-mens, bein that folk'd been observin the u.f.o. traffic just south o' the construcshun lot where ol' Andy's livin with his pappie in one o' them brown-stain'd houses folks didn't hardly believe fit fer no family.

Naw, if that don't beat all, said this'un. Naw, man, rubble an' ruinashun, cussidness an' bedevilry, said that'un.

An' it was after his pappie'd done been let out o' the pen an' come home that they's observin u.f.o. traffic up above the hills just south o' the construcshun lot.

A long time. Kinda sorta standin still.

He come home. The jake-leg feller with his magical brushbroom an' his flyin carpet too. An' the u.f.o. traffic ratchited up like you wouldn't believe, man.

But anyhow. It wutn't ol' Andy they drug out an' as fur as I know he wutn't never kidnapp'd by no u.f.o.-mens nuther.

But them u.f.o.'s. I seen 'em a long time after his pappie'd done been let out o' the pen an' come home an' ol' Andy he seen the u.f.o.'s too. Ol' Andy an' me we both seen the u.f.o.'s but they said we's tellin a tall tale, ol' Pucky Paul an' ol' KurtSquirt an' ol' Rattlebones Roger. They said we's tellin a big'un.

U.f.o.'s, holler'd ol' Andy. You remember them u.f.o.'s?

Who me?

Yeah, you. You.

Me. Sure I remember them u.f.o.'s. Couldn't a-been more'n a week ago since I last seen 'em.

Shut the hell up, ol' Pucky Paul yell'd. I'll be a hog molly if I's gon' listen to ye flappin yer gums about them dadblasted u.f.o.'s.

But I's tellin ye we seen 'em. We done tolt ye plenty o' times. An' we's still seein 'em. Sure as we's settin here we seen 'em. Cadgy. O. I's cadgy as a ol' tomcat.

Shut up. Shut up. Shut up.

Ah ah ah.

Is ye carsick, Squirty? Is ye carsick? Cadgy cadgy cadgy.

He ain't gon' be vommickin, not in my veehickle, that's fer goddamn sure.

Stop. I . . . I . . . I's fixin to . . .

An' ol' Rattlebones Roger he crack'd his joints an' took to flingin his arms agin an' ol' KurtSquirt's cheeks was a-bulgin an' I give ol' Rattlebones Roger a piece o' my elbow an' ol' Pucky Paul's a-hollerin an' ol' Andy's a-laffin an' ol' KurtSquirt's a-holtin the vommick in an' the veehickle it flew on down the wood-hole, down down into the late summer night wi' the beer bottles a-clinkin an' a-clankin inside the crate an' the tote bags an' the shotgun an' bucket an' flashlight all goin donk donk an' everthang's prob'ly fixin to be toss'd round an' round an' round in the trunk back there before . . .

Stop? A dead stop?

Ol' Pucky Paul he stopp'd the motor, switch'd off the headlights got hisself out o' the veehickle shov'd the driverseat down so it knock'd bang on the styairin wheel an' took aholt o' KurtSquirt's hair fer to jerk his head toward hisself an' jump out o' the way just as the vommick come a-spewin out like a waterfall from ol' KurtSquirt's inspir'd limerick-spoutin beak.

A wood-troll who grow'd up in Gran,
Guzzlin cod-liver oil of tran,
He felt queasy an' barfulous,
Sobful an' querulous.
Then he spew'd in the forests of Pan.

Ah. Ah ah ah.

. . .

Hush. A eerie hush where the veehickle'd done come to a stop. A minute or two pass'd. Maybe more. Don't matter nohow. Time. Kinda sorta. Standin still. Still an' dark. Late summer night dark. An' ol' Rattlebones Roger he rais'd up his arm fer to fiddle wi' the ceilin light they was some kind o' tecknickal problems with an' it said clickclack clickclack an' they was light enuff so we's finally able to see a body, we who was still settin in the veehickle. Yep. We could. We sure could.

. . .

Come on.

The rest o' the gang out o' the veehickle too an' ol' Andy he said: *Come on.*

Do whut now? Ye ain't fixin to jack yerself now is ye? Is ye gon' jack it? ast ol' Pucky Paul standin by his open cardoor an' in whut little light they was comin from the ceilin lamp he took to studyin the locks o' hair his fingers was still wrapp'd up in.

Naw. Come on.

But where? I cain't just be leavin this here veehickle out in the middle o' the road.

The road? They ain't no more road out here. This the end o' the road. Come on.

Do whut now? The end? The road goes on from here, tho', don't it?

Shut up. Git back in the veehickle an' switch on the headlights so ye can see better.

Naw . . .

Come on. Come on now. An' go git the shotgun, Pucky Paul. Take the shotgun.

Okey.

An' the flashlight an' the bucket too.

Whut Andy was callin the end o' the road . . . was way down inside a hollow. A gorge. The Mare Cooter Canyon.

That's how I remember it. Flew down into the wood-hole, we did. Flew down an' ended up way down inside the Mare Cooter Canyon over by the Lunnerworld. That's where the veehickle stopp'd. Ol' Pucky Paul'd done switch'd off the motor at the very spot ol' Andy's callin the end o' the road. The very spot, man.

Come on. Ol' Andy's tellin everbody to come along an' ol' Pucky Paul let go o' KurtSquirt's hair an' they took the few steps to the back o' the veehickle, open'd the trunk an' fetch'd out the shotgun an' took the flashlight an' the bucket too.

Ol' KurtSquirt took off down the gravel path an' if anybody else was to come along with flashlights an' seen us now they'd sure be believin they's fixin to witness a summery execushun but naw, ol' KurtSquirt he gather'd his varius bodyparts tergither an' a seccun or two later he's standin tall an' broad-shoulder'd next to ol' Rattlebones Roger an' ol' Andy said come on an' in one hand he's holdin the flashlight an' in the other the bucket an' he's sayin he's fixin to lead the rest o' the way now that they wutn't no road no more an' he set his nebbynose toward the sky an' sniff'd the air, ol' Andy the Rat, sniffin like a stress'd ol' harehound on a leesh while he took to trottin on' up a slope with ol' Pucky Paul at his heels wi' the shotgun.

Okey. Ol' Pucky Paul he said okey. Prob'ly thankin the BossMan had some kinda plan figgur'd out.

Prob'ly.

Prob'ly thankin somethin along them lines, ol' Pucky Paul, ol' Paul Pucky, ol' Hoss-Pucky Paul, that ol' mucky munchkin who'd done been threatn'd with a whuppin by some mussleheads the summer he turn'd nine lessun' he munch'd down a delicate pile o' steamin fresh hoss-pucky an' now he's trottin, trottin on after the harehound. (Ha ha. A hare (or a beever) trottin *after* the harehound. Ha ha.) The shotgun. Ol' Andy's shotgun: carryin it on outstretch'd arms was ol' Hoss-Pucky Paul, who just prior to the wood-troll's innards turnin theirselves inside-out had been drivin like a god, that ol' Hoss-Pucky Gobbler, carryin ol' Andy's shotgun on outstretch'd arms like a playmobil-figureen, trottin like some overeager pinguin up the slope while the Boss-Man, ol' Andy the Rat, who at this point had done turn'd into a harehound, goed a-sniffin an' a-sniffin an' a-sniffin.

Come on, I said. So we trotted on after 'em too, ol' KurtSquirt an' ol' Rattlebones Roger an' me. Them. Us. The backseat kids. We trotted on after 'em, us backseat kids.

If that don't beat all. That on a late summer night a long time ago, in the way-back-when, I's trottin tergither with ol' KurtSquirt an' ol' Rattlebones Roger up a slope someplace or other down in the hollow, this volcanick gorge of a wood-hole down by the Lunnerworld that'd been call'd the Mare Cooter Canyon because folks belongin to the race o' humans who know'd durn well whut was whut an' never was tickl'd more'n when they's repeatin somethin they'd done heard here an' there an' all around in ever' nook an' cranny an' cranny-nook, in ever' house an' cabin, an' in ever' lean-to, them folks, them human-folks, they set their eyes on a poor soul an' open'd their gossipin lips, sayin:

Now let me tell ye all about it. That night the canyon got its name, the Mare Cooter Canyon, that woulda been the night they learn'd whut ol' KillerHenry was gittin up to over in his stable, that's right, whut he's gittin up to, boy . . . Ginormous. He was ginormous, ol' KillerHenry. Of the race o' sasquatches, he was. Next to him a Arab hoss look'd no bigger'n a lil' ol' Iceland pony. Yep, that ol' KillerHenry . . .

> The fugitive from Swedish forests
> Walk'd a spell out toward the West an'
> Said he'd done been walkin long an'
> Trod o'er branches, limbs an' mosses,
> Said he had to chop down timber:
> Lumber fer the boat he's buildin,
> Lawd-a-mercy build the boat an'
> Sail out over the open ocean
> Lawd-a-mercy, prophesyin,
> Prophesyin water water . . .
> Big diluvy . . . water water . . .

And? So he ended up in these here parts, the Prophet, ol' KillerHenry? *Yep. Here. Down in the Canyon.* The Prophet? They's callin him KillerHenry before they's callin him the Prophet? *Yep.* The Prophet on account o' him peerin into the future an' seein a new great flood? *Yep.* Ol' KillerHenry? *Yep.* Ol' KillerHenry, the feller they caught redhanded in the stable? *Yep.* S'whut they said. Said they'd done caught him redhanded in the stable, wutn't it? *Yep, 'swhut they said. Redhanded. Caught him redhanded.* But *he* was sayin somethin entairly diff'rent than whut they kep' on sayin an' repeatin over an' over an' over. They's talkin talkin talkin but *he* was sayin somethin entairly diff'rent. Whut he said, was:

Stable? That's my boat, that is.

Yer boat?

Yep, my boat.

Say whut now? The hell you need that sorta voluminus boat down in the Canyon fer? Ain't like they's much water in these parts fer it to float on. Sailboat? Is that a sailboat you's buildin? But then when's the last time they's any wind to speak of down in the Canyon? An' as fer water . . . ain't no water to brag about nuther . . . snow in the winter . . . plenty o' snow an' the snowmeltins whut set many a bubblin brook a-flowin, soakin the myre, drenchin the bog-hole to the very roots . . . an' wutn't they a girl who goed missin who wutn't never found? That girl. They said she'd done gone to the bog-hole. They said the sodden Canyon done took her. Said she couldn't resist. Somebody musta call'd her out to the bog-hole, they said . . . callin, callin, like callin the cows home . . . yep . . . snowmeltins . . . but a-diddelydattendoo, man, ain't no water to brag about . . .

One late summer night, late summer night
She couldn't resist, she couldn't fight
Found her a treasure, a purty sight
One late summer night, late summer night . . .

But sailin? Wi' that kinda voluminus boat down in the Canyon? Ho-no, boy. Ain't no water fer to sail with down here, boy . . . so whut'n the hell you need that sorta voluminus boat fer?

KillerHenry. He pointed up at the sky an' said: Rain . . .

He said: Rain . . . gully-whoppers . . . big diluvy . . . rain . . . rain rain rain.

Him. The Prophet. God hisself had done spoke to him. 'Swhut he said, the Prophet. The rain. Gully-whoppers. Big diluvy. Yep, he said it was God hisself who'd done spoke to him. God hisself an' troops o' angels. Okey. The voices. The voices way down inside his noggin. They said it was these chaintooth voices way down inside his sasquatch noggin whut was talkin to him. They. They said. They's talkin but ol' KillerHenry he tolt a diff'rent story. A whole other kinda story altergither. God. Angels. Rain. Gully-whoppers. Big diluvy. Ol' KillerHenry, the Prophet, he peer'd into the future an' seen a new great flood an' God knows whut it was whut reelly happen'd that evenin when a few snoopin rubes from the other side o' the Garter Strap Ridge who sure didn't have no bisniss bein in the Lunnerworld was able to git into such a fine mess almost all by theirselves down, down in the Canyon, bout four or five of 'em an' one of 'em's carryin a shotgun, carryin it, the shotgun, like it's some kinda trofy he's carryin, the durn'd fool, a trofy, a dadblam'd trofy. An' ol' Pucky Paul, it was *him* carryin the shotgun now, we's trottin after him an' ol' Andy he's trottin in front o' ol' Pucky Paul. The hosses. Ol' KillerHenry he said he's gon' take the hosses with him. The boat. The stable. The hosses. The holy hosses. An' one o' them hosses . . . it was a mare with a white strip down her muzzle, a mare he felt such warm an' fuzzies toward . . . the hosses. The holy hosses. Ain't none of 'em gon' be drown'd. Ain't none . . .

None?

None.

Yep. I'd done heard how they's talkin. KillerHenry. The real story bout this sasquatch, the Prophet, the fugitive from Swedish forests . . . yes, one day he come crashin thru all of a sudden, ol' KillerHenry. Crashin thru with all his might. Woah how the trees they did crack an' they teeter'd. Woah went the thunderment all thru the woods down by the Lunnerworld. A woful destructiousness. Woah. *Whut in the world?* An' the human-folks they's flyin an' flappin an' flailin an' jumpin an' hoppin an' trippin an' floppin an' screamin an' raisin cain an' all the flappin jaws took to churnin before anybody know'd to thank better of it an' the human-folks, they's wantin to know whut in the world done happen'd . . . Well, that story I'd done heard. Many a time I'd done heard it . . . Mister Principal, Miss Teacher, the Preacher, the Sheriff, ol' Andy's pappie, my mama, my sister plus a heap o' other chatterboxes I know have gone around addin a bit here an' subtractin a bit there till they all done glom'd tergither in one big fat equasion . . . They *lik'd* tellin the tale o' ol' KillerHenry.

Mister Principal. I remember him tellin:

My grandpappie, the one grandpappie o' mine, he come a-runnin out o' the Swedish forests too. My grandpappie. Didn't have a red cent to his name, I tell ye. Not one red cent to his name when he settl'd here. Not one thang. Didn't have one thang. Y'all hear that?

An' Miss Teacher. I remember her tellin:

KillerHenry. Sorta quare an' skeery name, don't y'all thank? But the reason he was call'd KillerHenry, was on account o' him bein so big, so big . . . cain't say as I ever heard tell o' him killin nobody.

The Preacher. He said:

The Prophet. They nam'd him fer the Prophet. An' it might've been yes it might coulda been he was a prophet sent from God hisself. Because he built hisself a ark that's right he built hisself a ark. The good Lawd, he said. The good Lawd had done spoke to him. Spoke to him about a new great flood.

The Sheriff. He said:

They tried arrestin him, about four or five hurlyburlies from the shootin range. But dammit, how in the hell's they spos'd to carry him off? Blow his brains out an' cut him into ittybitty bits an' stuff the bits in big burlap sacks an' haul it back all hunch'd over an' back-broke?

Ol' Andy's pappie. He said:

Sheeit. Some ol' sheeit whut wutn't worth diddly squat. But goddamn . . . Ye can say that agin, pardner. Like hell. Like hell, payin fer it. I'll prob'ly git this sheeit sold too, one way or another.

Skeer 'em. Force 'em. Boo. Boo boo boo. Here come ol' KillerHenry crashin on down. On his brushbroom. Ha ha ha. An' his napsack plumb full o' sheeit.

My mama too. She said:

Naw, don't believe me? I seen him. I seen him one evenin I's pickin lingonberries up on Dilly-Dally Hill. Lingonberries, oh me. Bless my bones... Say whut, now? Ye don't believe me? I seen him. Couldn't a-been a day older'n fifteen. I seen him. Ol' KillerHenry. He'd done cut his beard an' comb'd his hair. Yes an' I'll own he was a fine-lookin feller that evenin too.

An' my sister, she said:

Once upon a time they's a giant nam'd KillerHenry. That's right. KillerHenry. Hosses. He sure did love hosses an' they was one in pertic'lar he's lovin a lil' extra, a mare he'd done bought off a profeshunal hoss thief some time before he was hang'd... the hoss thief, that is, it was the hoss thief who got hisself hang'd. Extra lovin ... he give that mare a lil' extra lovin, ol' KillerHenry. An' one night ... naw, ye'd never guess whut they did see, these snoopin rubes. In the stable. Well ol' KillerHenry he's in there puttin a baby to his mare. That's right. Ol' KillerHenry. KillerHenry.

That sort o' thang. This an' that an' that an' this sort o' thang. An' a heap o' other chatterboxes. Their talk. How they did talk an' talk an' I heard all the talkin, I did.

Not one thang. Didn't have one thang. Y'all hear that?

I did hear.

Cain't say as I e'er heard tell o' him killin nobody.

I heard everthang whut was said.

Mighta coulda been he was a prophet sent from God hisself.

So I heard.

But dammit, how in the hell's they spos'd to carry him off?

I heard.

Some ol' sheeit whut wutn't worth diddly squat.
Heard.
I seen him.
Heard.
Yep. Ol' KillerHenry. KillerHenry.

The noggin. The warsh-tub noggin. Tarnatious amount o' activity now. Ol' Andy leadin the way. Trottin. Sniffin. Carryin the flashlight an' showin the way. An' ol' Pucky Paul right at his heels. The shotgun. On his outstretch'd arms. Trottin. An' if he'd a-been a hare or a hedgehog or a playmobil-figureen well then . . . just thank. An' ol' KurtSquirt an' ol' Rattlebones Roger an' me. We's trottin along too. *Foller 'em foller 'em. Ain't n n no other way. Ah ah ah.* An' I heard 'em talkin, I heard . . .

Up an' up . . . Up the slope, down the canyon.

Up the driveway, boys. Up up up the driveway.

Driveway? Course it would be ol' Andy who said so. But a driveway? Ain't nuthin but a trail here. A ordnary steep narrer trail in the woods on a late summer night. But that was just like him, comin out with stuff like 'at. A driveway. An' up at the top of this here driveway, he said, *they's a house with a garden.*

H h house with a garden.

'Swhut he said. Course he did.

H h house with a garden. H h house with a ga ha harden. Ain't much futher to go, now.

Rest. Take a breather on this here hill. A fur piece up the slope now. Up an' up. Steep. An' it done got a lot steeper an' narrerer an' craggier an' a sight more problematickal an' one by one the boys'd done left off the trottin. Steppin slow now. Poke-easy. One by one.

Rest. Ol' Andy's voice. Hollerin. Commandin. Ol' Boss-Man, he done stopp'd, turn'd, an' pointed the beam at the others an' he sees 'em clumblin an' stumblin on after him an' he cusses at 'em an' tells 'em to hesh up now an' then he turns off the light. Shadows. The Boss-Man an' his cowboys have done turn'd into clumsy stumblin shadows on a godfersaken late summer night.

The moon? Whut happen'd to the moon? The man in the moon?

Rest. Take a breather on this here hill.

How m m much futher? somebody pipes up complainin. How m m much futher has we got to go, man?

The Boss-Man. He cusses an' tells him to hesh up an' says: Up. On up, boys. We'll be there dreckly.

Dr dr dreckly? G g goddammit, Andy. Goddammit.

Hesh up. Cut it out, Squirty. You hush now. You'll make it. Just like everbody else. But now we's gon' take a breather on this here hill. A breather, ye hear. Rest a spell. Breathe. An' cut out the dadgum yappin.

If ye ast me it's a overgrow'd tropickal rainforest we's takin a breather in.

Shet it, Pucky. Shet it. Hesh up.

Naw you hesh. Ye's *hollerin*, fer cryin out loud. An' all that gravel in that bucket o' yourn. Gravel.

Shet it. Hesh hesh hesh.

You hesh.

The shotgun. A honor an' a priv'lege, carryin the shotgun . . . an' ol' Pucky Paul's the one who got the job, natcherly. An' now he's standin there huffin an' puffin on these here slopes on account o' him havin to go swearin an' sweatin thru the confounded bushbrambles an' it was him who got to carry the shotgun an' he is a-huffin an' puffin fer sure but not nowhere nair as much as ol' KurtSquirt's a-huffin an'a-puffin. Aggervated. Tucker'd out. Now he's standin on the slopes on a godfersaken late summer night a-protestin, the shadow o' ol' Pucky Paul is.

I see him now, the shadow. I see somethin whut's mergin tergither wi' the black spruces but still lookin like a human fer all that. The playmobil-figureen wi' the shotgun. Or maybe he look'd more like a beever. Or a hare. Beever with a shotgun. Hare with a shotgun. Pinguin. Don't make no diff'rence nohow but the shadow it's carryin a shotgun an' I know I done thunk to myself the thought *but whut I cain't explain to ye is how come I's a-thankin it:*

Shoot him. Shoot him now. I know ye done loaded the shotgun so shoot him. Blow his head clean off. Blow that rat mother's head off. Blow it to hell . . .

. . . but I cain't explain to ye how come how come how come . . .

Come on. Ol' Andy he said come on an' so next thang I know we's off clumblin an' stumblin agin. The air. Sure was chilly. I felt it. My sweaty ol' husk was feelin it. The chill in the air. Air, o the air. Shadows. Branches, grass, needles an' nettles. Rocks. Ye's hearin sounds an' ye know'd it was sounds ye coulda heard on a slope out in the jungal. Swish swoosh crunch cronch stamp stomp. Yep them boys was a-clumblin an' stumblin on up. The expedishun was nearin the end. The house. The garden.

Welcome.

Do whut now?

Welcome, said ol' Andy an' they had to've been somebody other'n us boys he's sayin it to. *Welcome*. Because he had his narrer back turn'd toward us an' I realiz'd he'd done set down the bucket o' gravel an' he reach'd out his lil' spindley but otherwise perfeckly normal right hand before bowin an' bendin his knees a little, this shadow o' hisn. Who? Who in the hell's he talkin to now? Nobody. Wutn't nobody there. Or was they? *Welcome.*

We'd done arrov'd. An' we's waitin fer ol' Andy to tell us cowboys whut in tarnashun we's doin here.

Sheeit. I stood right where I was. Hidin behind a big ol' rock.

Course I know'd. Know'd it was best to stay hid. I know'd it almost soon as ol' Andy stopp'd an' his shadow took shape as a meckanickal stop-moshun push-puppet man, right outta Ivo Caprino, just like me (only I ain't only a push-puppet, I's always been a push-puppet gnome-doll man). Big ol' rocks. They's big ol' rocks up in these parts. I peek'd out slow an' cyairful. The shadow. The shape the Boss-Man took. Naw. Somethin wutn't right. *Shoot him*, I's thankin. *Shoot him*. But the fennomenon whut was carryin the shotgun, human or beever or hare or whutever it was . . . they wutn't nuthin, man, not a thang whut would indicate the rat-head's fixin to be blow'd away, now, on this very speshul late summer night. *Coward*. I's thankin: *Coward*. But if I's thankin that about Pucky Paul or my own self . . . don't make no diff'rence. I stood there. Peek'd out. Air was chilly. Rain. Rain? Tonight? The boat. The ark. Natcherly. Natcherly it would be here ol' KillerHenry come to build his boat, up on this here hillside. A ha. Natcherly. Because why go a-buildin the new ark way down in the Canyon? If they's one thang they's right about, Mister Principal an' Miss Teacher an' the Preacher an' all them other chatterboxes, it's that it don't make a lick o' sense mannin the ship at the bottom o' no canyon while the big storm's a-ragin an' somehow expectin everthang to work out fine an' dandy. The great flood come an' ol' KillerHenry he's mannin the ship down in the Canyon while the hosses is a-neighin an' a-buckin an' that ark gits smash'd to smithereens down at the bottom o' the Canyon with a swish-swooshin splish-splashin old-testamentary boom. Naw. it wutn't like that. That's a whole diff'rent story than this'un. The stable . . . why that was just a blind, ye see. Them snoopin rubes from the other side o' the Garter Strap Ridge who after they'd done manag'd to git into such a fine mess almost all by theirselves had done caught him redhanded in the stable: man, they couldn't hardly stutter an' stammer a word right then but later, man, later they's talkin an' talkin. An' my sister . . . she had a head fer deetails an' she gobble'd up ever' word they's servin up. Coffee. Ye better git that coffeepot churnin agin boy. Coffee. An' one night . . . naw, ye'd never guess whut they did see, them snoopin rubes. In the stable. Well ol' KillerHenry he's in there puttin a baby to his mare. Coffee. More coffee. The fellers in the labbarinth is wantin them some coffee. Kid Clipclop he's wonderin whuther I plumb fergot all about him. Yep, there he was, puttin a baby to his mare, the giant. Okey. Coffee. More coffee. That was my sister tellin me that fairy tale. Me. I's maybe five or six then. Maybe. I's layin in bed. My room. Home. Back when I sang in the choir, sang in my sleep. Sang. I could just see it. The giant plowin his mare an' all their jaws hittin the ground an' they's havin the livin daylights skeer'd out of 'em, the snoopin rubes. Wooooah nelly. Ain't never seen the like of it. The sorcerer with his mare. Never, boy.

Why, just imagine it, my sister she said. Savorin ever' deetail. *Imagine. Just imagine.*

Ahhhhhh right. Coffee. Okey. But it was a blind. An' it was a trap.

Ol' KillerHenry. He know'd whut he had to do.

He trod over branches, limbs an' mosses an' claim'd hisself a spot up on the hillside, a spot where at one time there liv'd a herd o' twolegged creturs, humans or wood-trolls or gnomes or space creturs. Hmm. Ol' KillerHenry he survey'd the mossy rock formashuns. Heap'd rocks. A foundashun wall, too. Naw. Whut's left of the foundashun wall. Hmm. Couldn't a-been a very spashious room fer receivin no company. But big enuff, sure, big enuff fer shelterin a couple o' grow'd-up toilers an' each kid they'd gifted the gift o' toil on the mornin or the afternoon or the evenin or the night he or she was born an' who'd liv'd to grow up an' be a real toiler his- or herself. An' ol' KillerHenry, he know'd whut all the toil was about. Swedish woods. Wutn't easy livin in them dark woods o' Sweden, nuther. He remember'd how it was. Bark. They stripp'd the bark off o' trees an' they put the bark over the fire an' in their one kettle the bark-mush was a-bubblin an' a-bilin an' they et up the bark. They drunk up the bark too, course they did, 'cause in the other kettle they's bilin an' brewin the coffee, a speshul blend o' many vintage bark-pulvers ginerously perporshun'd an' mix'd all tergither. Coffee. Serve the coffee. Take a turn thru the labbarinth, yep, finish yer round an' don't fergit another round in a hour. Yuh-huh, they been complainin a-plenty, the Minister o' Justice an' Kid Clipclop an' that toughie who matterfactually come santerin on down an' extanded his right hand an' said whut his name was: Rambo, he said, the name's Rambo an' you, you must be the new idiot around here, the new idiot, he said, this here Rambo, I didn't make no anser, they wutn't nuthin to say, I's playactin, actin the stone-deef Hobblestiltskin an' the artifisshul right hand bein extended by this here stone-deef Hobblestiltskin it trembl'd, trembl'd somethin fierce boy. I's settin by my desk an' the artifisshul right hand it's tremblin an' bout two-three days later this here Rambo took to complainin, him an' the Minister o' Justice an' Kid Clipclop. Coffee wutn't tastin like it's spos'd to. So they's complainin an' complainin an' cussin an' the stone-deef Hobblestiltskin took to thankin an' thankin bout the late summer night. *Welcome.* Ol' Andy he said Welcome. I seen his shadow. Hid myself behind a big ol' rock an' seen ol' Pucky Paul's shadow too. I seen the cowboy carryin the shotgun.

Welcome, said ol' Andy, loud an' clear. Welcome. Welcome to this here coffeeclatch. We's fixin to sample some o' ol' KillerHenry's barkbrew'd coffee.

KillerHenry?

That's right, Pucky. KillerHenry hisself. An' ye's fixin to sample his barkbrew'd coffee.

Say whut now? Whut'n the hell you mean?

Whut I mean, Pucky, is, that it was *here*, on this very spot, ol' KillerHenry built hisself the ark.

Here?

Right here. He built it here. Waited here, by dod. That night. That very night, Pucky. That very night. This very place.

Ol' KillerHenry an' ol' Pucky Paul. I heard whut all they said. I's hidin behind a big ol' rock but still able to pick up whut they's sayin. Heard whut kinda secret this here shadow whut done led us up the slope decided to inisherate the shadow carryin the shotgun into. Secret? Yeah, well. Wutn't the fust time he'd menshun'd all this, ol' Andy. I rickolect one evenin down in the rumpus room. He up an' plow'd a path with his pipecleanerlegs (clutter, he's knee-high in his own clutter, plowin a path thru it) all whiles a-babblin an' talkin an' in a instant ol' Pucky Paul's up an' follerin him on the path, in a instant, trampin in ol' Andy's tracks, round an' round they's stampin an' plowin like a couple o' fidgity Indians round a invizable totempole an' ol' Andy he was babblin, talkin, said he never woulda believ'd it, never believ'd ol' KillerHenry woulda built a ark at the bottom o' the Mare Cooter Canyon.

At the bottom? Naw, up on the hillside. Up on the hillside, that's where he built it. Up on the hillside fer to wait on the gully-whopper, the great flood, the big diluvy.

Natcherly. I's thankin, while I sat on the beanbag chair, thankin an' a-mumblin: *Natcherly. Natcherly ol' KillerHenry'd done built hisself the boat up on the hillside. A ha.*

You say somethin?

I didn't say nuthin, Andy.

Okey okey okey. An' on he goed a-babblin an' talkin, ol' Andy, in circles:

. . . an' they's a house an' a garden there, house an' a garden an' a blah blah blah . . .

But did ol' Pucky Paul unnerstand whut was goin on when he took to trampin in ol' Andy's tracks like some dang-ol' tag-along lil' brother? Don't thank so. Nor do I thank he unnerstood a lick o' whut was goin on now nuther, this late summer night, at the spot up on the hillside, after we'd done clumbl'd an' stumbl'd up the slope. Naw. Ol' Pucky Paul? Cain't say as I thank so, naw.

Pucky Paul. Maybe the only one o' us who dar'd talk back to ol' Andy. Could be he was the only one who wutn't afear'd o' him. That's how I remember him. Ol' Pucky Paul. A gnawer who maybe sorta look'd like somebody's asskissin lil' brother but he sure wutn't no asskissin lil' brother, ol' Pucky Paul. The Driver. The dude with the razor-edg'd opinions. An' protestin, the art o' protestin, that was a art he'd done master'd better'n my sister an' my mama both an' I remember whut they said, my sister an' my mama, that time a old she-gossip come by to personally deliver a report on the topic of who'd been drivin around drunk as a skunk an' wound up smack on somebody's roof, why it was none other'n ol' Gury an' Cory's son, that feller Paul, yes him that ol' razortooth Paul an' then my sister an' my mama they's talkin over each other sayin how that lil' ring-around-the-rosy shoulda oughta taught him a lesson he ain't like'ta fergit, bein how they wutn't no denyin it nor no protestin nuther, drivin around drunk as a skunk, he done done it. Yep. Ol' Pucky Paul. An' it was only a few days before I's carry'd off by these mussleheads that that ol' she-gossip come an' deliver her report an' I might coulda been thankin, mumblin:

Quick as a hickory with his backjaw, sure. But ol' Pucky Paul, he ain't none too bright.

Say whut now? KillerHenry? Did you say *KillerHenry?*

I said KillerHenry, Pucky. KillerHenry.

Lawd a mercy. I declare, you reelly *believe* this sheeit.

Believe? This here's a house an' garden. Ain't nobody livin in it no more. Gone to pot. C'mon an' let's keep goin.

An' off they goed agin. An' I seen the shadows movin. Fust two shadows an' the one shadow hadn't forgot to bring the bucket. Then another two shadows. The shadows four they's goin . . . goin . . . gone into the darkness . . .

An' the moon? Was he out? D'ye thank the man in the moon was keepin a close watch? Do ye? Yeah, you. You. Whut do you thank?

Big ol' rock. Prob'ly best to stay standin where I'd done been standin the past few minutes. House? Garden? Coffeeclatch at ol' Killer-Henry's? Wouldn't that be somethin. Ain't ever' day ye git serv'd coffee by a haint. Once upon a time . . . My sister's tellin that fairy tale. Once upon a time they's a giant who . . . an' my mama's pickin lingonberries . . . said he'd done cut his beard an' comb'd his hair. An' then they was all them others who'd talk'd about him. Ol' Andy's pappie an' the Sheriff an' the Preacher an' Miss Teacher an' Mister Principal an' yes . . . them. All them folks. The voices. Way down inside . . . Naw. Best to stay standin here . . . Coffee? No thankee. Nope. Done already had too much as it is. An' maybe they'd be right, ol' Rambo an' the Minister o' Justice an' Kid Clipclop, prob'ly the Professor too if ye was to go an' ast him about it. About the coffee not tastin like it's spos'd to. Naw, hell with it. It was there I stood an' there I stay'd standin, standin hidin back behind a big ol' rock. Money. The money ol' Pucky Paul said ol' Andy'd done stole off his pappie. Five thousan' kroners. Five thousan'. Sheeit. He ain't worth a flip ol' Andy nor his pappie nuther. The Sheriff ain't the only one who'll attest to that. My mama an' my sister an' . . . them. Still them. An' my cables, connectors, fuses . . . got to be now or never. An' one day folks just as hurly an' just as burly as them fellers from the shootin range is gon' come an' carry me off, gon' take holt o' my man-husk an' drag it off an' shut it in an' say it's fer the best an' all the domehead doctors an' snoopin rubes an' robot-riffraff from this side o' the county line is gon' come peer down inside my wide-open gap. Okey. It's okey. Cause this here barn gnome's a entairly diff'rent sort o' barn gnome than one o' them fairly ordnary overpertic'lar barn gnomes. Meckanickal. Yer fairly ordnary meckanickal barn gnome. Entairly diff'rent sort than one o' them fairly ordnary overpertic'lar ones. Yessir, entairly diff'rent . . . But them human-folks, they have a hard time unnerstandin just how ordnary a meckanickal barn gnome matterfactually is, man. Now it could be they unnerstood *a little bit* back when they's sayin the meckanickal barn gnome-young'un oughtta be in the childern's choir. Could be . . . Naw. Big ol' rock. Funny how easy it was to stay hid back there. I dissappear'd. *Swish swoosh.* They wutn't hollerin fer me nuther. Funny how nobody was callin fer me. Andy. Pucky Paul. Nobody. Funny too how ol' Andy hadn't switch'd his flashlight back on.

But now I hear 'em. The voices. Fur off in the darkness. *Rain.* Ol' Andy he says rain. Whut he means is, hard rain's a-comin.

Any minute now, boys.

Any minute, Andy? Any minute? Any minute now whut?

Shet it, Pucky.

You shet it.

Rain, Pucky. Rain. It's fixin to rain. Now. Hard rain's a-comin.

The hell it is. It ain't gon' rain tonight, Andy.

Rain. Ol' Andy was waitin on the rain. That's how come he was wantin to come up here so bad. He was wantin to stand on the spot where ol' KillerHenry built hisself the ark an' waited on the rain, ol' Andy did. So I believ'd. That's whut I believ'd he was wantin to do.

The gully-whopper. Great flood. Big diluvy.

KurtSquirt. His voice. Sayin somethin, ol' KurtSquirt. But they wutn't no hearin whut he was sayin.

Big ol' rock. I's standin there. I's hidin. I's shakin. They's gravel in the metal warsh-tub an' the shakin turn'd into rattlin like somebody'd just pick'd up my head an' took to swingin it back an' futh an' round an' round an' these chaintooth voices, man . . . naw, they ain't too happy bout the gravel, *why it's a goddamn twister in here*, they's screamin. The lady. O. That lady. Many a year later it would be *her* who was fiddlin around with my noggin an' I imagin'd myself young an' strappin agin an' I's able to give her a plowin or two on the couch in my livin room, round an' round, back an' futh. He'p. I's yellin he'p he'p he'p. Reelly. *They reelly was somebody fiddlin around with my metal warsh-tub noggin back behind the big ol' rock.*

He'p. Y'all hear me? Boys?

Nobody.

Fur off in the darkness.

Nobody.

Andy. Pucky Paul. KurtSquirt. Rattlebones Roger.

Nobody.

But in my metal warsh-tub noggin . . . Gravel. Noises.

He'p.

It ain't like he hadn't seen a heap o' weird stuff too, now. It wutn't him an' him alone they's always pickin out as the culprit. Diner's a mess. Wall to wall with cups an' glasses an' other breakables. One o' us. Skeer'd. Enrag'd. Had to git hisself up off his chair because whut all the secont feller was sayin wutn't right. Say whut now? Wutn't me wutn't me wutn't me it was him comin here flingin gravel in my face comin here sayin all that. An' a thud feller said: Come here? Here cowie cowie coooowie.

A mess. A mess inside the metal warsh-tub noggin.

An' he kep' holdin on . . . big ol' rock . . . kep' holdin on . . . round an' round an' back an' futh an' coffeeclatch yes coffeeclatch wouldn't that be somethin an' I cain't say as I remember how long it took before I's realizin whut done . . . big ol' rock . . . an' a house an' a garden prob'ly fur off in the darkness an' maybe ol' Andy he's considerate enuff to knock on the door knock knock an' he opens the door an' asts whuther anybody's home an' is they awake in the middle o' the night an' the playmobil-figureen holdin the shotgun mumbles somethin like I'll be durn'd if this don't beat all fer foolishness an' he's wantin to peek inside the front door but ol' Andy hadn't turn'd the flashlight back on an' the house is all dark inside an' ol' KillerHenry . . . big ol' rock . . . knock knock . . . is anybody home an' is they awake . . . knock knock an' back an' futh an' ol' KillerHenry he woke up . . . woke up from the dead, man . . . woke up . . . ol' KillerHenry . . . by jingum he'd done woke up from the dead, man . . . ol' Andy was waitin on the rain an' they coulda been a couple o' drops but . . . ol' KillerHenry . . . he woke up from the dead only to notice the man-husk that was clingin close to him an' he took holt o' the man-husk an' lifted it up an' it was my metal warsh-tub noggin he'd done grab'd aholt of.

I holler'd fer he'p. Wutn't nuthin else to do 'cept holler fer he'p . . . big ol' rock . . .

He holler'd fer he'p. We heard him. Heard him hollerin fer he'p. His voice. Out there. Like the voice o' ol' Jens in that Carius an' Bactus cartoon of old. Out there. Up there. But in reality it come from down there an' wound its way thru us. The breath whut carry'd his hollerin, it come from down there, below us, slidin thru us in waves, the breath that is, an' went out thru the door, the wide-open door. He'p. An' one o' us had done stopp'd flailin around. Just after the fust holler. Stay'd standin. Kinda sorta froze. Coffee cup in one hand.

He'p.

He'p? Hesh up. Hesh up, Dead Feller.

Dead Feller? I ain't no . . .

Hesh up, Dead Feller, just you hesh up. This here's my spot an' ye ain't spos'd to be here. Now git.

Git?

Hesh.

An' he set me down. Feet on the ground. Best do whut he done tolt me to do. I goed. Goed off to where all the others had done goed even tho' I know'd ol' KillerHenry's fixin to fall back asleep.

He'p me.

The boys. The shadows. I hover'd toward 'em an' they hover'd toward me. They'd done been fur off in the darkness before turnin back.

An' I heard sounds. Dingdong dingdong. Low sounds. Dingdong dingdong dingalingalingalong. An' some kinda rattlin noise. Rough pebbles. Gravel.

More shadows. Shadows movin an' mergin tergither wi' the walkin cowboy shadows.

Dingalingalingalong dingdong.

An' ol' Andy took to callin the cows:

Here cowie cowie cowie. Hyeeere cowie cowie cowie.

Oh sheeit.

Ol' KillerHenry wakin from the dead an' swingin me back an' futh a little an' callin me the Dead Feller . . . naw, that ain't diddly compar'd to this lil' prosesshun whut come hoverin toward me at that spot an' sure as I's settin here in my crannynook I could give a slick chicken turd about them fellers in their fancyfied costy suits with sand in their craw (they been bellerin in my ear, ol' Rambo an' the Minister o' Justice an' Kid Clipclop), yep, sure as I's settin here . . . it's almost like I's got me a humongus screen too, just like the others, a humongus screen on my desk instead o' piles o' pencil shavins an' heaps o' paper an' now it's movie time here in my crannynook, an' this'un's a black an' white cowboy film, boy, an' a talkie too.

Hyeeere cowie cowie cowie. Hyeeere cowie cowie.

Dingalingalingalong.

Naw man, a giant wakin from the dead an' swingin ye back an' futh . . . A flesh an' blood human woulda had the everlovin daylights skeer'd clean out of him. A barn gnome on the other hand an' espesh'ly a barn gnome o' the meckanickal vurriety . . . he's used to that kinda thang. Ain't no more'n yer ever'day fuckery to him. But he'll own to bein surpris'd, that barn gnome, surpris'd too the moment somethin big take aholt of him. Big ol' rock. Towerin big rock. I wutn't payin attenshun enuff. Shoulda hid myself better. Shoulda just stay'd hid an' nuthin else. Never woulda dreem'd that the rock I's hidin behind could become such a ginormous livin giant, man. Nuh-uh. I jump'd. I holler'd fer he'p. Was my instinct whut holler'd.

But I could give a flyin turd about all that.

An' about all them coffee-depriv'd fellers in their fancyfied costy suits.

Like hell.

O.

Ol' Andy. O.

Coooowie. Hyeeere cowie cowie.

An' now I seen it. I seen it with my own two gnome eyeballs. The bucket. Of course. Ol' Andy was carryin the bucket. An' ol' Andy was shakin that bucket. That's how come the cattle was follerin him. They thought they's somethin fer 'em to eat in the bucket. Maybe ol' Andy's cattlecall was part of it too but if ye can git 'em to thank they's somethin fer 'em to eat in the bucket then they's gon' foller ye boy an' them plumb fool animals they foller'd after him. Hoverin. I was hoverin toward them an' they was hoverin toward me. Ol' Andy he carry'd the bucket. Callin 'em. Bigger an' bigger they grow'd, the cowboys an' the cattle. Bigger an' bigger an' side by side now, me an' them. I's fixin to ast 'em whuther they'd done found the house an' garden, whuther the coffeeclatch was still happ'nin or not, I look'd at the glowy numbers on my wristwatch an' seen they's plenty o' time yet fer all the cowboys to set theirselves down an' guzzle a whole cup o' pipin'-hot barkbrew'd coffee, I'd done been standin a few minutes behind a big ol' rock an' ol' KillerHenry'd done woke up an' even more minutes had done tick'd an' tock'd on by. *Y'all find the garden? The house? Is we gon' have the coffeeclatch now, cowboys?* But I didn't ast 'em, I's tongue-tied an' couldn't git no questions out, naw. Whut'n the hell was goin on? Ah, the cowboys an' the cattle, they was hoverin jam on by me. Didn't even see me. I stopp'd, stood still, was fixin to ast 'em but they's hoverin jam on by. Shadows. Shadows, all of 'em. The hoverin prosesshun. A sort o' swayin gait. Cattle gait. An' they hover'd jam on by.

Dingalingalingalong.

Hyeeere cowie cowie. Coooowie.

I stood right where I was. Manag'd to turn the metal warsh-tub noggin an' seen 'em with my own two gnome eyeballs, seen em gittin smaller an' smaller, the cowboys an' the cattle. Smaller an' smaller before they just about merg'd clean into the black trees whut look'd like a overgrow'd hedge in betwixt the aforemenshun'd spot an' the heel o' the steep hill. *Hyeeere cowie cowie.* Yep, ol' Andy he was leadin the way. Bound an' determin'd. Down the same steep narrer trail. They's gon' go back down now. The cowboys'd done clumbl'd an' stumbl'd on up here, been turn'd into shadows in the dark o' the late summer night an' now it was back down agin.

Okey.

Guess I'll mosey on down agin too.

Hyeeere cowie cowie.

Craggy. An' so god-dang'd steep. It stands to reason. If ye done made it up the slope, why ye already know whut to expect on yer way down. Ye know where to go steppin an' how to go about the steppin an' if ye plumb fergot to thank about it on the way up why now ye know that ye shoulda oughtta know'd better cause it's too late now that ye's comin back down. Naw. Ain't no way to go a-hoverin down the hill. Not even fer a shadow. Ain't that simple, boy.

An' ol' Andy . . . he shook the bucket an' kep' on callin the cows an' the sounds o' the shakin an' callin an' the the sound o' the cow-bells faded on down down down. An' how I wonder'd how come ol' Andy hadn't turn'd on the flashlight agin.

Ain't no way in the world none o' this is gon' turn out well.

Ain't no way.

An' I seem to remember somebody wisperin in my ear. KillerHenry, maybe. Maybe he couldn't fall back asleep after bein woke up by whut he thought was the Dead Feller an' so he come creepin after me an' now he's wisperin in my ear. Maybe.

But I could give a flyin turd about all that.

An' about the coffee an' about ol' KillerHenry too. A flyin turd.

I notic'd I's a good deal more cumflutter'd than I ordnarily would be in a critickal sitcherashun like this'un where they wutn't no use in broadcastin to everbody else how good ye was at puttin one foot in front o' the other. I started goin down an' I's just barely able to make out the prosesshun down below, tho' I could still hear ol' Andy' shakin the bucket an' callin the cows an' the bells clangin. Steep. Turrible steep. Cumflutter'd. An' then . . . An' that's when I decided to use the ol' rear end fer a sled, to git on down on my rear end an' go sleddin on down the rest o' the way in the late summer night darkness . . . an' *that's* when everthang took a turn fer the wust.

Fust, a awful bad roar. Ol' Andy. Ol' Andy was roarin somethin awful. I know'd his voice an' it was him whut was roarin, that rat mother, roarin the same way a big ol' b'ar'll roar after he done been shot in a cowboy movie. An' then a scream, a piercin scream, prob'ly comin from ol' KurtSquirt. An' then a shot. The shotgun. *Pucky Paul. Ol' Pucky Paul he's firin.* An' I sledded, sledded on down, fer many a yard I sledded on down an' a voice it shot thru me: *Pucky Paul he's firin he's blowin somebody's head clean off.*

More roarin. More screamin.

An' mooin. Cattle was mooin.

Roarin an' screamin an' mooin. One hell of a racket.

Fellers o fellers, is they fallin thru air?
Say, high on the hillside, whut's happ'nin up here?
Say whut ye know, all they is fer the knowin
Cause folks git to astin, an' they ain't tip-toein
An' out o' their asses the smoke comes a-blowin.
Smoke is a-blowin, smoke is a-blowin
An' that ain't the only thang whut's rodeoin.

Fellers o fellers, tergither they crashes:
The ol' pilot glasses an' pencil-moustaches,
The ol' leather jacket an' his slip-on shoes,

An' marbledy squeezins in the britches does ooze.
Ne'er in this world did ye smell such a smell-o
Cause the bunghole is full an' the turds they is yellow
An' swellin an' smellin from springtime to yule
The turds they is yellow an' that ain't no fool,
An' swellin an' smellin from springtime to yule.
But folks is gon' read in the paper an' all
Bout the humptydump fellers whut had a great fall.

The humptydump fellers whut had a great fall?
Say, high on the hillside, whut's happ'nin up here?
Is they fallin, them fellers, fallin thru air?
Say whut ye know, all they is fer the knowin
Cause folks git to astin, an' they ain't tip-toein
An' out o' their asses the smoke comes a-blowin.
Smoke is a-blowin, smoke is a-blowin
So say whut ye's knowin. An' say it now now now.

Fellers o fellers, they's fallin thru air,
With a hop down the hole, it's happ'nin there.

They's fallin thru air. Fellers o fellers they's fallin thru air. Cowboys. Slip-ons an' runnin shoes. An' the cattle. The cattle's fallin thru air too. Bout four or five animals.

Four cowboys. The fith cowboy was sleddin down on his rear end before doin a few somersalts an' crashin into a tree, took a hard hit an' his rear end was out o' order. Like a rimreck'd bikewheel he'd done tombl'd an' tombl'd, faster an' faster. An' they was roarin an' screamin an' mooin an' in the middle of it all he's prayin, prayin that . . . that he wouldn't lose that one tatter'd shoe, that one velcro runnin shoe with a big wad o' cash hid unnerneath the sole.

Light.

Bright as all-git-out.

Open up, now. Say ahhh.

Ol' Andy he's blindin me with his flashlight an' ye couldn't see yer own self nor much o' anythang else mirror'd in them steelrimm'd ding'd-up glasses o' hisn, Good heavens. That flashlight. Ol' Andy'd done turn'd on the flashlight agin, man. I lay on my back in the blueberry bush an' if ye's able then ye's welcome to try to reconstruct the seequinse of events an' imagine ol' Andy kneelin right next to me holdin the flashlight by his cheek an' stretchin his pipecleanerneck as fur fo'ward as it would go an' me feelin his breath as it's seepin into my nostrils an' him commandin me to open up an' say ahhh.

Gunshots. Here come another one. Four or five of 'em, now. Ol' Pucky Paul blowin the head off o' one dumb animal after the other.

Open up, now. Say ahhh.

An' I open up wider an' wider.

They ye go.

Ahhh.

They ye go. Yep.

. . .

An' ol' Pucky Paul he come along an' ast whut it was we was up to an' he set the shotgun on the ground an' ye can imagine him kneelin too. Kneelin just like the Boss-Man.

Lookie here, Pucky. Lookie here. Cables.

Durn'd fool.

No foolin. Cables. They's cables in this here man-husk. Lookit.

Cables, like hell. Cables.

But lookit, Pucky. Lookit. Ain't ye got one o' them swissarmy knives with a screwdriver? In yer coat pocket? I's needin to squimmy out one o' these here cables o' hisn.

Okey.

An' the cattle? They all dead now?

Course they is.

All right. Open up. Wider, now.

Ahhh.

They ye go. Naw. Wider.

Ahhh.

If that don't beat all.

. . .

How in the hell is we spos'd to fix all this? Open. Open wide now.

. . .

Pucky?

Yeah.

Screwdriver.

Okey.

Lookit.

. . .

Whut d'ye reckon bout this'un here, Pucky? Whut say ye? Ye reckon we oughtta . . .

Hesh up, Andy. Hesh up. Doin my best here.

Open up. Come on now, wider. Yer teeth's in the way. An' looka there, smoke. Still smokin.

Reckon we better pull them teeth o' hisn. Squirty, ye got a pair o' pliers in yer pocket? Reckon . . .

Ahhh.

Quit yer complainin, now. Ye done heard whut ol' Pucky Paul said. We got to pull them teeth o' yourn.

Squirty, pliers.

Pliers? Ain't got no puh puh pliers, boys.

Troll o' the woods. Ye done heard whut ol' Pucky Paul said. Go fetch us some pliers.

Ahhh.

I already done tolt ye how the others didn't end up pullin my teeth nohow. Nuthin come of that ideer an' praise the Lawd it didn't . . . ol' Andy's flashlight. Blindin me, didn't help I's still feelin dizzy an' when they started talkin bout the light, ol' Andy an' ol' Pucky Paul, I thought it was the flashlight they's talkin bout. Woo boy had I done took a lickin. Took one heck of a tryin tomble to put it mildly an' I wutn't as lucky as them other cowboys, ol' Andy he straighted his aviater glasses an' said they'd had a gardian angel, yep, a angel whut dove down from heaven the seccun betwixt ol' KurtSquirt screamin an' ol' Rattlebones Roger trippin over the shotgun an' the bang whut skeer'd the cattle sendin 'em jumpin an' hoppin an' trippin an' floppin an' draggin the cowboys aroun' an' they's floppin an' trippin an' the cattle they's shittin an' the cowboys was slippin an' slidin in shit floppin smack on the ground.

Gardian angel, said ol' Andy. My glasses. Hale an' shiny. Stay'd put on my nose. An' my chain too. Still hangin round my neck. Gardian angel, boys.

The cattle took to mooin produsin some o' the grusomest tones ye ever did hear an' their bells was ringadingdingin fur off into the night, clankin an' clunkin. That's how I remember it. S'whut I remember. The clankin an' clunkin the cattle brung futh in one big concert fur down there an' ol' Andy roarin an' ol' KurtSquirt screamin an' ol' Pucky Paul roarin an' ol' Rattlebones Roger, who'd done tripp'd over the shotgun . . . that part, buddy, that part I learn'd about later, how ol' KurtSquirt had slipp'd, sendin his troll-body smack dab into ol' Andy an' ol' Andy smack dab into ol' Pucky Paul an' *that's* how come the shotgun slipp'd out o' his hands an' the feller who tripp'd over the shotgun an' caus'd it to fire, why *that* was ol' Rattlebones Roger . . . I do remember that. Ol' Rattlebones

Roger screamin too, I mean. Wutn't screamin fer he'p, he wutn't. But he was screamin all right, ol' Rattlebones Roger. Screamin just like ol' KurtSquirt was screamin an' ol' Pucky Paul was roarin an' ol' Andy was roarin an' as fer that cow concert it wutn't the sort o' concert ye'd hear on no audiocasette tape fer use as a musical cure aginst wet-blanketism an' all manner o' ailments worser still than wet-blanketism, they was always carpin on about that, a couple o' them robots some domehead doctor had done sent over to cyare fer me bout a month after the cowboys an' cattle had done tumbl'd an' tumbl'd down into the Mare Cooter Canyon raisin hell an' tarnashun in one big jamboree, yeah, they kep' on carpin about it, them robots, the cure aginst wet-blanketism: sick, is ye sick, is ye soul sick . . . music, music, listen to morose music the moroser the better cause only the morostest'll do, now . . . cure, cure, that'll cure ye, they said, them robots said, them robots I hadn't yet met on the night I goed tomblin an' tumblin an' *rollin*, rollin down into the Mare Cooter Canyon, I's a rimreck'd bikewheel accompany'd by a cattle concert no fissical thurrapist in the world would e'er have had on no audiocassette tape nor e'er used fer no musical cure aginst wet-blanketyblankism an' ailments worser still an' I's rollin on down into the Mare Cooter Canyon an' in the one tatter'd velcro runnin shoe, unnerneath the sole, I had five thousan' kroners hid in a big wad o' roll'd-up an' well-trampl'd bills an' I hadn't yet met them musical robots but that presumpturous robot-riffraff group ol' Andy said must've squimmy'd out more'n seven cables, now *them* robots I know'd purty well at that pertic'lar time, yep.

Puh.

Down at the bottom.

Got me a dent. Crash'd into a tree, metal warsh-tub ding'd.

Gardian angel, said ol' Andy.

Angel. Heavenly cretur.

Got me a dent. But okey. The cattle, them animals the cowboys done stole when they shoulda oughta been drankin ol' KillerHenry's barkbrew'd coffee an' waitin on the rain; naw, this here angel didn't git there in time fer to save none o' them cattle. Wutn't none of 'em able to git back up agin. Took a bad hurt, they did, more'n likely a case o' complex bone fracshures an' all.

Nuthin else ye can do, said ol' Andy. Blow the heads off of 'em, Pucky.

An' Pucky Paul he blow'd the heads off of 'em an' that ended the cattle concert.

An' I lay in the blueberry bush with my mouth wide open.

The flashlight. The screwdriver. The pliers.

A skinny lil' skiver o' smoke curlin up out o' my wide-open gap.

An' they wutn't no seein yer own self nor much o' anythang else mirror'd in them glasses o' Andy's an' the cowboys started talkin bout the light.

Dizzy. I thought they meant the flashlight. Ol' Andy's flashlight.

Blindin me, that flashlight. An' them cowboys was talkin bout the light.

Come on, now, said ol' Andy. Git yerself up. Git up. Must be a lamp o' some sort. Come on. We's fixin to go now. Don't fergit the shotgun, Pucky. Just leave the bucket. An' Rattley, you take that flashlight an' woe betide if ye turn it on.

An' on we goed. Into the late summer night forest down at the bottom o' the Mare Cooter Canyon. An' inside there was a lamp. Musta been a lamp o' some sort.

More'n a hantle full o' folk in here, I tell ye whut. Days like this ye wonder whuther the village is done got overpopulated. Blatherin old folks, rambunkshus kids off school. An' new-minted mamas who done arrang'd a meetin fer to talk about diapers an' sheeit an' it's all gone to sheeit with their strollers takin up all the room makin it hard fer a coffeethirsty body to reach the front counter an' the lady, the lady who's workin here, he thanks she's purty an' after he done made his way over there he's slouchin maybe blushin a little too an' he's astin her all old-timey-like whuther she'd be so kind as to please give him a refill.

No foolin, said ol' Andy. No foolin.

The light. Trod over branches, limbs an' mosses, we did. Thru the thick woods. Clearin us a path, man. Shoulda had us knives, some o' them vikingswordstiff knives wielded by folks in safarihelmets an' khakishorts slashin wide arcs thru the jungal.

No foolin.

The light. Lamp o' some sort.

An' there it was. A parafin lamp like a lil'bitty star in a universe you's able to observe now that ye's done crept right up to the glass a-snoopin like the snoopin rubes they is.

The cabin. Wutn't that big. Fairly ordnary cabin out in the woods.

KillerHenry, said ol' Andy. KillerHenry.

Speakin softly.

KillerHenry? I said, softly. But I didn't menshun nuthin bout whut happen'd earlier wi' the big ol' rock.

So this is where ye is, said ol' Andy. Stable. It's a cabin . . . Now, boys . . . *now's* the time fer the barkbrew'd coffee . . . now.

An' ol' Andy he crept all the way over right next to the glass . . .

Yeah?

Next to the glass. Ol' Andy he crept all the way over, right next to the glass.

Yeah?

Whut happen'd next, ye mean?

Well, yeah . . .

I ain't rightly itchin to tell whut comes next, tell the truth. If the Boss-Man an' the Secertary was to stop by my crannynook then they's gon' hear a tune of a diff'rent sort altergither an' if they was to force me to cough up more why then they's gon' hear about whut happen'd later behind the SportsMart.

An' the Dead Feller. The Boss-Man an' the Secertary they know all manner o' wild stories about that there Dead Feller, fur as I can tell. That's how come, if the Boss-Man an' the Secertary's to go toddlin on up to this plum-rotted man-husk o' mine, I's gon' tell 'em how thangs got hairy fer ol' Andy an' them other cowboys, they had to git theirselves gone, up an' out o' the Mare Cooter Canyon *up up up out out out . . .*

BOSS-MAN: How come? How come they had to come up outta there?
SECERTARY: Yeah how come they had to come up outta there?

. . . because they thought they's hearin the Dead Feller sangin . . .

Yes. In the version I's tellin now the cowboys thought they's hearin the sangin.

Thought. They thought . . .

Yes. In this here version I's tellin.

Okey enuff.

. . . but man whut a woeful ballit. An' the chaintooth voice whut sang it.

> O the girlie, the girlie, she went out a-walkin'
> An' the foxie, the foxie, in wait was a-stalkin . . .

Thick woods. Ye was havin to clear a path now too. Try an' clear faster. Ow. Ow ow ow. Woods was thicker'n all-git-out. Darker'n all-git-out. Branches whippin ye in the face.

An' the Dead Feller sang.

A breath from a tree right behind ye. An' then from another tree. Then another an' another. A breath. Somethin strange an' mystickal like a breath from the dead.

A song.

Trees fill'd with song. Ever' breath is a tone an' ever' tone is piercin an' shrill.

Ow.

Ow ow ow.

Like it's a briar patch ye got to fight yer way thru.

Ow.

Briars. Clingin. Clangin. Tones.

Ow.

> An' the foxie he sang
> Sang a song.
> An' the girlie she wept
> The whole night long.

Later. The Tavern. We arrov'd just a hair before closin time. Or, naw. They wutn't too strict about the closin time, the folks who run the Tavern that is an' ol' Pucky Paul'd done been burnin rubber a-plenty over the past year an' it wutn't nuthin new fer ol' Andy to go ahead an' staggel out o' the veehickle while ol' Pucky Paul goed lookin fer a place to park an' ol' Andy's seat clapp'd fo'ward an' out ooz'd the backseat kids an' ol' Pucky Paul he staggle'd out too, maybe he remember'd to lock his door an' the other doors too an' even tho' the folks who run the Tavern shoulda stopp'd servin half a-hour ago an' closin down fer the night they wutn't no bouncers or other toughies tellin us to git ourselves gone, nope, so we wobbl'd right on in, one after the other. Music. Smoke. Wimmenfolks an' menfolks talkin over each other. Drankin an' toastin an' drankin. Some folks was dancin an' some folks was neckin an' some folks was vommickin in the co'ner an' some folks ye can just about bet the farm was lookin to kill somebody. *Hey an'a ho an'a hey daddy-o.* The Tavern.

Whut is it you's wantin me to say? Nuthin. Pretendin, actin like nuthin done happen'd. That was the name o' the game fer us right then. Pretendin, actin like nuthin done happen'd at'oll. Ol' Andy an' ol' Pucky Paul an' ol' KurtSquirt an' ol' Rattlebones Roger an' me. The gang. The cowboys. Course we could pretend like nuthin done happen'd. Play up the playactin one more time. Rattlebones Roger. He sure was a quare sort, ol' Rattlebones Roger. No matter whut kinda power ye was dealin with, whether that power took an' dragg'd him thisaway an' thataway an' upways an' downways . . . naw, nobody who know'd him or leastways know'd the sorta oddball he was woulda open'd their trap after studyin the way he carried hisself an' said *now somethin done happen'd whut never shoulda happen'd, an'he was a part of it, done got hisself swept right up in it*, naw, nobody who took the time to study him an' the cowhockey he was cover'd in . . . *naw, he ain't the only one cover'd in cowhockey . . . an'besides he's always been a quare sort, that ol'Rattlebones Roger.*

An' ol' KurtSquirt. Nervous as all-git-out. Always had been. Wutn't a bit unusual fer the ginormous troll o' the woods to go around bleary-eye'd an' quaky an' havin to all appairances a bad case o' the fan-tods. That was ol' KurtSquirt to a tee, that was. Ol' Sob-n-Blubber. He'd a-got hisself a royal ass-kickin if he'd a-been more everbody else's size. But seein he was bigger'n everbody else all the toughies they wutn't inclin'd to go messin with him, an' steer'd clear o' him. Troll o' the woods, ginormous troll o' the woods . . . an' as fer the cowhockey he was cover'd in . . . *naw, ain't a bit unusual fer a troll o' the woods to be cover'd in cowhockey.*

Durn straight he can pretend like nuthin done happen'd, ol' KurtSquirt. Ol' Rattlebones Roger too. That's the ideer, that two-headed troll gon' play up the playactin one more time.

Ol' Pucky Paul. Wutn't just cowhockey he's cover'd in, naw. He'd done stood too close when he was dispatchin the cattle, fur too close, an' got hisself a good splatterin o' blood, one time, two times, naw, prob'ly fer as many o' them infernal shotgun shells as he'd sent showerin in the direcshun o' that cussid cattle choir. But okey enuff. He didn't give a diddly damn one way or the other, ol' Pucky Paul. Not one diddly damn. About lookin fer all the world like a butcher from some dang-ol' horrorfilm, naw, not one diddly damn. An' they wutn't no livin soul inside the Tavern fixin to give a hoot, nuther. Ain't that right? Naw, why in the hell would they? Everbody 'cept fer the longhair'd feller behind the bar had had more'n whut even them lib'ral folks down at the Y would consider a acceptible amount to have in one evenin an' ol' Pucky Paul he slid hisself right into the crowd because it didn't make no diff'rence whether they'd been a-fightin fist an' skull or whut: the Tavern was full to bustin, so goddang'd overflowin that while ye's tryin to make yer way in a zigzaggin waltz thru a maze o' mullets, leather jackets, jean jackets, perms an' cleevidge you's like'ta be greeted with one horrorfilmhorror after the other such as a tennisballsiz'd shiner with a oozy slit fer a eye-sockit somebody'd done ding'd in with a hammer an' chisel an' a scabby fishbone-lookin crater where ye'd have expected to see a fur more operashunal bulbulous nose an' a swole-up an' chappy unnerlip that speakin o' ol' Tennisballeye might've reminded ye of one o' them pigskins ye must'ave seen in a ol' Amurrican movie where miniskirtclad girlies with long legs an' white boots was whirlygiggin round an' round an' was ever so captivatin to watch fer the simple reason that they's shakin some kind o' rainbow-ribbon'd thingamajigs in both hands, round an' round an' round an' I tell ye it's so goddang'd overflowin in here an' ye's tryin to make yer way in a zigzaggin waltz thru a maze o' mullets, leather jackets, jean jackets, perms an' cleevidge an' they's a blood-smell in here, a blood-smell inside the Tavern mix'd all tergither with smoke an' piss an' vommick an' all manner o' sheeit.

He's pretendin like nuthin done happen'd, ol' Pucky Paul. Playin up the playactin one more time, he is.

Andy. He was fightin mad. Fightin mad. An' still havin to pretend like nuthin done happen'd. An' *I's* havin to pretend like nuthin done happen'd, mmhmm, if they's *anybody* whut's havin to play up the playactin, it was me, boss. *The money*. Ol' Andy was itchin to git all that money back. He was wantin them five thousan' kroners he'd done stole off his pappie because ol' Helena . . . *Helena* . . . He was fightin mad, boy. Ol' Pucky Paul'd done drove at a such turrible speed an' after throwin hisself a hissy-fit when ol' Andy's wantin to jack off in his veehickle an' after directin ol' KurtSquirt's meat-n-potater stew off to the side o' the road . . . Pucky Paul didn't give one diddly damn now about the inventory bein cover'd in cowhockey an' blood an' ol' Andy he was fightin mad an' his ladyvoice blended tergither with the reverberashun from another voice, another chaintooth voice . . . *The money. My money*. You sank down in the backseat. You. Yeah, you. You know'd full well whut happen'd to that wad o' bills. But go to ol' Andy an' tell him to hesh up before fessin up like a repennant sinner? No thankee. A barn gnome holds his life dearer'n 'at. Him bein meckanickal don't mean he's just gon' go an' throw his life away like that. He was fightin mad. Itchin to git all that money back, ol' Andy. An' he was gon' git that shotgun o' hisn back too. An' he was gon' kill 'em both.

Kill who both? Whut d'ye mean?

That there Helena. That there' Calfy.

We'll I'll be . . .

But ain't like he cain't pretend like nuthin's done happen'd, ol' Andy. He's havin to play up the playactin one more time too.

I's gon' kill 'em both. Kill 'em kill 'em kill 'em.

Simmer down, now.

The Driver tellin the Boss-Man to simmer down.

I sank sank sank down in the backseat.

Dammit, Pucky. I's gon' kill 'em. I's gon' kill 'em both.

My money. Shotgun.

Simmer down.

You simmer down. Sheeit. Yesyesyesyesyes-sirree. Just you watch me. Gon' kill 'em. Kill 'em both. Right right right. List'n up, boys. In the Tavern . . . in the Tavern we play hushmouth, each an' ever' one o' us. Pretend like nuthin. That's the name o' the game now. Pretend like nuthin done happen'd.

That means you too, Andy. You too.

Yesyesyesyesyes-sirree, Pucky. Yesyesyesyesyes. Sheeit. Gon' kill 'em. Kill 'em both.

Ol' Andy. Course *he* was the one who shoulda oughtta gone to school fer profeshunal drumatic playactin. Him stidder me, stidder you. Course he should. Because when he goed ahead an' staggl'd out o' the veehickle while ol' Pucky Paul goed lookin fer a place to park an' the backseat kids took to wobblin after him after they'd done been squose'd out o' that toothpastetube of a veehickle . . . Hmm. Fightin mad? Nuh-uh. He wutn't fightin mad now, ol' Andy. Now. *Swish swoosh.* Diff'rent sort o' role. Diff'rent sort o' talk. Wobblin fo'ward an' gigglin an' pointin at the Tavern an' praisin to the skies all the ambrosial bev'ridges inside.

Ha ha ha. Boys. Ha ha ha.

An' that was the name o' the game. Pretend like nuthin done happen'd. Play up the playactin.

Whut is it you's wantin me to say?

The Janitor. I thank it was him I heard rummagin around in one o' the cubicals right around the co'ner from my crannynook. Coulda been yesterday, coulda been the day before. Pencils. Paper. Crannynook was cramm'd with all the work they give me. I mean it, boy, cramm'd. Stack'd a mile high. Pencil shavins. Heaps o' paper. All of it stack'd a mile high an' I's thankin an' thankin bout the late summer night an' I remember'd whut that lady done tolt me, that lady settin over in the one recliner who give me a pamflit, I's mumblin, I's wailin. I's just wantin to write down a sinnence or two but bein that they'd done come so many goddang'd pencils an' so much goddang'd paper . . . Pshaw. The beanbag chair too. The mintgreen beanbag chair look'd like a poop'd-out pack-mule lit'rally saggin unner the weight of a overly cumbersome encumbermint, yep, puttin it lit'rally, overly cumbersome, just go an' ast that ugly-lookin hunchback, the feller they call'd the Professor, go an' ast him whut it looks like an' he'll like as not tell ye that beanbag chair looks to him like that pack mule. The Professor. They made him take off that bluestrip'd 'nittid sweater an' his britches an' unnerbritches too. Coulda been yesterday, coulda been the day before. He's wailin an' whimperin but they's standin firm bein that they'd done adopted a resolushun an' I heard 'em say the Boss-Man done give this resolushun his full support an' so did the Secertary. Doojiggers. They said he had to shove two or three of 'em up his cornhole. They's gon' analyze the effickasy of it, they said. The effickasy. *Naw naw naw*, he wail'd an' whimper'd, the Professor. Naw

naw naw. But they wouldn't let up. An' it might coulda been I heard the rummagin right after that. In one o' the cubicals right around the co'ner. An' the rummager . . . that was the Janitor. I thank so, anyhow.

Burrup fer us, Professor. Better burrup fer us.

Comin round wi' the coffee. That's how come I witness'd the in-voluntery medicating. Wutn't no partishuns standin in the way now. Them fellers had all gather'd round him an' wi' the artifisshul right hand a-tremblin I slowly but surely an' without spillin a drop crept into the gatherin an' serv'd pipin hot coffee, cause they had to have it now that they'd done made the Professor take off his bluestrip'd 'nittid sweater an' his britches an' unnerbritches too.

Coffee?

Muchablige.

Coffee?

A smidge. Naw. Fill 'er up.

Coffee?

Now yer talkin, boy.

Coffee?

Muchablige.

Naw. Naw naw naw. I won't I won't I won't.

Runnin around like some lil' snotnos'd kid, that Professor. Snifflin an' snivellin an' beggin to be let go. But by jiminy, it ain't like he done had it worse'n anybody else. Shovin doojiggers up yer corn-hole? Two or three o' them boogers an' ye's havin a good time. All peacified in yer soul. So why go a-snifflin an' snivellin, beggin to be let go? They's gather'd round him. They done gather'd round him an' one of 'em done put his coffee cup down an' took to clappin his hands, clappin in time to all the other chaintooth voices:

Cornhole cornhole
Up yer cornhole.
Cornhole cornhole
Up yer cornhole.

The Professor. Says he don't want to. Lopper-jaw'd, ball'd-up. Or naw: a movin collecshun of meaty gobs. Ye can see it now, without the sweater an' britches an' unnerbritches, how that hump o' hisn is just one of sev'ral meat-gobs he's doom'd to carry round an' ain't never gon' be spar'd from carryin around (bein that he's doom'd) down here in the unnerworld. An' he's beggin *fer to be spar'd*. Ha ha ha. Ye done put it in? But ye can see it now. How he's a movin collechun o' meaty gobs. Meat, man. Yucko. One o' these suit-wairin fellers is clappin two-by-two an' all the voices is sayin stick the doo-jigger up yer cornhole. His cornhole? Which one o' them gobs ye figgure is his rear end? Ha ha. This'un, or maybe that'un, or whut about this here? Ha. He ain't standin still. He's a movin collecshun o' meat-gobs an' they ain't no tellin which part from the other.

The Minister o' Justice. O how I was a-tremblin when I come round fer his refill. The artifishul right hand trembl'd. Ever' bit o' me trembl'd, trembl'd an' trembl'd an' it mighta drew some o' the fellers' attenshun away from the Professor an' over to me. I notic'd how the clappin slow'd e'er so little. The feller clappin he lost the rhythm an' I heard somebody say *up* while everbody else was sayin *cornhole*. The Minister o' Justice was a-bilin. I's tremblin an' I's refillin his coffee an' even tho' I wutn't lookin dreckly at his face on account o' tryin to consentrate on the coffeepot an' the cup in front o' me I sure did see all they was fer the seein: a pair o' savage eyebrows an' a broad nose an' a mouth pinch'd shut the tendons tens'd tight all thru his jaw . . . I seen all . . . all they was fer the seein

. . . the Minister o' Justice . . . bilin . . . it trembl'd an' trembl'd an' maybe . . . rhythm . . . they's all back in rhythm agin an' before I turn to his neighbor fer to refill his neighbor's cup . . . yes . . . I turn the beat-up metal warsh-tub noggin e'er so slightly an' see all they is fer the seein: a movin collection o' meaty gobs.

The cabin. The cabin out in the woods down in the Mare Cooter Canyon.

Naw, I believe I's gon' skip over this part.

Okey.

Okey?

Aw, skip it. Ye can skip over the norratin. Pretend like nuthin done happen'd.

Like nuthin . . .

But okey enuff. Okey. The cabin . . .

. . . out in the woods down in the Mare Cooter Canyon. They's light comin from a lamp.

Just a itty bitty cabin, a fairly ordnary cabin out in the woods an' a light comin from the parafin lamp an' the light it sorta o'pn'd the wender an' streak'd futh. A star. *A star out in the woods down in the Mare Cooter Canyon . . . how'd it end up here? U.f.o.-mens. They could be u.f.o.-mens, space creturs who done took a turn thru the woods, scatterin stardust . . . Or whut do you thank? D'ye thank . . . My how it do shine, that lamp. The light streakin futh.* Yep, the light it streak'd futh thru the woods. Ye's clearin a path, follerin the star, you an' the others. Thick woods. Needles an' nettles. Clearin a path but without raisin too much of a racket since ain't none o' y'all know'd whut lay up ahead where the star was. A racket . . . well, oopsie daisy, now. Everthang whut had ears down in the Mare Cooter Canyon woulda heard the cow concert an' the yowlin an' the screamin an' the bellerin, the shotgun . . . Ain't no matter. Ol' Andy's leadin us, clearin a path an' you an' three other plug-ugly oddballs is clearin the path too.

The star. The light. The lamp.

The cabin.

Somebody's in there.

Durn straight, said ol' Andy. Durn straight.

Talkin soft as could be.

An' ol' Pucky Paul he said:

Who in the heck? They's someone in there. Somebody's in there.

Hesh, Pucky. Hesh. Hand me the shotgun.

Here ye go.

Durn straight. Durn straight. KillerHenry . . .

KillerHenry?

Keep quiet, man. Keep yer mouth shut, man. Last thang we need, fer you to go vommickin all them cables o' yourn . . . Durn straight. So this is where ye is . . . Boys . . . now . . . *now* we's fixin to have that barkbrew'd coffee . . . now.

An' ol' Andy he crept all the way over right next to the glass.

With his narrer back turn'd toward us he straddles them pipecleaner-legs o' hisn while holdin the shotgun wi' the barrel pointin straight up an' to the cowboys who's standin wide-eye'd an' watchful behind him it looks like that barrel's a-growin slanchways out o' his left shoulder an' he peeks into the wender an' the light from the parafin lamp done give him a halo an' the cowboys done fasten'd their eyes on the back o' his halo'd head an' he fires a shot an' he takes to roarin, not like a big ol' b'ar'll roar after he done been shot but roarin like the devil hisself.

Helena.

Her name. Explodin. Her name. He roars out her name an' that devilroar o' hisn is a explosion a sight worse'n the shotgun blast itself an' the skinny pipecleanercretur kicks the door open an' he's inside the cabin an' the cowboys they go stormin in after him.

Helena. Helena Bunnykins. She's yowlin. Yowlin yowlin yowlin. Ol' Helena she's yowlin.

Helena. O yes. Ol' Helena was in there. Strange but true. Bleach'd perm an' all. Prominint eyebrows, big blue eyes. Ittybitty snub nose. Poutin lips. It was Helena, all right.

An' time it kinda sorta stood still. Kinda sorta. Helena.

An' she'd done put on her pink puffer jacket. Zipper zipp'd all the way up to her chin. Late summer night down in the Mare Cooter Canyon, down in the chilly an' some would say freezin Canyon . . . an' when she stood in front o' the mirror back earlier in the shank o' the evenin gittin ready she prob'ly thought to herself: *Might could git chilly tonight better bring me some warm clothes.*

Them bubbies o' hern. Kinda flatten'd, lookta me like. Cause the jacket was mighty small an' tight on her whut with the zipper she'd done zipp'd all the way up to her chin.

Helena Helena whut in the hell is you doin Helena?

Naw Andy naw Andy this ain't nuthin to do with you Andy.

An' it wutn't just the zipper on that there puffer jacket whut was pull'd up fur as it could go. Skyblue britches. Pull'd up fur as they could go too. Them tight britches o' hern. Tightn'd with a pink leather belt whut lay like a boa constricter round her waist, the belt, just vizable unner the earthwormskinny white edge along the bottom o' the jacket. An' the bottom cuff o' them bluejeans, it was also as fur up as it'd go. Both of 'em brighter'n the skyblue pants-cuff. An' them tennissocks. Pull'd up as fur as they'd go, the one sock just like the other with two green strips where the elastic band was tight an' (I'd imagine) leavin a imprint on her skin.

An' the velcro runnin shoes. Pink. Bog-soak'd. She musta fell in somewhere.

Yep.

But still . . .

Goddammit Helena goddammit.

Naw Andy naw.

But he crosses his arms, the feller who's there, in the cabin, tergither with ol' Helena. He's standin next to her an' he crosses his arms an' he takes two steps fo'ward an' two to the side an' he posishuns hisself so she can hide behind him. An' she hides an' she yowls an' if they's wantin to git aholt o' her they's gon' have to go thru him fust, the feller who's there tergither with ol' Helena, standin there with his arms cross'd.

KillerHenry? But that ain't ol' KillerHenry, him there. That feller there, why, that's none other than that ol' watersogg'd Calf, man. The Calf.

The Calf? Did you reelly say *the Calf*?

S'whut I said. The Calf.

But . . .

> Curiosity she had, the girl
> Dancin down the path, she
> Plum fergot herself an' the fox,
> The poet,
> In wait was a-stalkin'
> In wait was a-stalkin.

Sing,
Sing that girl a song,
A whisperin song. You's
Dreemin, man, you's
Dreemin, an' it's
Inside ye,
Inside ye,
It's . . .

The Calf. The star done led us to the Calf. The Calf an' ol' Helena. The Calf an' ol' Helena in that bright shinin cabin. Believe it or not. The watersogg'd Calf. The u.f.o.-boy hisself. A cretur from a teetotally diff'rent planit than the one Mister Principal come from. An' Miss Teacher an' the Preacher an' the Sheriff an' ol' Andy's pappie. An' my mama an' my sister. An' the Farmer an' his ol' lady. An' Domehead Doctor. None o' them had the faintiest noshun whut it was like livin an' breathin on the planit regarded by the Calf as the paradyce o' the universe. The Calf. The Calf. Yep, believe it or not. The Calf tergither with ol' Helena.

Naw.

Her voice.

Naw Andy naw.

An' ol' Andy he's roarin like the devil hisself:

Whut in the goddamn hell is you doin?

The Calf. Arm's cross'd. Protectin her, he's her brick wall, the Calf is. A watersogg'd brick wall but a brick wall fer sure. An' he's eyeballin the one who's roarin, the one who done fire'd a shotgun blast an' kick'd the door open an' storm'd inside . . .

I got it Helena I done got me the cash it's me it's me who . . .

An' ol Pucky Paul has the gumpshun to grab the shotgun from him now that he's fixin to git his money out, ol' Andy, the money he done stole fer to give to ol' Helena because that way she'd let him nibble them bubbies o' hern an' like as not throw in a lil' extra natcherly an' he unzips a pocket on his brown dewkie-smear'd leather jacket an' digs around turnin it inside-out spillin sigarett-butts an' all manner o' nastyness an' a couple o' matches out onto the floor an' he unzips the other pocket an' digs around turnin it inside-out spillin more sigarett-butts an' more nastyness an' a couple more matches out onto the floor.

Farkin sheeit my money my money.

Ol' Helena she ain't yowlin now. She stays put an' watches from behind her watersogg'd brick wall.

My money my money.

An' his hands is diggin now unner his miniskirt-lookin pocoloco sweater an' they's diggin diggin turnin ever' cowhockeysmear'd locopoco pants pocket o' hisn inside out.

Handful o' coins. An' he snatches up faster'n a-hoot-a-hollerin.

God farkin dammit.

An' Pucky Paul he takes to diggin in his pocket too. But it ain't no money he's diggin fer. Ol' Pucky Paul's diggin fer shotshells an' he finds one an' loads the shotgun.

Naw Pucky naw, yowls ol' Helena.

An' ol' Andy he clenches his ittybitty fists an' he's jumpin up an' down an' he takes to threat'nin the Calf with a whuppin, that ol' Calfy who done turn'd into a brick wall:

It's you done took my money. Come on now, Calfy, come on.

The Calf. Arms cross'd. Eyeballin this bellerin feller who's threat'nin him.

An' ol' Helena done took to yowlin agin.

An' ol' Pucky Paul's a playmobil-figureen holdin the shotgun on his outstretch'd arms.

An' ol KurtSquirt . . .

An' ol' Rattlebones Roger holdin the switch'd-off flashlight . . .

An' me . . . this must be right before I piss myself, piss an' piss an' the piss it runs down both legs an' soakin it thru an' thru, soakin the big wad o' cash hid unnerneath the sole of one o' my tatter'd velcro runnin shoes.

Roarin.

Yowlin.

An' ol' Andy he demands his money an' he demands Helena to come out from where she's hidin behind the brick wall an' he orders Pucky Paul to point the shotgun at that big ol' watersogg'd Calfy.

If I don't git my money then shoot him.

Naw Pucky naw.

Shet it Helena shet it . . . it's me it's me who . . . me not him . . . my money give it back Calfy or else . . .

Naw. Whut is it you's wantin me to say? That everthang got all hush'd all of a sudden?

Hush'd. Inside the cabin. Such a eerie hush inside the cabin all of a sudden. Like somebody'd done found the switch fer turnin off both the roarin an' the yowlin all at once.

Hush'd.

Such a eerie hush.

Such a eerie hush in a bright-shinin cabin deep in dark woods far down a gorge, a hollow, a wood-hole, a canyon, one speshul late summer night . . . yes, a eerie hush inside the cabin because they's strange noises comin in from the outside to fill up the tiny room in here.

The cloudcuckoo. The cloudcuckoo, just a-coo-coo-cooin, they said. Long after, many years after, that's whut they said: *The cloud-cuckoo, just a-coo-coo-cooin.*

Cloudcuckoo?

Naw, man. Wutn't no cuckoo. Wutn't no nightowl, nuther.

The Calf.

An' he took two steps fo'ward, the Calf did. Two steps. Steppin so soft, this watersogg'd brick-wall space cretur, soft, so soft, an' I wonder if it wutn't me an' me alone who seen he was movin, movin fo'ward.

Steppin so soft. Eerie hush inside. Strange noises from outside. An' they turn'd e'er so little to look at the door, at the wender right next to the door, then the other wender, then the other other wender, look'd up toward the ceilin an' down toward the floorin, their eyes was wide-open an' their ears was sharpen'd just like the pointy gnome-ears I know'd so well, an' wutn't none of 'em hardly darin to breathe, ol' Andy an' ol' KurtSquirt an' ol' Rattlebones Roger an' ol' Helena over there, not one of 'em hardly darin to breathe an' the Calf took two steps fo'ward an' even tho' they's strange noises tryin to seep on in an' fill up the room an' time kinda sorta stood still, he's breathin slow, slow an' easy an' his eyes they wutn't wide-open, nor his ears sharpen'd nuther.

Noises. Strange noises from outside.

Fust a cracklin an' the cracklin become humm'd notes an' the hummin become song.

Louder. Louder. Seepin on in. Fillin the room. A woeful ballit.

A ballit. An' now it was in the room, that woeful ballit. Now it was in the cabin an' it was just like it was twistin an' twinin, twinin an' twistin all thru-out the room like a cretur made o' fog or smoke or magical vapors. A cretur one late summer night in a cabin down in a gorge, a hollow, a wood-hole, a canyon, one night in the pit where the lava had come a-bubblin up in the beginnin times, bubblin an' bubblin an' the dinos they's roarin an' the ballit it grow'd an' flow'd all thru the room all wavywindin gently caressin an' the song it got louder louder louder an' it was a chaintooth voice, ye know it, man, a chaintooth voice whut was sangin. I remember it now. Remember how everthang started tremblin, the floorin an' the walls an' the ceilin all a-tremblin, just like everthang was a-tremblin back behind the big ol' rock an' ol' Andy he was tremblin an' ol' Pucky Paul an' ol' KurtSquirt an' ol' Rattlebones Roger an' ol' Helena they's all tremblin an' tremblin . . .

Naw, you just hold yer hosses now ye hear. That ain't how it was at'oll when all this talk about the planit an' the space cretur got around to us by an' by. Might as well tell ye how all that got started. Comparin. That's all it was. Comparin. They's light all around this poor sucker an' they said it was glowin all around him. Like a space cretur who done took a wrong turn somewhere, they said, they was a funny sort o' light a-glowin all around him. Like. Like a space cretur . . . an' they threw in somethin bout stardust too . . . so you just hold yer hosses, now. You hold 'em.

O. I git me the gooseflesh just thankin bout that bit o' theater takin place inside o' this cabin all them years ago. Theater. The song. The song sung by the Dead Feller . . .

I tried to fergit. Fer a long long time I tried to fergit. They come an' took me. They said it was best thataway an' their long snaky fingers slid squishin down my wide-open gap an' they's sqwippin an' sqwuppin fer to squimmy out the right cable an' I realiz'd I'd best be fergittin.

The money. I's the one who got the money. I's the one who stole the money ol' Pucky Paul said ol' Andy'd done stole off his pappie. But fess up an' say it was me? Hell naw, pardner. The woeful ballit it flow'd thru wavywindin gently caressin, the song it got louder an' louder, everthang's all a-tremble an' the big wad o' cash I had it unnerneath the sole o' my tatter'd velcro runnin shoe an' settin here now in my crannynook I can feel the hairs on' my artifisshul arms standin straight up, I git me the gooseflesh just thankin . . . thankin . . . An' I tried to fergit. Fer a long long time.

A long time? Hell, d'ye figgure he has a noshun o'time? Time . . . the beginnin times. The way-back-when. An' the time after the way-back-when. The past few days . . .

Listen to him. Listen to him.

How talkified he done got all of a sudden.

But d'ye reckon he has a noshun o'time? Or knows anythang at'oll about thems that's still follerin along? D'ye reckon he knows about us?

Gooseflesh. Theater. An' I remember the goose in the play I seen in my mama's mirror. Bedroom. Wall. Mirror. That funny kid who was jumpin up an' down on the bed sayin I oughtta go to school fer profeshunal drumatic playactin, yep, that funny ol' kid: he's jumpin up an' down an' all of a sudden them creemyeller corderoy britches o' hisn split clean down the middle an' in the mirror I seen him freeze up an' he look to me like a broody ol' goose . . . an' time . . .

O how we'd been a-laffin. An' they wutn't no more laffin that day nuther . . .

But theater, they's theater a-plenty, from beginnin to end. The goose put on a play. I watch'd that play in my mama's mirror. The mirror on the wall in her bedroom. A play in the mirror, an' the playactor he jump'd on the bed an' laff'd an' said I oughtta go in fer playactin too. Shame. A goll-durn'd shame it is that that playactor ain't a part o' the norration, this here norration bout the late summer night, bout the Calf, bout these last few days. Shame. Cause if he'd been there in the cabin too, the playactor, then they mighta been a diff'rent endin to the ballit than the one we all got serv'd.

Coffee?

Naw, more coffee already? Naw naw naw.

Or the Farmer's ol' lady? If *she'd* had a more sintral role in this here norration? She woulda been hollerin, the ol' hag. Woulda took off all her clothes an' stood there hollerin while the woeful ballit it flow'd thru wavywindin gently caressin an' the song got louder an' louder with everthang all a-tremble an' Farmer a-gruntin an' a-oinkin, tryin to sang along . . .

Or whut about Mister Principal? Or Miss Teacher? Or the Preacher or the Sheriff? Ol' Domehead Doctor?

Or whut if ol' Andy's pappie, the jake-leg feller, had had a more sintral role? Or my mama? Or my sister?

Pshaw.

Or, naw . . .

Ain't no tellin why everthang shook out like it did.

The Calf. Took two steps fo'ward an' ol' Pucky Paul didn't realize it. He look'd at the door, ol' Pucky Paul. He turn'd his noggin an' look'd at the door. He trembl'd an' trembl'd an' the shotgun was tremblin an' he twisted his noggin around fer to look at the door, at the wender right next to the door, then the other wender, then the other other wender, look'd up toward the ceilin an' down toward the floorin, his eyes was wide-open an' his ears was sharpen'd an' he twisted an' twisted his noggin around an' the song it got louder an' louder an' he twisted an' twisted his noggin till his whole body was twisted an' unjointed, ol' Pucky Paul he got all twisted an' unjointed an' wrench'd an' wrung an' he open'd his mouth but they wutn't no hearin him just then cause the song had done fill'd the whole room an' he lay on the floor with his eyes just about bustin out 'o his skull like a couple o' bouncy balls bouncin smack into the one who'd done twisted an' unjointed an' wrench'd an' wrung him. The Calf, that is.

The Calf holdin the shotgun in his hand.

Wutn't holdin his arms cross'd now, boy.

The shotgun. The shotgun in his hand.

He took two steps fo'ward, snatchin the shotgun from ol' Pucky Paul with one hand while layin him smack on the floor wi' the other. Yep, he twisted an' unjointed an' wrench'd an' wrung him an' he'p'd hisself to the shotgun too. The Calf. Like that. Lickety-split he took it, the shotgun. An' lookit ol' Pucky Paul now. His eyes is like two bouncy balls an' he's layin there skeer'd half to death.

An' lookit ol' Andy. Lookit him. O that needle-thin ol' booger, that ol' Rat. So pittiful all of a sudden.

Pipecleaners. He reelly is made out o' pipecleaners an' maybe it's *now* he up an' benastied his britches. The chestnutbrown streak addin a purty nice touch to the cowhockey already smear'd on the seat o' his locopoco britches.

An' lookit ol' KurtSquirt. An' ol' Rattlebones Roger. Lookit that twoheaded troll tremble.

Her lips, ol' Helena. Poutin lips. Now she sets to hollerin. Ol' Helena. But the song's done fill'd up the room. They ain't no hearin 'whut she's a-hollerin just now.

They ain't?

Well. Wouldn't want to exaggerate too much, now would we? Ol' Helena, she's hollerin somethin like:

Shoot shoot shoot the whole gang now shoot.

Naw, how d'ye figgure that? Would she reelly?

She's hollerin somethin like it, I said. Somethin like:

Shoot the whole gang shoot shoot shoot the whole gang.

An' the Dead Feller sang. The cowboys finally got to hear the Dead Feller sangin. Down in the Mare Cooter Canyon that late summer night. *That's where it happen'd. That's* where the Dead Feller was sangin.

An' he'd been flyin an' flyin an' flappin an' flyin fur too long. Flyin an' flyin an' flappin an' leavin behind only a few traces, all very innerestin natcherly in an' of theirselves. That was how come they said he was still flyin an' flyin an' flappin an' flailin fer so long after he'd done busted out o' his coffin an' dug hisself a tunnel an' crawl'd out an' set off runnin out o' the graveyard. On account o' the traces he's leavin behind. On account o' that.

The burial cloth. Hangin from a pinetree branch.

The burial cloth. Fram'd up in a museeum.

The burial cloth. They stare'd an' studied an' fell to wonderin, them human-folks. They's prob'ly thankin he shoulda stay'd put, the Dead Feller. They's prob'ly thankin so but this here was some kinda miracle an' they's talkin an' talkin an' writin to the newspaper an' talkin more an' the years is done gallop'd by an' the clock's been a-tickin an' tockin an' maybe he'd done hid hisself in a house with a garden outside, a big house, a creemcusterd layercake castle.

An' he's pale, pale as that ol' burial cloth, the Minister o' Justice is, the feller who ain't never been no logbuster. He's pale as the burial cloth but I's paler an' the Calf he's paler'n me.

Green space creturs? Naw, man, the space cretur *I's* seein, he's paler'n the palest corpse.

There.

Down there?

Up there. Lookit . . .

. . . the space cretur's hoverin up there with his nebbynose pointin down an' he knows it so incredible well, the man-husk does, knows that it's mirrors, it's mirrors they done put up on the ceilin an' he stretches hisself out, the man-husk stretches hisself from top to toe an' he's nekkid an' they ain't no beanbag chair to lay in back behind the SportsMart an' he's bleedin, the man-husk is bleedin bleedin an' the strongest toughie his legs is so far apart with his sluggerfied doublearm risin up so high an' I see him up in the mirror turn'd upside-down but still standin stout, the ol' wide-leg, stout as a big ol' rock up on the hillside, the biggest o' all big ol' rocks an' course he's of the race o' sasquatches an' he howls, the strongest toughie o' the bunch, he howls an' with all the howlin this is whut he says:

This is whut'll happen if ye go stealin my mare.

Helena. Helena Bunnykins. So she was a mare too.

La illa holla illo alla,
La illa holla illo alla,
La illa holla illo alla . . .

The Tavern. Like nuthin. Just pretend like nuthin done happen'd. Course we could pretend like nuthin done happen'd.

Ol' Rattlebones Roger an' ol' KurtSquirt an' ol' Pucky Paul. They slid theirselves into the crowd an' sorta seem'd to dissappear. Just like them who'd done clumbl'd an' stumbl'd up the slope an' turn'd into them satanical shadows an' sorta seem'd to dissappear.

An' by jiminy I declare luck was on my side too. Slid myself into the crowd an' sorta dissappear'd.

An' ol Andy . . .

Course he was the one who shoulda oughta gone to school fer profeshunal drumatic playactin.

Ol' Andy Ol' Andy . . .

O.

We'd done heard the Dead Feller sangin.

An' liv'd. Liv'd to tell the tale.

The Calf. The Calf holdin the shotgun in his hand.

O.

Aw, sheeit.

Run.

Had to git ourselves out o' there, us cowboys. Run fer the door. Twoheaded troll in front, foller'd by ol' Andy with a meckanickal barn gnome in tow an' ol' Pucky Paul he bounc'd up eyes an' all from the floor an' run fer the door after the rest.

Run run run.

An' the Calf stood there in the magical lamplight.

The Calf an' ol' Helena.

Them two.

An' the Dead Feller sang. Sang an' sang.

Run run run.

Embarrassin as all-git-out.

Runnin away like that.

Swish swoosh swish.

So goll-dang'd embarrassin.

The Tavern. Music. Thunderin music. Boomin. One crack o' thunder after the other. Only now did I hear how the music did thunder an' boom inside the Tavern. Only now . . . after the Song o' the Dead Feller wutn't full-soundin in my ears like it was down in the Mare Cooter Canyon an' then after in Pucky Paul's veehickle. Thank ye gods. O thank ye.

One crack o' thunder after the other.

An' ol' Andy . . .

Course he was the one. Playactor.

Used to be a tavern here back in the way-back-when. Somebody who has the gift o' smell wrinkles their nose an' sniffs the air an' swears it's still there in the walls. The smell. Smoke beer likker piss sheeit vommick blood . . .

Okey enuff.

. . . an' it prob'ly wutn't easy fer the warsh-wommon back then. Scrubbin an' scrubbin. Floor walls ceilin . . .

But the Diner . . . that Diner become the place to be, man. An' if they's a little smell still left in here . . . they ain't that much else to remind ye o' that den o' inickwitty regardless . . . Yessir . . . But thems was the days, man. Thems was the days . . .

Hey, who done turn'd off the music, now? Who done turn'd on the light? *Who is it wantin to chase them unnerworldly creturs off an' make 'em run run run?*

Shet it. Shet yer goddang custerd hole.

An' them unnerworldly creturs they hesh up real quick. Cause this here voice that's tellin 'em to shet it, why it's a voice they know all too well, many's the time it's been compar'd to the howl of a wolf whut gits whut it wants whenever it takes to a-howlin.

Shet yer goddang custard ho-oo-oo-le.

Hush'd. All eerie an' hush'd in the Tavern.

. . .

The voice. The wolf:

Welcome. Welcome, Andy. It me you's lookin fer?

Hush'd.

. . .

Who me? says the piddly lil' voice of a pipecleanerpipsqueak who all the troll-eyes in the now-lit-up room is turn'd toward.

Who me? Naw, I . . .

The wolf. He's leanin aginst the bar with his bleach'd mullet an' it's the baddest-ass mullet ye ever did see an' a lit filter sigarett's hangin from the co'ner o' his mouth an' boy is he ever so badass an' tough-lookin in his black leather jacket . . .

It's him. It's him. The strongest toughie o' the bunch.

My my, Andy, my my . . .

I . . . Naw, I mean . . .

Barkbrewins? How about some o' them barkbrewins? Hey, fetch ol' Andy here a barkbrew'd cup o' joe.

An' now we's able to laff. An' them unnerworldly creturs they laff just like them meckanickal puppetmens an' meckanickal puppetladies laff in the Ivo Caprino movies but ain't nobody got no barkbrew'd coffee to serve.

Shet yer dang custerd hole.

Hush'd.

. . .

An' whut about the rain, Andy? You's waitin on the rain, ain't ye? But d'ye thank it's fixin to rain now? Great flood . . . big diluvy . . . Aw, Andy boy, Andy boy . . . Runnin around plannin . . . A plan. Tell me now, have ye done cook'd up up a plan fer me? O, I's hongry. Where's the plan ye done cook'd up up fer me? Say whut?

I mean . . . I . . .

Shet that custard hole o' yourn right now. Shet it. Tell ye whut. Got ye a few drops o' yer big diluvy right here . . .

An' the longhair'd feller behind the bar who knows where this is headed goes to fetch a beer from the tap an' the glass is full in a jiffy an' the strongest toughie waves ol' Andy over an' says in his wolf's voice:

Drank up now. You's the one always drankin an' havin yerself a good 'ol time. Drank up. Waitin on that big diluvy . . .

An' the pipecleanerpipsqueak he dranks an' he's havin to empty the whole glass in one big swaller.

Holt up, now. Holt up . . . Now empty the rest of it over yer noggin . . . They ye go . . . Looky there. A few drops o' that big diluvy you's waitin on.

An' now we's able to let out some more meckanickal laffin.

Shet 'em. Y'all shet all y'all's goddang custerd holes right now.

An' ol' Andy he fluffs an' scruffs his fingers thru his hair an' the spikes is stickin straight up agin an' he's havin to push his aviater glasses futher up his nose an' now ol' Andy he's reelly pushin it:

Thank ye much. Thanks fer the drank.

Thanks? Ha ha. Why yer welcome, Andy. Yer mighty welcome . . . thank ye. Danky shayn. But pray tell . . . before I stomp ye flat . . . pray tell . . . whut about my cattle, Andy? You's a real cowboy, now ain't ye? Ye been takin real good cyair o' my cattle tonight, have ye? I see ye done been slidin in cowhockey . . . not that it makes no diff'rence one way or the other . . . I ain't lookin to cause no trubble, now . . . an' ye ain't the only one who done been slidin in cowhockey, I see . . . don't want no trubble, ye see . . . cowhockey an' blood . . . But pray tell . . . My cabin . . . You bein the shagnasty's boy an' all . . . you ain't been breakin into my cabin, now have ye? Pray tell . . . Ye ain't been . . . breakin into . . . the stable? An' whut about the boat? An' one last thang, naw *two* thangs . . . About my money, Andy boy . . . I thank somebody's done up an' stole my money. Lots of it, too . . . Y'all heard anythang? Seen anythang? Well have ye? My money. Big wad o' bills. Done up with a rubber band. An' Andy, boy . . . I'd got to know, pray tell, where ye done hid my mare . . .

Mirrors. They done put up mirrors in here an' it's just like the fairy tale of old. Ye can hear whut they's sayin, thems that's inside the mirror. I hear the wolf's voice an' I hear ol' Andy's lady voice an' I hear the ladies all weepin an' wailin an' all them other chaintooth voices from the time they says is over an' done with an' accordin'ly they call it the way-back-when. Talkin. They was talkin an' talkin an' the Dead Feller he was sangin an' on an' on they goed wi' the talkin. An' all of a sudden here they is agin, boy. In the mirror. Above me. An' they's hoverin just like them shadows was hoverin an' dancin on that forestclad late summer night. Hoverin an' dancin dance my lil' dollie an' on an' on he goes, that strongest toughie o' the bunch:

Where'd ye hide my mare? Where'd ye hide my mare? Where'd ye hide my mare? An' whut about my money? My money? My money?

An' ol' Andy . . .

Maybe it's *now* he up an' benastied his britches?

Hell if I know.

But then . . .

. . . them . . . them two . . . they's there . . . in the Tavern . . . in the lit-up barroom . . . lit up . . . not with daylight . . . but a flickerin sort of elecktrick light . . . them . . . no shotgun . . . naw, ain't holdin no shotgun but in her hand . . . goin hand in hand . . . is ol' Helena tergither with that ol' watersogg'd Calfy.

The mare an' the space cretur.

They come.

The strongest toughie o' the bunch was fixin to stomp ol' Andy flat an' then they come, goin hand in hand, the mare an' the space cretur . . .

O the girlie, the girlie, she went out a-walkin
An' the foxie, the foxie, in wait was a-stalkin . . .

Yep. An' that's all she wrote . . . Yep. You know how the fairy tale ended, don't ye?

Yep.

An' one o' us says: We's gon' play hushmouth. Any o' us says somethin why then it'll be our turn. They know'd we was there. Course they know'd it an' they know who I is an' who y'all is an' who we is an' if they was to catch wind about all that other stuff, why it'd be the death of each an' ever' one o' us. The death of all o' us. Now... right now they believe it's him whut done all of it an' they's gon' keep on believin it I tell ye whut.

An' another one he took to snifflin an' weepin an' boohooin. They, they, they n n know who we is. Yeah they know who we is. They, they, they n n know...

An' the shotgun? The money?

He prob'ly found the shotgun somewhere down in the Mare Cooter Canyon sometime after, ol' Andy. That an' the bucket. An' the flashlight somebody else had took with 'em. But the money...

Yeah?

She said somethin or other about the money, the lady over in the one recliner, the lady who give me a pamflit. She said somethin or other about the money.

Don't ye recognize me? she said. Then somethin about the money. Yeah, somethin or other. An' she said somethin bout a rope somebody'd done tied 'round a big ol' pinetree whut was standin all by herself, a long rope, a long long long rope. An' I mean to remember she's dress'd fer winter on the late summer night an' she had a mark on her forehead, a scar or a tattoo an' no foolin, she was talkin bout life on another planit. An' she said:

We need ritcherals. We need religion.

Yep. S'whut she said. Meckanickal barn gnome's surtin of it, s'whut she said. But the money. Naw, the money? He'd done hid them big bills, that ol' gnome, boy. Hid 'em good. An' he kep' well hid whut he had inside hisself an' nuthin e'er become o' most of it, he' dreem'd an' fantasiz'd but nuthin e'er become o' whut he's dreemin an' fantasizin bout, in the way-back-when. An' ol' Helena . . . Whutever become o' her? Somebody said she went poof an' goed up in smoke. *Poof.* In the Tavern. *Poof.* An' the man in the moon . . .

Ahhhhhh right.

Do whut now?

Woah nelly, whut kind o' picklement you go an' git yerself into? Is you standin there stuck inside the mirror cabinet?

It all goed to hell, my friend. Only thang left to do now is play the optimist better'n ever before, man. Paper. Pencils. Ain't gon' run out o' no pencils or paper anytime soon. An' maybe, just maybe, termorrow or next week, they's gon' be plenty o' apples fer the havin durin lunch break.

GRANAVOLLEN,
2019

Translator's afterword: *Desophisticating translation*

Our modern English words *barbarity*, *barbarian*, *barbaric* derive from the Ancient Greek βάρβαρος, which means, roughly, *them folks who come from way off yonder and talk real funny*. At least, this was how it was put by a Classics professor whose class on Ancient Greek culture I took at the University of Georgia in the early 2000s. What struck me then–and must be why I've remembered it all these years–is that this was not how the professor normally spoke. True, he seemed a wizened old Southern gentleman of the old, genteel variety, with his dark brown three-piece suit it was hard to imagine him ever going without. You half expected him to take out a monocle, a pocket watch on a chain, and a meerschaum pipe to complete the picture. I also remember his frequently expressed fondness for scotch, and a desire for class to be over so that he could go home to drink it. To him belonged a genteel air of sophistication that in former times must have been an unremarkable sight on college campuses in the Deep South. He spoke in the measured tones appropriate to the role, too. He did speak with a clear Southern twang, but his speech was urbane rather than suggestive of the hills.

That changed suddenly on this day when he was explaining the Greek root from which, for instance, Whitman has his "barbaric yawp." *Them folks who come from way off yonder and talk real funny*: was he invoking this hillbilly-speak with an intention to mock, to look down upon the hoi polloi with their unsophisticated speech? I think not. Rather, this was the professor's way of demonstrating the word's derivation from the language of common people. These were common, ordinary Greeks, who said something like *ba-ba-ba-ba* in imitation of the incomprehensible languages of foreign peoples: hence *βάρβαρος*, or *blahblah-er*, to give it the most literal translation possible. It is a word that does not merely *signify* the non-Greek, but immediately and unpretentiously *imitates* what sounds, to the Greek's ear, like babble.

This professor, then, who normally spoke in the neutral, measured, sober tones appropriate to a learned disquisition on this or that, suddenly adopted an Appalachian bluntness when he wanted to demonstrate, in the most concrete and unmetaphorical way, how so many of our abstract usages derive from the everyday parlance of common people. This puts us squarely in the realm of what Dante (in Latin, ironically enough) called *vulgari eloquentia*. The eloquence of the vulgar: this is what my professor was invoking, consciously or not, when he made his imaginary ancient Athenian adopt the speech and manner of a Southern Appalachian.

Twenty years later, I sit here, trying to recall the language of the old South which I heard all around me growing up, all because of one book called *Kælven*, by Leif Høghaug, which I now put before you as *The Calf*. Høghaug's is a novel that tries to tap into that same eloquence of the vulgar, to harness the sound, the rhythm, the inventive energy, the generative possibility inherent within the colloquial. Like my professor's Ancient Greek commoner, the narrator of Høghaug's novel remains every bit who he is—a *fjøsnisse* or barn gnome, a figure of Norwegian folklore, albeit in Høghaug's telling a mechanical creature who speaks the local dialect (*hadelandsk*) of the author's home region of Hadeland–even as, in my translation, he adopts the speech of a native of the hills of Appalachia. This is a translation, in other words, that seeks not to appropriate or subsume the foreign text to the receiving culture's official standards in a seamless transfer, but rather to harness the subversive potential of the *as if*. In my translation, the mechanical barn gnome comes to us *as if* his dialect were that of the Appalachian commoner. He tells us, after all, this barn gnome, that he has a knack for acting; from the very first page, we learn that it will require some goodwill on the part of us readers to see him for the mechanical barn gnome that he is.

So allow me, as the translator, to beg along with that mechanical barn gnome narrator: "You'll indulge that goodwill, won't ye?"

As a darkly comic cock-and-bull tale, combining elements of cowboy westerns, science fiction, Old Testament myth, and 80s camp horror, *The Calf* is hardly a text that takes itself too seriously. But neither does it divulge its secrets easily. It is a challenging text, and I have done my best to preserve its obscurities in my translation. Much like a text central to *The Calf*–Joyce's *Finnegans Wake*, to which I'll return–some readers may find the following "skeleton key" of sorts useful.

The setting is the Eastern Norwegian region of Hadeland. Our narrator, the mechanical barn gnome, has an old metal bucket for a head and innards consisting of wires, circuits, nuts and bolts, etc. He is employed at an underground office landscape where he performs an array of meaningless tasks: shredding paper, sharpening pencils, and ensuring a constant stream of piping-hot coffee for his unquenchable superiors. The company he works for apparently produces some kind of gadget that users are supposed to either swallow as a pill or shove up themselves as a suppository in order to alleviate anxiety and stress.

In the meantime our narrator's thoughts keep returning to a murky but traumatic event in the 1980s on a "late summer night" at a place far off in the woods which the locals have dubbed the "Mare Cooter Canyon." His memories go back and forth without a lot of guideposts for the reader, which is further complicated by the fact that he hears a multitude of "chaintooth voices" in his head, making it hard for us to discern exactly which one is speaking at any given time. Whether these voices represent real figures or are mere figments of a traumatized imagination is not very easy to determine, either. Whether real or imagined or some mix between the two, however, a whole cast of characters emerges in connection with the mysterious late summer night, including "the cowboys"–the narrator, Andy, Rattlebones Roger, Pucky Paul, KurtSquirt–a group of adolescent boys who fancy themselves as tough guys but are more like a loose collection of incels whose main pastimes are drinking beer, smoking weed, jerking off. Then there is the Lady, a mysterious figure, seemingly a kind of social worker who arranges for the narrator to take the underground office job. She may (or may not) be the same figure as Helena, who exploits the cowboys' lust by dangling promises of sexual favors in exchange for large sums of money. The Dead Feller and KillerHenry are two quasi-biblical figures, the Dead Feller a kind of Lazarus rising from the grave, KillerHenry a modern-day Noah building a boat by the Mare Cooter Canyon in anticipation of a great flood. And finally, the Calf: the title character is apparently a space alien from a distant planet who arrives by UFO in 1980s Norway. The Calf's physical appearance is rather mysterious, though he is described as "watersogg'd." This has its origins in the character's real-life namesake: a small lake in Hadeland which connects to a much larger lake as if it were the latter's baby. An open question which the novel leaves unanswered is whether the narrator and the Calf are one and the same figure.

To the novel's mishmash of personalities and voices, Høghaug also adds a number of references to Norwegian pop culture that would have blended together in the average Norwegian teenager's mental landscape in the 1980s. Within the first few pages, for instance, our barn-gnome narrator describes himself as "A stop-moshun push-puppet gnome-doll man, right outta Ivo Caprino." Ivo Caprino (1920-2001) was a Norwegian director of stop-motion animated films based on Norwegian folk tales. With this reference Høghaug is trying to make us see the barn gnome in terms of the jerky, cartoonish, artificial-seeming action in these films. Another reference comes with the hairy, mulleted jock who beats up the Calf behind the sporting goods store, who is partially inspired by Titi Suru, the protagonist of the 1976 French-Soviet-Romanian musical *Rock 'n Roll Wolf.* Helena gets referred to as *Hellene Harafrøken* ("Helena Bunnykins"), a nod to a song by the beloved children's troubadour Alf Prøysen (1914-1970) whose direct influence on the novel's action can be seen in this stanza (with my translation):

Helene Harefrøken brisker seg	Helena Bunnykins bats her eyes,
Og tripper lett og glad på skolevei	Skipping fancy-free, to school she flies.
Jeger Bom-Bom kommer, børse har han med	The hunter Bom-Bom comes, with his shotgun he hurries
Helene blir så redd, hun hopper fort av sted	Helena gets scared, and away she scurries
Brun over, og grå under, og lyselyserød på snuten	Brown fur on top, grey fur below, and a ittybitty pink nose in front.

Another of her namesakes is Helen of Troy, the face who launched thousands of warships; similarly, the novel's Helena (with her oft-mentioned physical charms) launches the cowboys on their ill-fated expedition to the Mare Cooter Canyon.

A salient feature of the original text is that it is written in the author's local dialect, *hadelandsk*. This is entirely different from writing in one of the two written variants of modern Norwegian, *bokmål* and *nynorsk*, both of which are standardized languages that are written the same regardless of individual users' spoken dialect. In contrast, the language of *The Calf* is a visual representation of speech. In that sense it is thoroughly non-standard, though of course it has its own linguistic features and conventions. These include so called "eye-dialect" (where words are spelled the way they sound, like "thru" instead of "through"), elision (like "I dunno" for "I don't know"), as well as grammatical and lexical peculiarities native to Hadeland (think of US regionalisms like "y'all" or "y'uns" for the 2nd-person plural pronoun).

The choice to write in a non-standard Norwegian permits Høghaug to take a much more playful and generative approach to language than rigid, official norms would allow. One example is when the narrator looks at an old, worn-out sock sticking out of someone's sneakers and thinks it looks like a *bikkjetongefille*, a compound word working on several different levels:

> *bikkje*: a dog
> *fillebikkje*: a more contemptuous word for a dog, like "cur" or "mutt"
> *fille*: an old rag or scrap of cloth
> *tonge*: tongue

So what he imagines is the tattered, threadbare sock (*fille*) sticking out of the shoehole like the tongue (*tonge*) hanging out of the mouth of a mutt (*fillebikkje*).

No discussion of this novel and its language is complete without mentioning that Høghaug is currently translating *Finnegans Wake* into Norwegian; as of 2025, the first chapter of the translation has been published in chapbook form, with the rest coming (let us hope and pray) by the end of the decade. In the author's own telling, *The Calf* is something of a footnote to his *Wake* translation, for the *hadelandsk* which lends *The Calf* so much of its restless verbal energy is also the backbone of Høghaug's rendering of Joyce's epic. The choice to use a local dialect of Norwegian to translate Joyce is no accident. Remember that, despite the *Wake*'s obvious difficulties, borrowing as it does from dozens of different tongues, the foundation of its bizarre dream-language is a rather ordinary spoken variety of Irish English. Take the following sentence:

> Well, you know or don't you kennet or haven't I told you every telling has a taling and that's the he and the she of it. (*FW* 213)

In this line–the overheard gossip between two washerwomen on the banks of the river Liffey–the actual sense of the words is almost less important than the sonic, rhythmic, musical quality of the language itself. By deploying the sing-songy qualities of Hiberno-English, Joyce aspires to free language from the strictures of straightforwardly narrative prose to become something like music in and of itself. It is a language that aims less for comprehension than to be *listened to* and *heard*–even for a reader sitting and reading the book in silence.

"Here words are not the polite contortions of 20th-century printer's ink. They are alive. They elbow their way on to the page, and glow and blaze and fade and disappear." Samuel Beckett's verdict on

Finnegans Wake applies equally to *The Calf*, I think. Which means that this book will demand an entirely different translation strategy than the staid old paradigms of "fidelity" and "accuracy." If, as Mr. Beckett informs us, "Mr. Joyce has desophisticated language," then what I've attempted here is something like a corresponding desophistication in the art of translation.

In more ways than one, the book you hold in your hand is the work of a translator. The original was authored by a translator, arising out of his experience translating one of the most radically experimental novels in the English language. Certain passages in *The Calf* are themselves "translations" or at least echoes of passages from *Finnegans Wake*. The novel exists between languages, in the unpredictable, unruly slippages between them. Translation, for Høghaug and *The Calf*, is not merely the thing that is nice to have but ultimately of no consequence to the original as such. It is more like the very ground and soil out of which the original grows and flourishes.

A main point for me as the translator of *The Calf* is to approximate what the reading experience would be for a Norwegian reader of the original. A primary aspect of the Norwegian text, I take it, is that the text looks *weird*, and not only because of its approach to dialect and the non-standard. Because of its verbal invention, the permeability of its different characters' identities, and its rapid shifts in time and place, this is a text that demands a learning curve of sorts as the reader becomes accustomed to the novel's linguistic and narrative landscape. In short, the text should demand some effort.

Early on I decided to experiment with the Southern American dialect I heard all around me growing up as I did in Georgia. I chose this dialect, quite simply, because it was available to me. In fact, my overarching strategy has been to read the original and imagine how my dad, with his heavy Southern dialect, would say it–which seems appropriate, too, as Leif tells me the *hadelandsk* of the novel is more or less that of his own father. My ear sense of my father's voice is therefore by and large what I've attempted to replicate in the translation.

The advantages of this approach have been numerous. Southern American English has its own distinctive grammar and vocabulary, plus a wide register of highly concrete and often onomatopoeic vocabulary, such as "gully-whopper" for a bad thunderstorm (a word that comes close to the hundred-letter evocations of crashing thunder scattered through *Finnegans Wake*). Indeed, a range of colorful expressions are often available in Southern American English to talk about the same thing, like these phrases, all of which mean basically to teach someone a lesson they won't soon forget: "I'm a-knock a knot on yer fat head," "I's fixin' to slap ye windin," "I'll give ye the whut-fer," "I'm gon' beat the everlovin' daylights out o' you, ye dad-blasted sumbitch."

As I think these examples show, Southern American English has its own inborn capacity for inventive locutions, just as much as Høghaug's *hadelandsk* or Joyce's Hiberno-English. Besides the use of Southern dialect, my translation strategy is one based on sound, on free association, on the brash energy of metonymy rather than a cautious one-to-one transfer of meaning. Hence, in the very first paragraph, we get introduced to the narrator's *kråsåfarne blekkspænnhue*, literally a "weather-beaten tin-bucket head." In my translation this becomes a "wore-out metal warsh-tub noggin." The full phrase gets repeated a lot throughout the novel as one of its recurring leitmotifs, which is why I aimed to impart a certain percussive quality to it. Inside the narrator's metal head is the constant churning of *skjærandes stæmmen* (literally cutting or slicing voices), which I noticed Høghaug rendered as "chainsaw voices" in a short sample translation prior to my involvement in the project. The

Norwegian word for chainsaw (*motorsag*) appears nowhere in the passage; presumably, it appears in Leif's sample for its sonic force, perhaps even for its evocation of *The Texas Chain Saw Massacre* (a not-too-distant possibility given the book's reliance on the American camp horror tradition; the "chucky-doll out o' some horrorfilm" [*skrækkfilmakti dokkemænn*] is an explicit reference to the *Child's Play* franchise). I decided to take the association one step further in my translation with "chaintooth voices," which evokes the cutting teeth on the chain, while also suggesting the gnashing teeth in the mouths that utter these voices.

Continuing the conceit of this translation–that a creature from Norwegian folk legend might "play-act" as a Southern American–I resorted to a couple of specifically American references, for instance in the paragraph on page 81 where the mulleted jock is laying into the Calf with a baseball bat. This scene takes place behind a sporting goods store, and the Norwegian word for mullet–*hockeysveis*– evokes the Swedish hockey stars of the 70s and 80s who popularized the 'do in Norway. When the mullet-man (the "strongest toughie o' the bunch") brandishes the bat, it appears to the gnome-narrator as if the arm itself has extended in size, almost like that of a cyborg from *Transformers* or the T-1000 robot from *Terminator 2: Judgment Day*. In the original, Høghaug simply has *bælltrearm*, "baseball-bat arm." But there is a certain *umph* I feel is lost in the transition from *bælltre* to *baseball bat*, the latter of which drops with a listless thud rather than a powerful whomp. And that whomp is essential. To preserve the whomp, I introduced a reference to the venerable Louisville Slugger brand of baseball bat and morphed *bælltrearmen* into "sluggerfied doublearm," the two words themselves almost a pictographic representation of an arm that's doubled in length.

As for "sasquatch sonofabitch," Høghaug has *jotunjævel*, a

compound word composed of *jotun* (the race of giants in Norse mythology) and *jævel* (literally devil, but also a coarse term of abuse à la bastard/s.o.b./fucker). Here I thought it important, first, to preserve the alliteration in the compound word, and second, to retain the mythological resonance of *jotun*, meaning the generic and commonplace "giant" wouldn't work. I considered "goliath-goon," but Goliath from the Bible is an individual, not a race, and *goon* rather too tame in comparison with the much rougher *jævel*. The solution came to me when I considered those mythological giants that haunt the modern imagination, the apelike humanoid variously known in North America as Bigfoot, the Abominable Snowman, Sasquatch. This beast also dovetails with general air of the paranormal that permeates the book, with its UFO sightings and alien visitations (those particularly 80s obsessions, in Norway apparently as much as the United States of my childhood).

The insertion of American references also raises the question of what to do with specifically Norwegian ones. Despite the dialectal conceit of my translation, the book's landscape is still very much that of Norway. Helena's price for the cowboys to enjoy her bosom remains 5000 kroner, not 500 bucks or whatever the current exchange rate would have it. This extends to place names as well, with a nod to how foreign they might sound to Anglo ears. When the Calf ends up in the nearest hospital in Gjøvik, it gets mangled in translation as "Gorvik." And then there is the matter of the *lusekofte*, a particular kind of sweater in Norway dotted with a pattern said to resemble lice (*lus*). Here, I recalled the Netflix sitcom *Lilyhammer*, whose title comes courtesy of the show's American gangster protagonist and his chilly exile to Lillehammer, Norway. I opted for a similar malapropism with "looseykoftee sweater". With that, I assume the curious reader should still be able to suss out the meaning, at least judging from my brief experimentation on Google (try entering "looseykoftee sweater" and it will show results for the *lusekofte*).

Besides my father's speech, I've relied upon several sources for the grammar and vocabulary of Southern American English, most notably Montgomery and Heinmiller's magisterial *Dictionary of Southern Appalachian English* (2005). Literary sources have been important, too, including Mark Twain's *Adventures of Huckleberry Finn*. In the end, however, my translation is intended less an accurate representation of Southern American English than an attempt to exploit the generative possibilities inherent to the non-standard. We can see this, for instance, in my choice of "big diluvy" to denote the great flood predicted by the novel's quasi-biblical prophet, KillerHenry. Is "diluvy" a word that lodged itself in my teenage consciousness after being thundered from the pulpit on a sleepy Southern Baptist Sunday morning in the waning months of the 90s? No. Actually, I discovered the word only recently in the *OED*'s Historical Thesaurus, where, far from being documented as a Southern American usage at all, it is listed as an archaism, having fallen out of the English language entirely by around 1546. (Mid-16th-century sample: "Soche vnspekable fylthynesse . . . as brought vpon them the great dyluuye or vnyuersall flod.") Happily, the four syllables of "big diluvy" are a perfect metrical match with the source text's *syndefloden* (lit. "the sin flood"), a perfectly ordinary biblical term in the Norwegian which would have only sounded clunky and bad if translated literally or with the safer and more prosaic modern English equivalent of "the deluge" or something similar. The little trochaic tetrameter ditty on page 154 of the translation shows why the metrical equivalency here is paramount:

Rømlingen frå svænskeskøvven
gikk i rætning Væsterlænnet,
sa'n hadde tri så lenge,
tri og tråkke, kvist og måså,
sa'n måtte felle trea, ælle trea, bygge båten.
Jøssda mænn sku bygge båten
fara over havet sku'n sann,
Jøssda mænn hæn hadde skjønt'e.
skjønt at vatn vatn vatn . . .
syndefloden . . . vatn vatn . . .

The fugitive from Swedish forests
Walk'd a spell out toward the West an'
Said he'd done been walkin' long an'
Trod o'er branches, limbs an' mosses,
Said he had to chop down timber:
Lumber fer the boat he's buildin',
Lawd-a-mercy build the boat an'
Sail out o'er the op'n ocean.
Lawd-a-mercy, prophesyin',
Prophesyin' water water . . .
Big diluvy . . . water water . . .

In many ways, my strategy represents an attempt to reinsert the physical into translation, to concretize, aurally and visually, my own lived and felt experience of Leif Høghaug's novel. As it is nigh-universally conceived, translation exists for the sake of the reader who lacks access to the original language. For that reader, the original is experienced as an absence, a mute, missing center that the translation can do little but helplessly encircle as its ghostly afterimage. But surely this misses something about *The Calf*, preoccupied as it is with the physical, the bodily, populated by figures with mechanical innards and pipe-cleaner limbs whose rickety joints creak across every page. In this text, where the bodies of the living and the dead are jockeying for space, making themselves felt, brooking no denial: isn't it natural that this text should have a highly physical, sensual feel, even in the translation? The musical flourish provided by "big diluvy," for instance, is emblematic of *how I hear* this novel, a record of the sonic resonances awakened in me as I undertook to translate Leif's text, turning it over, sounding it out, word by word.

As should be evident at this point, this is not a text where the staid old translation paradigms of faithfulness and accuracy will apply. I am tempted to riff on Twain's note to the reader in *Huckleberry Finn* (to wit, that any persons seeking accuracy in this translation shall be shot), but as this sort of get-off-my-lawn vigilance can be rather off-putting, especially in translation, where hospitality and the erotic are of the essence, I propose instead that we conceive a different role for the translator than the one we are accustomed to ascribing him. This role would be less the expert who has sucked all the meaning and marrow and life out of the text to offer up an empty shell of an artifact for our disinterested perusal, than as one reader (among others) who experiences the text, and attempts to convey, with all the creative means at his disposal, this lived and felt experience. For in the end, the choice of dialect to which to translate is, of course, arbitrary; why couldn't a translator from Dublin, Glasgow, East London, Harlem, or Bombay draw upon their own local Englishes to achieve a comparable marriage between musicality and invention as the one I've striven for? (Perhaps those translators will come someday; no translation is ever definitive–mine included.)

Because a final affordance of dialect is that it allows the novel to speak with its own unique *voice*. Perhaps no other aspect of this book is as important as getting the voice right. Admittedly, a hard notion to pin down. But think, again, of Huck Finn. Think of the Ishmael of *Moby-Dick*. Voices so memorable as to evoke a whole world. The voice of *The Calf* ought to be just as unmistakable–or come pretty damn close. I see no reason why a translation ought not aim to leave such an indelible imprint on the reader's consciousness. And it's an aim that would have been wholly unattainable if I'd hewed to a placeless "ideal" English for the sake of an impossible one-to-one accuracy. Give me a translation that takes risks, that risks the occasional extravagance in service to a greater gain, a gain impossible if we wallow in perpetual mourning over what's "lost" in translation. If I could sum up my guiding principle as this work's translator, it would be: Go big or go home.

–DS

Glossary

Given the strange hybrid of this translation–combining American hillbilly-speak with the hyperlocal Norwegian references of the original–some readers may find the following glossary useful.

The greater part of the glossary is devoted to Southern American usages, in which my chief source has been Montgomery and Heinmiller's *Dictionary of Southern Appalachian English* (University of North Carolina Press, 2021). Certain literary sources, chiefly Mark Twain and William Faulkner, have also provided a handful of words. If no other source is indicated for a term, it likely derives from my own memory of the regionalisms I heard growing up in the US state of Georgia.

Apart from the nonstandard morphology of certain verbs, I have not gone into the grammar and syntax of Southern US English. The preface to Montgomery and Heinmiller provides an extensive treatment of the subject for those readers interested.

The glossary also includes some specifically Norwegian references (and their "countrification" in my translation). Finally, words of my own invention are also indicated, so as to not send the unsuspecting reader on a fruitless Google excursion for one of my *hapax legomena* . . .

If the process of flipping back and forth to this glossary becomes too cumbersome, my advice would be to not worry too much about pinning down exact meanings in each instance. As I've indicated in my afterword, this is a text where sound is equally as important as sense. As such, it is perhaps best appreciated in a mood of relaxed revery, where images, associations wash over the reader, like the waters of the River Liffey, or the aqueous figure of some alien visitor from another planet . . .

–DS

aholt–Ahold.
allfar'd–All-fired, i.e. complete, utter, thorough (DSAE).
all-git-out–Something extreme in degree or intensity (DSAE).
always-ago–A long time ago (DSAE).
arrer–Arrow.
arrove–Arrive.
arthur–Arthritis.
ast–To ask. Used as infinitive/present/simple past/past participle.
ballhootin–Originally, to slide, roll, pull, or shoot (a log) down an incline (DSAE); here, to fly headlong or precipitously as in a car or on a bicycle.
ballit–Ballad, or song more generally.
bangest–Most extraordinary (DSAE).
b'ar–A bear.
beat–In the phrase *beat all fer*: used to express something that surpasses every other instance (as in, "That sure beat all fer luck" for a very lucky occurrence).
beller–To bellow (DSAE).
bilin–Boiling.
billfold–Wallet.
birkie-biner–*Birkebeiner*, a member of the legendary warrior clan who skied the infant heir apparent, Haakon Haakonsson, to safety during the medieval civil war period in Norway.
blatherskite–One who talks nonsense (DSAE).
broody–Of fowls: inclined to sit or incubate (OED Historical Thesaurus).
bug dust–Cheap smoking tobacco (DSAE).
burlyhurly–A muscular tough guy (neologism formed by reversing the term *hurly burly*, a commotion or hubbub)

burrup–To belch, or to do something that is accompanied by a belch-like sound like raring up a motor (neologism, onomatopoetic).
busseyroll–Imagined Southern US dialect pronunciation of *busserull*, a traditional Norwegian work shirt.
cadgy–Sexually aroused, lustful (DSAE).
calm daylight–Full daylight following or preceding darkness (DSAE).
Carius an' Bactus–Two "tooth trolls" that wreak havoc in the mouth of Jens, a little boy who doesn't brush his teeth, in a 1955 animated short by Ivo Caprino (about whom, see entry further below in glossary).
catamount–A lynx, wildcat (DSAE).
catch learnin–To learn or become informed about something (DSAE).
cattycorner'd–Slantways, askew (DSAE).
chaw–1) Verb: to chew 2) Noun: chewing tobacco.
clart–Feces (DSAE).
clumb–Simple past and past participle of *climb*.
cods–Testicles (DSAE).
coffee barefoot–Black coffee, no sugar or cream (DSAE).
coffeeclatch–From German *Kaffeeklatsch*, a gathering or conversation around coffee.
constitushun day–May 17th (*syttende mai*), celebrated as Constitution Day in Norway.
crannynook–A hidden-away corner or refuge (neologism, from the idiom "nook and cranny").
cumflutter'd–Excited, flustered. Variant: **cumfluster'd** (DSAE).
cussid–Infernal, outrageous. Usually *cussed*, but spelled here so as to indicate the two-syllable pronunciation.
dadgum–A mild oath, interjection, or intensifier expressing anger or exasperation.
daydown-sun–The sun in the evening, sunset (DSAE).
diluvy–Deluge, flood (*OED Historical Thesaurus*); see also translator's afterword.
doddle–To toddle, move slowly about (DSAE).
doins–Doings, business.
dreckly–Directly, here meaning immediately, at once.
drumly–Of weather: gloomy (DSAE).
durn'd if–A shortening of the phrase "I'll be darned if . . ."; in other words, expressive of a strong negative.
ellavater–Elevator.
et–To eat. Used as present/simple past/past participle.
fan-tods–A state of nervous tension or discomfort (Twain, *Adventures of Huckleberry Finn*)

fare-thee-well–In the phrase *to a fare-thee-well*: to a finish, to perfection or completely (DSAE).
fast as a hen a-peckin'–Very fast (DSAE).
fer to–In order to.
ferrididdle–Red squirrel (DSAE).
fightyfied–Pugnacious, raring for a fight (DSAE).
flim-flammin–Deception or fraud (cf. *The Flim-Flam Man*, a 1967 film starring George C. Scott as a con artist in the American South).
forestclad–Wooded, sylvan (literal translation of Nor. *skøvvklædd*)
fun–(Verb) To joke, kid, or mess around with (as in, "I'm just funnin' with you") (DSAE).
fur–1) Fair 2) In the phrase *a fur piece*: a long way (Faulkner, *Light in August*)
gashful–Ghastly, horrible (*OED Historical Thesaurus*).
gashly–Ghastly, horrible (Twain, *Adventures of Huckleberry Finn*)
gin around–To potter around with various activities (DSAE).
ginormous–Gigantic, enormous.
git 'er done–I.e. "Get the job done," a catchphrase originally popularized by the American comedian Larry the Cable Guy.
gnat's heel–In the phrase *to a gnat's heel*: very small or precise (DSAE).
goozle–To guzzle, drink rapidly (DSAE).
Gorvik–Imagined Southern US dialect pronunciation of Gjøvik, a town near Hadeland, Norway.
gullick–The gullet (DSAE).
gullup–Gulp, swallow (DSAE).
gully-whopper–A thunderstorm.
haint–A ghost, apparition.
hale–Whole, sound, healthy.
halesome–Wholesome.
hantle–In the phrase *only a hantle full*: only a small crowd or number of people (DSAE).
hear tell–To be informed, find out from someone.
he'p–Help, pronounced sans *l*.
hesh–Hush, often issued as a command (*Hesh up* = shut up, be quiet).
hi-kaflutin–Fancy, pretentious, overly formal (DSAE).
Hobblestiltskin–Combination of "hobble" and the Grimm fairy tale, *Rumpelstiltskin* (taken and adapted from *Der Kälberich*, Matthias Friedrich's German translation of *The Calf*).
hogback–A mountain ridge that slopes sharply on each side and often has jutting rocks, resembling the high, narrow back of a wild hog (DSAE).

hold yer hosses–"Hold your horses," an idiom meaning "Wait a moment" or "Slow down."
Honerfoss–Imagined Southern US dialect pronunciation of Hønefoss, a town near Hadeland, Norway.
hove–Simple past and past participle of *heave.*
Ivo Caprino–Norwegian director of children's stop-motion animated films (1920–2001). See also translator's afterword.
jake-leg–Paralysis or incapacitation of the legs caused by drinking low-quality (usually wood) alcohol (DSAE). A slightly different condition than that described in the original, *røykebein* or vascular claudication, which is more associated with smoking and lacks a colloquial equivalent in English.
jam–In the phrase *jam on by*: completely, entirely, as in "He went jam on by without seeing us" (DSAE).
Janitor– A character based on one made famous by Trond-Viggo Torgersen in various Norwegian sketch comedy shows during the 1980s and 90s.
journey jaunt–A venture, trip (DSAE).
keepin–(Noun) Condition, shape.
kendalgreen–My translation of Nor. *myrgrønn* (literally, moor- or bog-green) is a Shakespearean reference; in *Henry IV Part I*, Falstaff is going to rob some travelers on the highway but is himself robbed by Prince Hal and Poins under cover of darkness. Later he tells a story that he has been attacked by a gang dressed in "Kendal green," a gang whose numbers keep increasing in his telling so that he will seem even more heroic for having fended them all off.
lessun–Unless (DSAE).
lick–In the phrase *a lick of*: a bit of, a small amount of.
like'ta–1) Probably 2) almost, as in "I like'ta died when I found out."
like'at–Like that.
lippin' full–Full to capacity (DSAE).
looseykoftee–Imagined Southern US dialect pronunciation of *lusekofte*, a Norwegian knit sweater with a spotted pattern said to resemble lice (*lus*).
lopper-jaw'd–Lopsided, crooked, askew (DSAE).
louieville slugger–Louisville Slugger, a famous American brand of baseball bat; see also translator's afterword.
Lunnerworld–Combination of *underworld* (or *unnerworld* in dialect pronunciation) and Lunner, a municipality in the district of Hadeland in Norway.
mommix'd–Confused, bewildered (DSAE).
muchablige–Much obliged, i.e. an expression of gratitude.
narrer–Narrow (DSAE).
needcessity–Necessity (DSAE).

norration–Narration, story, tale.
nuther–1) Neither 2) another 3) in the phrase *no nuther*: "no other," here intended as a kind of spoonerism.
own–To admit to, acknowledge.
peart–Lively, spirited (DSAE).
peckerwood–Originally a derogatory term for poor white people (DSAE); here used as a more general term of abuse without racial or economic overtones.
picklement–A difficult or awkward situation (DSAE).
pigskin–Slang for an American football.
pitcher–Picture, photo.
plag take it–Mild expletive (DSAE).
plugg'd nickel–In the phrase *ain't worth a plugg'd nickel*: utterly worthless.
plum–1) As adjective: Total, absolute, major 2) As adverb: Extremely, totally.
Pocoloco–A brand of clothing that was the "it" brand among Norwegian teenagers of the 1980s.
poot–Fart.
pucky–Dung, feces.
purty nair–Pretty near, i.e. pretty close, almost.
pussle-gutted–Fat, obese (DSAE).
quare–1) Queer, in the sense of "weird" or "uncanny" 2) Excellent, as in "a quare good plan" (DSAE).
quietus–In the phrase *put the quietus on*: to cause something to stop, put an end to something.
Rand-fyord–Randsfjorden, Norway's fourth-largest lake.
rimreck'd–Damaged beyond repair (DSAE).
ritcherals–Rituals.
rumpus room–A room set aside for recreational activities (gaming, television etc.), typically on the lower ground floor/basement of a house.
rustling–Stealing livestock.
sasquatch–Mythological North American humanoid beast; see also translator's afterword.
sassprilluh–Sarsaparilla, a soft drink like root beer (Faulkner, *The Sound and the Fury*, explanation from the annotated Folio Society edition, 2016)
shackl'ty–(Adj.) Appearing as ready to collapse at any moment; rickety (DSAE).
shagnasty–An unkempt, disorderly, or disagreeable person (DSAE).
shank o' the eve'nin–The period late in or toward the close of the day (DSAE).
shuck–Escape, go away.
since heck was a pup–For a long time (DSAE).
sitcherated–Situated.

skedaddle–To go or leave promptly.
skiver–A small amount or portion (DSAE).
slanchways–Slanting, crooked (DSAE).
slap–(Adv.) Exactly, precisely.
slop-dozzler–One who carelessly spills something is said to "slop-dozzle" (DSAE).
smoke like a two-dollar stove–Originally, to smoke a lot (DSAE); here, to give off a lot of smoke.
spell–(Noun) A while, some period of time.
splendifferus–Splendid, magnificent.
springer–A cow that shows signs of calving (DSAE).
squimmy–To carefully extract (wires, cables etc.) by gently wiggling and pulling (neologism).
squose–Simple past and past participle of squeeze.
staggle–Stagger (DSAE).
stealborrow–Literal translation of Nor. *tjuvlåne*: to borrow something without asking the owner's permission under the presumption that the owner won't mind, while also acknowledging (to oneself, at least) that one is committing a form of theft after all.
steddle stones–Stone "feet" on which a small farmyard structure like a barn or shed is supported.
stidder–Instead of.
stoddle–Combination of toddle and stumble (neologism).
switch'd–In the phrase *I'll be switch'd*: an expression of surprise, like "I'll be damned."
swollop–To slap (DSAE).
tarnatious–Extreme, fearsome (DSAE).
tetched–In the phrase *tetched in the head*: deranged.
tetchy–Peevish, excessively sensitive.
that's all she wrote–Idiom to indicate the end of a story, that there is nothing more to add, etc.
this'un–This one.
tolt–Simple past and past participle of tell.
tucker'd out–Tired out, exhausted.
up–In the verb phrase *up and* (+verb): used to express a quick, sudden, or unexpected action, as in "He up and died on us."
vommick–Vomit (verb and noun) (DSAE).
wairy–Weary, tiresome.
wender–Window (US Southern dialect pronunciation).

wet-blanketism–Pessimism, dejection, being a killjoy (*OED Historical Thesaurus* has an entry for *wet-blanketiveness*, documented from 1834).
which from the other–One from another (DSAE).
whoop an' stave–To rage, throw a fit (DSAE).
whuppin'–(Noun) A beating, drubbing.
wingle–To wind and twist, meander (DSAE).
yulegoat–Traditional Scandinavian Christmas figure.

Translator's Acknowledgements

This translation was begun during a difficult period in 2023. I happened to be staying with Leif and his family on their property in Gran, Hadeland, where I was supposed to spend the summer collaborating with him on *The Calf* translation. This was cut short when my mother's cancer diagnosis took a turn for the worse. I quickly returned home to Georgia.

My work on *The Calf* was one of the few bright points for me in the aftermath of her passing. For over a year, Leif answered my questions via Messenger, about Hadeland dialect, about Norwegian pop culture, about the hundreds of other hidden literary references. It is rare to meet someone with such a depth of reading and a zeal for literature as Leif. As he wrote to me shortly after my premature departure: "Literature is always with us, also during the sad days—perhaps even more so then." My deepest gratitude is therefore owed to Leif Høghaug himself.

Many others were kind enough to read drafts and take an interest in what I was doing. Dean Krouk gave a lot of valuable feedback, both on the translation and the afterword, when I was his grad student at the University of Wisconsin-Madison. I am fortunate to have him both as a sensitive reader and a dear friend. This also goes for my colleagues from the Iowa Translation Workshop: Lizzie Buehler, Julia Conrad, Caroline Froh, Michael Overstreet, Abby Ryder-Huth. and Anthony Zilli.

Matthias Friedrich has been an important point of reference, too, with his German translation of *The Calf*.

Finally, I thank my father, Alton Donald Smith, for "lending" his voice to this translation. Thanks to him and my aunt Denise Merck for their support.

Leif Høghaug (born 1974) studied literature at the University of Oslo. Prior to debuting with his poetry collection, *Fama*, in 2012, he had worked in publishing, literary criticism, and academia. Since then he has been an author, translator, and teacher; his fourth book of poetry was published in 2025, to be followed by a biography of the Norwegian labor activist and poet, Rudolf Nilsen. His translations include names like Karl Marx, Slavoj Žižek, and James Joyce, the latter of which holds a special place in Høghaug's authorship. His major project at the moment is a Norwegian translation of *Finnegans Wake*, several excerpts of which have already been published. The influence of the *Wake* is strongly felt in Høghaug's first novel, *The Calf* (2019), where "the pftjschute of Finnegan" becomes a tumble through a twisted narrative about Høghaug's home region, Hadeland in Eastern Norway.

David M. Smith (born 1982) is an American translator of Norwegian prose fiction, with an MFA in literary translation from the University of Iowa. In addition to *The Calf*, his published and ongoing translation projects include names like Dag Solstad, Tarjei Vesaas, Thure Erik Lund, and Johan Harstad.

www.ingramcontent.com/pod-product-compliance
Lightning Source LLC
Chambersburg PA
CBHW051646080926
51108CB00037B/768